The Sting of the Bee

K.E. Lanning

DEDICATION

This novel is dedicated to all the souls who strive for a better life, and to my father, who always believed in me—no matter what.

Part I

Humans must have the vision of a New World in front of them—the necessity of a great quest is in our bones.

CHAPTER 1

John Barrous opened his eyes in the dim light of the hotel room. A pleasant voice said, "John, wake up, it's time to rise and shine."

With a yawn, he turned to his phone. "I'm awake. Thanks, P."

"I hope you slept well?"

He stared at the ceiling above the bed. "Not really." John threw the covers back and sat on the side of the bed, looking dully at the band of pale morning light framing the top of the curtained window.

"John, I thought you might be interested in today's news story on the Antarctic Land Rush."

Scratching his head, he mumbled, "I guess."

A smiling virtual newscaster appeared on the screen. "In our top story of the day, the stage is set for the Great Antarctic Land Rush. The final conference will be held today at the United Nations headquarters." From the corner of the screen popped a 3-D video running on a continuous loop, showing the melting ice cap of Antarctica, the huge glaciers flowing to the ocean, breaking off into the sea until the continent was bare. "People from around the world will be signing up for the adventure of a lifetime—"

A dull pain pulsed in his head. "I'd like some quiet now," he said, and the screen went blank. His hands trembled as he massaged his temples. He caught a whiff of brewing coffee and rose to grab a cup. Clasping the warm cup in his hands, he gulped the coffee, closing his eyes as the hot liquid stung his throat.

With a sigh, he walked to the window of the room, edging the curtain open on one side. Blinking against the slanted rays of the sun, he gazed out over the port city of Summit, New Jersey. Across the street, a myriad of flags fluttered in front of the newly completed United Nations building. His nerves tingled at the sight.

To the east, the sea shimmered in the dawn light, broken only by the tallest skyscrapers still visible above submerged New York City. He sipped his coffee and then shifted his gaze to the vast shanty town near the edge of the water. Tendrils of smoke rose from amidst ramshackle huts cobbled together from the scrap material washed onshore after the Melt.

The wealthy had fled the rising sea waters and built anew, but in the burgeoning lower classes, survival of the fittest had been their only choice. Massive refugee cities grew from the outcasts of society, abandoned on a shore of hardship. Years of pitiful conditions created an underclass filled with anger and resentment. Like stray dogs, savage gangs had proliferated, snatching crumbs from a world devastated by rising sea levels.

An emptiness punched him in the gut, and his lips parted like a drowning man trying to draw a breath. A moan escaped from the depths of his pain, and John glanced at his daughter Ginnie, snuggled in the other bed. He had not awakened her with his outburst.

Swaying, he turned back to the window, clutching the curtain. That underworld had murdered his beloved Helen.

*　　*　　*

John opened the door, blinking against the uproar of the ballroom. He and Ginnie stepped inside, and his nose twitched from a bouquet of scents: new carpet, perfume, and body odor. They threaded their way through a crowd in monotonous western clothes, dotted with purple and red saris, blue Sikh turbans, and white Bedouin robes.

Faces etched in desperation turned toward them. These were not the meek, waiting to inherit the Earth. These were the ones to seize it.

Men leered at Ginnie's fresh face. John wrapped his arm around her shoulders; she was only fifteen. He spotted two seats together and they made a dash for them.

Young men, couples, and families with children flowed into the overcrowded hall. John shifted on the hard metal chair, focusing on a three-dimensional image of Antarctica projected over the stage. The once-frozen continent, now unveiled by the Melt, was rich with green valleys and lofty mountain ranges.

"It's packed in here," Ginnie whispered. "Are all these people doing the Land Rush? Why doesn't the UN just hold a lottery?"

John leaned toward her. "The UN is holding on to Antarctica like the tail of a tiger. They've thrown this Land Rush together to ward off a global conflict between Russia, the U.S., China, and India—all wanting to break the international treaties and grab open land." With a smile, he shrugged. "Or maybe it's some crazy publicity stunt."

John sat back in his chair, trying to relax amidst the milling horde of people. He darted a nervous look sideways. A scruffy man stood next to him, grinning like a Cheshire Cat.

The man put out his hand and introduced himself. "Buck's the name. Homesteading?"

John replied with a guarded handshake and a "Yep."

Buck squatted next to him, jerking his head toward the hologram of the continent. "You know, it's going to be mighty rough on Antarctica. You're not really thinking of taking the young lady, are you?" He leaned closer and said in a hushed voice, "There's a group recruiting people to make a land claim for them, and then they pay your passage back. Make you a cool twenty grand and a free round trip to Antarctica. Maybe you'd be interested?"

With a curt shake of his head, John replied, "I'm not interested. We plan on making Antarctica our home." He narrowed his eyes at Buck. "My understanding is the Land Rush is for principals only—no brokers allowed." In a nonchalant tone he asked, "Who is this group?"

"I'd better find me a chair," Buck mumbled, and lost himself in the crowd.

A short man with jet-black hair walked to the center of the stage, gesturing at the audience. "Everybody find a seat. We've got a lot of material to cover today."

He waited until the crowd quieted. "I'm Paulo Rodriguez, the UN coordinator for the Antarctic Land Rush—welcome!" He pointed in the direction of the harbor. "I hope everyone has had a chance to admire the beautiful ocean liner, *Destiny*, docked in our new facilities. She's ready to carry you to the adventure of a lifetime."

"I'd like to show you a brief overview of Antarctica." He dimmed the lights.

The stunning video transported the audience over the barren terrain of the continent, peppered with shallow lakes and rocks, and mountains ranges covered in snow.

A narrator's melodious voice filled the hall. "Scientists who predicted the warming of the planet were right. A tipping point altered the oceanic currents and warm waters flowed past the Antarctic coastline, accelerating the melting of the southern ice cap. In the span of a century, Mother Nature revealed a rich, virgin continent for the human race to spill into."

John muttered under his breath, "More likely to screw up."

The video brought them to a small mining town perched on the coast. "After the melting of the ice cap, everything changed. Before, it wasn't economic to mine Antarctica, but now it's become feasible. Once the ice had retreated, a mining consortium set up facilities, extracting major quantities of iron, copper, and gold."

Rodriguez paused the video and grinned at the crowd. "That's the good news." He switched to a photo of a massive sinkhole. "The bad news is, we're having a nasty little problem with sinkholes as the permafrost melts—but not too many people have been lost so far!"

Sporadic laughter dribbled from the crowd.

He restarted the video and the audience cruised over a broad river valley. Honking geese skimmed over a meandering river while caribou grazed along the banks. "This is the Concordia Wildlife Refuge. Many fowl species already inhabit the continent, but naturalists are now introducing Arctic land animals."

Rodriguez brought up a map that detailed the Land Rush area. "Many of the regions of Antarctica are named for an explorer or ruler. We will dock in Prydz Bay in East Antarctica, and the Land Rush itself is on the foothills of the Napier Mountains."

He zoomed to the area everyone was anxious to see. The foothills came into view, and the camera glided over a series of valleys separated by low mountain ridges. Like a pearl necklace, streams meandered between shallow lakes along the valley floors, but the vegetation was limited to lichen, short grasses, and anemic, windswept trees.

The room was quiet gazing at the lovely yet stark landscape.

"The weather is still nippy, but livable. In Fahrenheit, the average temperatures range from the sixties in the summer to lows of minus twenty degrees in the winter. But nothing like the minus ninety-four degrees Fahrenheit when the ice cap was in place." He smiled. "I've heard rumors that some of the miners wear t-shirts in the summer."

He pointed to the coastline. "Since the Melt, the sea has encroached on the lowlands, but only temporarily as these areas are rising in elevation with the weight of the ice gone. The Land Rush will take place in the area on the continent with the best soil and most available water. As with all farmers, water will be one of your main concerns."

Rodriguez advanced to the next slide, with a grid of brilliant diamond shapes against a black sky over Antarctica.

"The UN engaged SpaceX to develop a mesh network of satellites, suspended one thousand kilometers over the continent, to provide free internet and also a source of light during the dark months." He moved to the next photo taken on the beach at Prydz Bay, children playing in the water, the idyllic scene lit by reflected sunlight. "It's not as strong as the rays of the sun, but it is brighter than moonlight. When it is 'nighttime,' the panels flip, to maintain a dark sky while everyone sleeps."

"Every Land Rush participant has been given a computer locking key." Rodriguez held up a small metallic object. "This will send a signal to the UN organizers of the winner of the parcel, and once in the stake, it cannot be removed by another homesteader."

Rodriguez clicked to a photo of a farm near the mining station. "The UN wants to settle the region in a peaceable fashion and prepare for immigrants following in your footsteps. As the first settlers, you will have to raise meat-producing animals and/or plant crops. We will provide subsidies and technologies for you to succeed. However, you have to show progress! For example, if you choose to plant crops, you will have three years to plant all of your land, but you must plant at least one third the first year."

John raised an eyebrow at Ginnie. "I just hope something will grow down there."

Rodriguez pointed to the hushed crowd. "The UN has designated Antarctica an organic continent, and therefore, no artificial pesticides or chemicals will be allowed. There will be community farm equipment available for your shared use, which will include teams of agribots to assist during all phases of your agricultural needs, so sign up for those in advance."

Someone from the audience called out in an Urdu accent, "What is an agribot, please?"

Rodriguez nodded. "They are specially designed agricultural robots programmed to aid in planting, weeding, and harvesting crops."

Ginnie mimicked pulling weeds like a robot and whispered, "Yippee for agribots!"

Rodriguez gazed across the audience. "I'll be straight with you. This is going to be the hardest work most of you have ever done. You will be required, and I stress the word *required*, to set up irrigation systems and to plant your homestead with at least three types of crops and a combination of fruit, deciduous, and evergreen trees—all of which have been adapted to thrive on Antarctica."

He shook his finger. "Remember, you will be on your own! Anyone who cannot perform will be sent back home immediately and their goods will be confiscated to pay for their passage."

Reacting to the news, a buzz of muffled conversations rose, and then sporadic arguments broke out. A scattering of people shuffled toward the doors.

"Why are people leaving—didn't they know that?" Ginnie asked.

"Many people sold everything they had for this chance for land. But perhaps a few folks are getting cold feet." He shrugged. "Or maybe they just didn't believe the UN would send them home with their tails between their legs."

John saw Buck in an intense discussion with one of the defectors near the exit, arms gesturing to embellish his point. His face brightened as the man nodded and he slapped him on the back—Buck had netted his man. Then Buck turned, nodding to someone across the room. John followed his gaze to a wiry man with a short beard standing in the corner.

John frowned as unease swam in his stomach. He didn't like the looks of this—too much was at stake. He grabbed Ginnie by the hand. "I've heard enough. Let's get out of here before we get roped into something shady."

CHAPTER 2

On a clear, warm day in late September, John and Ginnie waited on the dock to board the ship to Antarctica. Future pioneers, well-wishers, tourists, and news crews milled about, while food vendors of every ethnicity offered a final meal for the homesteaders, teasing them with the scents of civilization. They found a spot near one of the dock warehouses and leaned their gear against the metal wall. Seated on their bags, they watched people from across the globe ready themselves to invade a new land.

John gazed up at the tiny puffs of white clouds sailing across the sky, while Ginnie listened to music and messaged her friends. She giggled and John smiled as she showed him a funny picture her friend had sent.

He studied her face. She had been devastated by the loss of her mother—a role he could never fill. They had discussed her remaining with her grandparents, but she had insisted on coming with him. Was it a true desire for a new beginning, or just to keep what was left of the family together? He shook his head with a sigh. As her father, he alone was responsible; what would become of her on Antarctica?

The voice on the loudspeaker broke his reverie, calling them to board. John and Ginnie looked at each other and then silently gathered their items. This was it. Commitment time.

John stood and slung his pack over his shoulder. He glanced at Ginnie. "It's not too late to run."

Ginnie adjusted her backpack, shaking her head with a grin. "And miss seeing you stub your toe on Antarctica?"

The Antarctica Land Rush hucksters with their T-shirts, postcards, and souvenirs slapped Half Price! signs onto their booths to squeeze the last dollars from the crowd.

John waved Ginnie toward the dock and swallowed hard at the volume of people gathering on the wharf. Guards herded the crowd between plastic poles topped with small, fluttering UN flags. The incessant beeping of robo-lifts echoed across the wharf as they shifted the homesteaders' worldly possessions onto conveyor belts streaming into the hold.

John bit his lip. God help this horde of humanity, descending into the wilderness.

The crowd drifted like cattle toward the ship, murmuring quietly, until angry voices erupted.

A thin man with a crooked nose screamed in broken English at a large man next to him. "There's no place on board the ship for an asshole!"

Scowling, the big guy shoved him through the poles lining the entryway to the ship, and several of the UN flags fluttered to the ground. One landed on the thin man's head as he lay on the dock.

His eyes bright with anger, he brushed the flag off of his hair, and glared at his adversary. He sprang to his feet like a cat, edging toward the larger man. They circled each other, until the smaller man feinted toward the other, and then twisted away, dodging a deadly punch. Other men gathered and began to shout, tightening the knot around the fighters.

A myriad of voices rose from the crowd behind them.

John cocked his head toward the man next to him. "Now what's going on?"

The man shrugged. "Someone is yelling that there aren't enough spaces for everyone on the ship."

John snorted. "That's nuts. That ship is huge—it will hold all of us *and* our crap."

With a shake of his head, John looked behind them, and then turned to Ginnie. "Let's just hope the crowd settles down." With his hand, he shielded his eyes from the sun and scanned the disorderly groups of settlers behind them. The meager security force had moved nearer to the ramp of the ship, leaving the tail of the line unguarded.

A group of young men pressed forward to gain position in the line. A scuffle broke out, and a bulge formed around the men, stopping their advancement. Then the thugs shoved through the blockade and edged closer to the ship.

John turned toward the closest security guard and waved. "Sir—" Shouts behind him drew his attention back to the rear of the line. Another group momentarily stopped the band from moving up the queue, angrily tearing at their clothes and packs.

John felt a chill go up his spine as an ominous growl resonated across the wharf. He glanced at Ginnie, listening to music and oblivious to the growing volatility of the crowd. "Ginnie! Something is going on."

A ripple of panic tore through the mass. The crowd pulsed forward, and like the muscles of a striking snake, surged toward the ship. John reached out for Ginnie, but an Asian family shoved between them. He watched in horror as his daughter got swept away as if caught in a flash flood.

"Ginnie!" he shouted, throat tight with fear. He lost sight of her behind a swarm of running bodies.

A sharp pain slammed into his back, followed by the vision of asphalt meeting his face as a wall of humans bulldozed over him. He struggled to breathe as dozens of feet raced across his body, knocking the wind from his lungs. He covered his head with his arms and twisted out of the path of the churning stampede until he was free.

John scrambled to his feet and shook his head to clear it. He wiped the blood oozing into his eye and then sprinted after the crowd. His heart raced. *Where was Ginnie?*

Screams echoed along the canyon of warehouses as the tide of bodies accelerated toward the ramp. A band of settlers ascended the incline, knocking over the welcoming crewmembers. Through a megaphone, the captain's metallic voice boomed across the docks, ordering the settlers to stop.

Warning shots rang out from the upper deck. Helmeted military police raced to the access ramp with rifles, creating a wall of force to ebb the flow of the crowd.

A sergeant yelled into a bullhorn, "Let's have order!"

The line of MPs shoved the sea of crazed homesteaders back down the ramp. Guns ready, the guards blocked the access to the ship until the melee quieted.

Scattered like leaves after a storm, the wounded littered the dock, and the air filled with moans and cries of desperate families seeking their loved ones.

John pushed through the crowd, panic constricting his chest. At last he heard Ginnie's voice.

"Back off!" she shouted.

With a relieved smile, he waved to her. "Ginnie, over here."

Ginnie forced her way to him, giving menacing looks to those who wouldn't move out of her way. John enveloped her in a hug.

Ginnie exhaled and murmured, "Geez, that was scary. Almost as bad as donut day at school."

Laughing, John kissed her cheek, and straightened her jacket which had become rumpled in the fray. The screaming children quieted, and with a trembling hand, he smoothed Ginnie's hair.

Ginnie gasped at his bruised and bloodied forehead, and she touched his cheek. "Dad, are you okay?"

With a wry smile, he shrugged. "I'm fine, but I guess my head isn't as hard as my mother always told me it was."

Lights flashing, swat teams arrived in armored vehicles, and men and women in full riot gear swarmed out, lining up around the crowd. Angry settlers pointed fingers at the group who instigated the pandemonium, and they were dragged away in handcuffs.

The wail of ambulances deafened the crowd and paramedics spread out to care for the injured. Nearby, a wounded man leaned on a paramedic, his face twisted in pain as they assisted him to the ambulance.

Children sobbed inconsolably, terrified by the insanity of it all.

Heart thumping, John swallowed hard, glancing up at the welcoming banner with the image of Antarctica stretched across the gangway. The hair rose on his neck, and wrapping his arm around Ginnie, the reality of this venture struck him. Was he dragging his child into an existence that might, at best, bore her and, at worst, kill her?

A blast from the ship's horn boomed over the crowd and boarding resumed.

John and Ginnie reached the top of the ramp and struggled along the deck through the mob, grimacing against the raucous bullhorns directing people onto the ship. When they reached the bow, John leaned on the rail with a sigh. The adrenaline rush from the stampede abated, and he dully watched families gathering on the deck, patching their wounds. He lifted his hand to his throbbing head.

One of the ship's doctors and her nurse joined the passengers on the deck, offering medical attention where needed. She glanced toward John and stopped in front of him. With a gentle smile, she said, "Looks like you may need some medical attention, sir."

Shrugging, he turned away. "I'm fine."

She grinned. "That wasn't a request—I'm in charge here." She waved her nurse over, pulled a penlight from her pocket and examined his eyes. "Just checking for signs of a concussion." The nurse handed her an antiseptic cloth, and the doctor cleaned away the dried blood crusted above his eye, and finally, stretched a bandage over the cut. She said, "The bandage is infused with pain killer, so you should feel better soon."

"Thank you, doctor." John smiled. "I guess the Land Rush will be a walk in the park after this."

"Hope springs eternal." She looked at Ginnie. "Are you okay?"

Ginnie nodded. "Thank you for patching up Dad. Did any kids get hurt?"

With a sigh, the doctor shrugged. "Broken bones, but thank god, no one was fatally injured."

A woman called out for help, and the doctor and nurse moved along the deck to aid the next group. A small brass band in the parking lot struck up a rousing farewell piece as the ship cast off. "Bon Voyage!" drifted up from the waving crowd on the dock. Streamers filled the air, and John squeezed Ginnie's shoulder at the final blast of the ship's horn.

The *Destiny* cruised away from the dock and John relaxed as the pain in his forehead waned. In the distance they saw the skyscrapers of lower Manhattan, debris lapping against the glass windows of offices now filled with the fishes of the sea. With the echoes of their horns reverberating between the abandoned buildings, water taxis puttered along canals between the Empire State Building and the One World Trade Center—some of the few buildings still open on the upper floors.

An eerie quiet came over the deck as the ship edged away from civilization. The lyrical sendoff faded in the distance and the crowds on the dock meandered home. John glanced around at the earnest faces. Were these pioneers of a new world holding their collective breaths?

Ginnie gasped and turned toward him, pointing with a shaking finger. A tear crept down her cheek and she whispered, "Dad, look at her."

John grabbed the rail to steady himself. He clenched his jaw against the tears welling in his eyes. Waves splashing into her lovely face, the Statue of Liberty stared serenely over the white caps of the bay, raising her torch to a drowned world.

CHAPTER 3

In a quiet sea, *Destiny* neared the Equator. The evening was warm and wisps of clouds ambled across the sky. Sitting at a small table on the deck, Lowry sipped a glass of smooth Chardonnay before dinner.

The wind blew its salty scent over Lowry's face and she leaned back in complete surrender to the respite of the voyage. Her life was so hectic that she rarely had a quiet moment. She gazed at the blue sky, breathed deep, and closed her eyes. She emptied her mind, listening to the waves lap against the ship's hull.

A tinkle of glassware drew her attention and she opened one eye. A bartender was setting up the bar on the deck and another crewmember pushed a cart of table settings to the terrace. The crew was throwing a special dinner party for the passengers to celebrate the crossing into the Southern Hemisphere. Crewmembers scurried to complete the final touches for the event.

Lowry grimaced, thinking of the spectacle this maiden voyage to Antarctica had become. Earlier she had spotted the head of the UN giving an interview on the Land Rush. Celebrities and media types crawled all over the ship, closely shadowed by their entourages of fans and photographers. Everyone wanted to be a part of this historic event.

With a sigh, Lowry closed her eyes again. *And all I want is some quiet.* After almost a decade, she was returning to Antarctica, and the voyage was an opportunity to sort out her thoughts. Years ago, her veil of innocence had burned away. Lowry was not the immature girl who had left the mining camp in Antarctica. But the protective armor she had developed these last years had grown heavy; perhaps this homecoming would be her chance for renewal.

A shadow fell across her face. Through half-closed eyes, she saw a man looking at his phone searching for his virtual name card on the table.

"I guess we'll be dinner companions tonight." He stuck out his hand. "John Barrous."

Just when I was relaxing. She sat up and forced a smile. "Lowry Walker." At least he wasn't a pain to look at. She gestured for him to join her.

After an awkward moment of silence, she asked, "Are you a homesteader or, uh, tourist?" She realized she might have insulted him either way.

He laughed. "My daughter and I are insane enough to be homesteaders."

With a playful grin, Lowry quipped, "Speak for yourself. She probably didn't have a choice."

"She did have a choice, but I'm the crazy bastard."

"Is your daughter joining us for dinner?"

"No, she's at the 'Teen Pizza and a Movie Night.'" He lifted the wine from the cooler, and Lowry nodded at his questioning look. He topped Lowry's glass and then poured a glass for himself. He tilted his head and asked, "How about yourself?"

She'd been asked the same question numerous times on the voyage, and the reactions had always been the same. No one believed she was off to homestead in Antarctica by herself. She shrugged. "I know, what's a pretty girl like me doing in a place like this?"

John raised an eyebrow. "I don't remember saying pretty."

"Touché!" She chuckled. "I'm a lunatic homesteader too."

A waiter brought a large appetizer plate to the table. "Compliments of the chef."

Lowry scooted prosciutto and melon onto her plate. "My father came down after the opening of the mines. I grew up on Antarctica." She gazed at John. "But I'm planning on staking my own claim."

"Really, you lived on Antarctica!" John spooned a couple of avocado slices onto his plate. "Your parents immigrated with the first expedition?"

Lowry lowered her gaze. "My mother died when we were still in the States. After her death, my father decided that I needed to be with him." She sliced the melon with a knife and continued with a thin smile. "When I was twelve, I moved to the bottom of the world."

John's brows furrowed. "Oh, I'm very sorry."

Exhaling, she shrugged. "It's been a long time, but I was close to my mother."

"It must have been a tough transition for you."

"It was lonely for me as a child." She gazed at the open sea beyond the rail. "But I had time to think and the freedom to roam where I pleased."

He speared an asparagus. "You came back to civilization for college?"

"Yes, undergrad and graduate school in geophysics." Lowry absently drew her finger around the lip of the wine glass. For just having met him, she felt oddly comfortable with John, but discretion was the better part of valor. *No confessions of the past—at least not before dinner.* "After that, I worked in the States on a mapping project and traveled as much as I could."

With a broad smile, she raised an eyebrow. "I'm afraid I've become one of those irritating women who does what she pleases and damn the torpedoes."

The waiter brought the main course of Surf and Turf. He set the plates on the table. "Filet Mignon from the States and Antarctic lobster with clarified butter." With a slight bow, he said, "Bon Appétit."

Lowry cut a piece from the Filet Mignon and popped the tender beef into her mouth. "Yum, this is wonderful."

John stabbed a section of lobster, and dunked it into the bowl of butter, and chewed with a sigh. "It's been a long time since I had lobster."

She dabbed her mouth with her napkin, and with a slight tilt of her head, asked, "Why are you going to Antarctica?"

John's eye twitched. He stopped eating for a second, then finished chewing and swallowed the bite in his mouth. He put down his fork and brushed his mouth with his napkin. He cleared his throat, leaned back in his chair and stared over the railing at the ocean.

Lowry drank some water, wondering if he was going to answer her.

He glanced at her, opened his mouth for a second, and then closed it with a sigh. Then, with an odd grin, he tilted forward and whispered, "It was the drums."

She set her water glass on the table. She inclined her head, not sure she had heard him right, then repeated his words. "The drums?"

A lopsided smile sprang onto his face. "The incessant drumming of society." John drummed the table with his fingers. "Most people aren't even aware of them. They just dance, moving faster and faster to keep up with the pace of the drums." He said in a thin voice, "The drums were killing me."

With a slight nod of her head, she hummed in agreement. "Humans evolved in small groups. I don't think we were meant to live together in huge numbers." Figuring he needed to be aided and abetted, Lowry lifted the wine bottle and filled his wine glass.

John sipped his wine, and then set it in front of him, and abstractedly tapped the side of the glass with his finger. He picked up his fork and stared at his plate. With a quick stroke, he impaled the last piece of lobster and stuck it into his mouth. Chewing slowly, he shook his head. "There is no greater isolation than to live with a million or more other humans, fighting turf battles you didn't even know existed. I guess that's part of the appeal of homesteading. It'll be awhile before Antarctica gets to that point."

"Turf battles are a part of being human. A pack animal instinct, I'm afraid."

Shrugging, John replied, "Yes, but that assumes that you're in a pack."

The waiter pushed the dessert cart to their table. Lowry chose the dark chocolate cake and John a dish of brandied pears. A silence drifted between them as they ate their sweets. The waiter returned, cleared the table and presented them with two brandies.

John tasted the brandy and set it back in front of him. He glanced at her, then turned away, his eyes fixed on the horizon. He whispered as if talking to himself, "You think you see your life ahead of you. But life is stumbling through a cave with a lit match, threatening every second to burn out, never knowing whether there's a solid step under foot . . . or a crevasse."

Lowry studied him. There was more to John than what she first thought—either he was a deep thinker or as he had termed it, "a crazy bastard." Or maybe both.

During her ten years mapping the geology and water sources on Antarctica, she'd had limited opportunity for relationships. She had worked in a small office, with an older geologist and a young female technician. A few dates with a professor or two from the university underwriting their work, but nothing ever stuck. Early in her young adult life she'd been burned by a bad marriage and become cautious with her heart.

She caressed the stem of the brandy glass. John was definitely the most interesting man she'd met in years. But the jury was still out.

Lowry lifted her glass in a toast and said flippantly, "To the million-dollar question: Antarctica—solid step or crevasse?"

They clinked their glasses together. "To Antarctica."

CHAPTER 4

John stared vacantly into the night, moving with the gentle sway of the vessel. At this late hour, the ship was quiet, and he was alone on the observation deck. He gazed at the brilliant moon and inhaled the crisp air. He shook his head, but the thoughts plaguing him resurfaced. He hated to admit it, but he was thinking about Lowry.

She was an attractive woman, one with strength in her face. Full lips with eyes the color of bronzed pewter and long, dark hair that reached past her waist. He pursed his lips. *And her ass wasn't bad either.* He estimated she was in her mid-thirties. A dangerous age—young enough to be in her prime, old enough to be experienced.

Earlier that evening, after they had finished their brandies, the captain had announced over the intercom, "Folks, we have a pod of sperm whales off the starboard side."

Like a child, Lowry's eyes had lit up in excitement. Smiling, John had refilled their wine glasses and they strolled to the side of the ship. When the whales surfaced, Lowry shouted, "Thar she blows!" and laughed, her smile lighting up her face. The wind swept her hair from her face and her scent drifted over him.

Now, in the darkness of the top deck, John gripped the rail. It wasn't the time to get entangled in a relationship.

He saw something white flutter in the wind. *Shit.* It was Lowry, coming across the deck. He clenched his jaw, stifling his first urge to acknowledge her, but his alter ego surrendered. "Lowry, over here!"

She was startled at first, but then her smile shone in the pale light of the moon. "You can't sleep either, I see."

Lowry walked across the deck toward him, while her dress clung to various parts of her body at the whim of the shifting breeze. He dug his nails into the palms of his hands, but he couldn't think of anything but her, the nearby deck chair, and making love.

She stood watching him, then with a grin, said, "Cat got your tongue?"

Shrugging, he turned back toward the ocean. "Just thinking."

Lowry joined him on the rail. They gazed out over the lower deck and the smooth sea beyond.

He bit his lip. In the middle of the night, he sometimes awakened to the reoccurring nightmare of Helen's death, the grief wrenching his insides like a crowbar. And a heavy burden of guilt that he failed to protect his wife in a world gone mad.

Now Lowry. Was it a betrayal of his wife's memory and the mother of his child to be attracted to another woman so soon? Lowry probably assumed he was divorced, since he hadn't brought himself to tell her about Helen during dinner. He chewed the inside of his mouth. He realized he had to reveal his heartache to a woman he didn't know, but to whom he seemed to be irritatingly drawn.

John brushed his hair back and stared out at the ocean, shimmering in the moonlight. "You must be wondering where my wife is."

With a wag of her head, she replied, "Since you have a daughter, I assumed you had been married at some point."

John cleared his throat. His fingers tapped the rail, then he blurted out, "My wife was killed in a carjacking last year."

Lowry's mouth dropped open. "My god!"

His throat tightened, choking his words. "After the Melt, the crime rate in Pittsburgh skyrocketed. One night, on her drive home from work, a fake detour in the road led her to a trap. Then the gang pulled her from the car and shot her. They drove away, leaving her to die in the street." Dizzy, he closed his eyes, struggling to regain his composure. "My wife and I had planned to buy a farm in the country and take Ginnie away from the violence. But we waited too long—and now it's just my daughter and I."

Lowry's hand slid over his. "I'm so very sorry, John." Her fingers trembled as she squeezed his hand. "The human beast can be cruel." Her voice became taut. "But I don't understand how violence seems to have become a way of life."

John sighed, murmuring, "It's been especially hard on Ginnie."

Lowry squeezed his hand. "Yes"—exhaling—"like your heart was ripped out of you."

Turning his hand under hers, they held hands silently, two humans bonding at a juxtaposition of losses. *What heartbreak was Lowry remembering?*

His breath slowed and for the first time since Helen's death, he felt the lifting of his sorrow. Odd that this stranger could have such an effect on him.

The shushing sound of the vessel cutting through the water filled the quiet between them, and his heart calmed with the warmth of her hand.

Then Lowry flinched, her eyes directed at the deck below. "What is it?" he asked, turning toward her.

"Please, lower your voice," she whispered from the side of her mouth. "See those three men down there?"

He squinted in the darkness below, discerning three figures huddled in a circle on the main deck below. As a door opened beside them, the light cast over the group. One of them resembled Buck, the miscreant who tried to hustle him at the Land Rush conference, and the other looked like his partner, the lean man with the trimmed beard.

With a jerk, she withdrew her hand and glanced at John. "Sorry, I can't explain now. I'd better go."

His hand felt cold as she turned to leave, and he touched her arm, saying softly, "Why don't you stop by our cabin for a nightcap?"

With pinched eyebrows, she looked at him, and then smiled. "All right, but not for long."

They walked in silence to his cabin. John opened the door and waved her in.

Lowry navigated around the boxes on the floor.

John clapped his hands together. "What can I get you to drink? I have beer and a bottle of wine."

"I'll take some wine, if it's open."

"Please, make yourself at home." John knelt, opened the tiny fridge and pulled out a bottle of wine.

Lowry squeezed into the sliver of space on the couch between suitcases.

He handed her a glass of wine. "I guess it would help if I moved this junk." He lifted the suitcases off the couch and cleared a spot. "Now, you can be comfortable."

She peeked into an open box near the sofa. "You collect art?"

John shrugged. "Uh, yes, I do."

Leaning over, Lowry perused the small sculptures in the box, and then glanced up at him, tilting her head with a smile. "Tell me about them."

He picked up one of the sculptures and held the carved form up to the light, caressing it with his hand. "The color and form of an abstract piece can evoke emotion or an idea."

Lowry asked, "What is that material? In the light, it almost glows."

"It was carved from a book of mica, and fairly fragile, which is why I've kept it with us and not packed in our crate in the hold." He set the mica sculpture back into the box and picked up a jade Buddha encased in a cage. His voice softened as he rotated the sculpture in the light. "Some art is a call for justice or truth."

"These are wonderful, John. I'm quite impressed!" She prodded an open trunk beside her with her shoe. "You're shipping bound books?"

He nodded. "Yes, a few of the old classics; they're like gold to me. The rest of my library is there." He pointed to a small tablet on the desk.

"Someone who surrounds themselves with interesting things is usually an interesting person."

"I like things around me which provoke thought." He carefully placed the sculptures back into the box and sat in the chair facing her. John cleared his throat and asked the question on the tip of his tongue. "What was going on with those men on the deck?"

Lowry looked at him, with a raised eyebrow. "Next question."

Evasive answer. *Maybe she's a spy?* Then with a shrug, he asked, "Okay, onto question two." John leaned forward. "You lived on Antarctica; you may know a great deal about the area to be opened for homesteading. Can you give me the inside scoop?"

A smile darted over her face. "You know that info is worth gold. Only certain tracts have surface water."

"I do know. If you have information, perhaps I could work out something to make it worth your while."

Her eyes narrowed. "Let me think about it," she said with an enigmatic smile.

"Hey, Dad." Ginnie stuck her head out from behind the partition between her bed and the main cabin area.

John stood. "What are you doing up? I thought you were asleep. I hope we didn't wake you."

"No, I was listening to music." She strolled into the room and smiled at Lowry. "Hi."

John put his arm around her and introduced her to Lowry. "This is my daughter, Ginnie. Ginnie, this is Lowry Walker— she lived on Antarctica as a kid. Now she's doing the Land Rush."

Lowry shook her hand. "Very nice to meet you, Ginnie. Are you excited at the prospect of settling on Antarctica?"

Ginnie nodded. "There's a lot I'll miss in the States, but what other kid could say they homesteaded on Antarctica?"

Lowry laughed. "You remind me of me." She wagged a finger at Ginnie. "Say, I need to check the horses before I turn in. How would you two like to see the mares?"

Ginnie's eyes lit up. "I'd love to!"

John raised his eyebrows. "Horses?"

"The UN sponsors different breeding programs for animals to inhabit the new continent. Arabian horses from the desert adapt very well to the climate of Antarctica, and over the last several months, I've been buying broodmares."

They left the cabin and started down the narrow corridor.

With a puzzled look, Ginnie asked, "What about the stallions?"

Lowry said, "Stallions are a lot easier to transport since all we need is their sperm."

John cocked his head toward Lowry, and with a twinkle in his eye, whispered, "If I'd known that, I would have mailed myself to Antarctica."

Lowry smirked. "Perhaps I failed to mention we want only superior bloodlines."

Flinching, he grabbed his heart dramatically. "Ouch—that hurt."

*　　*　　*

The thrum of the engines met them as they walked down the steps to the lower deck. Lowry led the way through the crates and vehicles tightly packed into the cargo area. A dog barked as they approached the stalls.

"It's okay, Sparky, it's me, boy," Lowry called out.

Ginnie knelt, smiling at the furry face. "Can I pet him?"

"Sure. He gets lonely down here. Don't tell anyone, but sometimes I sneak him into my cabin for the night."

John knelt and stroked the dog's thick fur. "What breed is he?"

"He's mostly Norwegian Elkhound and some other distinguished breed apparently known for jumping fences." Lowry patted his shaggy head. "He was born on Antarctica. I got him after graduate school. He's a good boy."

The mares nickered as Lowry reached into a box and pulled out several dried horse treats. She gave a few to Ginnie and gestured to a white mare looking expectantly toward them. "This mare's name is Hadeel. Hold the treat on the flat of your hand, so they don't accidentally catch your finger with their teeth."

Ginnie smiled as the mare nibbled the treat from her palm. "She's so sweet!" She pointed to the mare in the stall next to Hadeel. "Isn't that mare kind of fat?"

With a smile, Lowry shook her head. "No, she's pregnant. She's the only one we purchased who was, but I really liked the stallion she was bred to, so it was an opportunity to bring those lines to Antarctica." With eyebrows raised, Lowry tilted her head toward John. "As I mentioned to your dad, we only choose animals with good bloodlines and dispositions."

Chuckling, John snapped his fingers. "Damn. My mother always said that my Danish and Puerto Rican ancestry meant that I was a product of hybrid vigor."

Ginnie grinned. "A mutt by any other name . . ."

He stuck his tongue out at her. "Back 'atcha, daughter."

"Mutts are preferred in dogs—and men."

Lowry picked up a couple of grooming brushes, handed one to Ginnie, and then showed her how to brush the horse. "Have you ever been around horses?"

Ginnie brushed Hadeel's white coat. "No, we lived in the city, but Mom had promised we'd buy a horse if we moved to a farm."

John felt Lowry glance at him, but he concentrated on scratching Hadeel's back.

Lowry combed the mare's mane. "When I moved to Antarctica as a kid, we bought a farm and the horses from an old man. He told us that when the mine was first opened, he trained the horses to search for victims in permafrost areas. Horses can sense the footing under them and get rescuers in and out safely. And in many rough areas, horses are the only means of travel."

Lowry gave Hadeel a final pat and they moved to the other stalls. She untangled the mares' forelocks while Ginnie fed them treats. One of the mares lay down, and Lowry smiled. "They're telling us it's time for bed." She threw a bone to Sparky.

John said, "While we're in the cargo hold, I'm going to check on our buggy. I heard someone's tires got slashed last night."

With a nod, Lowry said, "I'm afraid the UN hadn't counted on the fierceness of the competition. People are calling it the 'Mad Max' Land Rush."

When they returned to the cabin, John hugged Ginnie. "You'd better get to bed, Sweetie."

She turned to Lowry. "Code for 'go away.' It was nice meeting you."

Lowry grinned. "Likewise."

Ginnie pointed to an old brass mantel clock sitting on the bar. "Don't forget to wind the clock, Dad."

"Yeah, I forgot earlier."

With a yawn, Ginnie walked behind the screened-off section and went to bed.

John passed Lowry in the small confines of the cabin and caught a whiff of her scent. He motioned toward the small couch. "Please sit." With a smile, he wound the clock. "It's an old Danish clock passed down through my mother's side."

"It's beautiful."

The clock tick-tocked behind him as he sat facing Lowry. He cleared his parched throat and made a grab for his unfinished glass of wine sitting on a box.

Lowry turned toward him. "You mentioned some kind of trade for information. I do need help with something, but you must promise to keep it confidential, whether you decide to help me or not."

He blinked at her serious look, wondering what bomb was getting ready to drop. They'd only known each other a few hours, yet she seemed to trust him. "Of course, you have my word on it." He felt like a bug under a magnifying glass as she studied him without expression.

She exhaled, then said quietly, "My Uncle Nick, who's been working as a geologist on Antarctica since the Melt, discovered a scam connected to the Land Rush. He asked me to try and find out who was involved."

Lowry leaned in, her perfume and proximity making it hard for him to think clearly. "He believes they may be on this ship. With the Land Rush coming up, it appears there's a group recruiting sham homesteaders to make claims on key parcels, then sell the land back to them, for a nominal amount. Every lead winds up a dead end. But those three men on the deck? We think they're involved."

She sat back, drumming her fingers on the arm of the couch. "John, this is serious business. We believe they are funded by a multinational corporation, perhaps a shell—for Russian interests."

Staring at Lowry, John sat back and crossed his arms, swallowing hard as warning sirens screamed in his head. *All I wanted was to go on a date, not be thrown overboard by thugs . . . or the Russian mafia.*

Lowry pressed her point. "Less-than-savory persons in Russia were not pleased when the UN set up the Land Rush. The publicity of the race effectively blocked their plans to sneak into Antarctica behind the world's back. Rumor has it that they staged the fights on the dock as a poke in the UN's eye. But even if that's true, no one could have anticipated the resulting stampede. It was pure luck no one was killed."

She shook her head. "We're talking a mega-Monopoly game here. If this group controls the best land and transportation routes, it will skew the entire future of Antarctica in their favor and lay down a welcome mat for the oligarchy in Russia. We're trying to gather evidence to expose this group and break their influence. We know there's an Antarctic connection, because someone is giving them insider information on the best tracts and where the critical routes will be."

She fell silent. He stared at the floor, struggling to digest her words.

John looked at her with a furrowed brow. "Why is Russia the only player? What about the States and China in the great domination of Antarctica?"

"China is wrapped in territorial disputes with Japan and India because of human migrations away from the flooded lowlands." Lowry shrugged. "And Amerada? They're busy 'managing' the merger between the America and Canada— homesteading the northern regions and screwing the indigenous populations.

"Russia has a huge stake in Antarctica—it would give them a foothold in the southern hemisphere. The Russian mafia is their tool to get their fingers into Antarctica, and if they win, we are doomed."

She pointed at him with her finger. "We must stop the scam and the Russian interference. And we can make the case that the time is right for us to vote in our own government. The provisional, appointed government is corrupt—we have to clean house, and set Antarctica on a path to democracy."

John exhaled, sweeping his hand through his hair. *Lowry seems like a modern Joan of Arc and that didn't end well.* "Dare I ask how I can be of help to you?"

"We need someone to pose as one of the speculators to get the names of the principal people involved. We believe they're coaching the groups on board this ship. We need a video of one of their meetings—with the kingpins—to prove who the backers are. With that, we should have enough evidence to start an investigation. The UN can't help us if there's no concrete evidence against these 'buddies' of the Kremlin."

John shifted in his chair. *Another fine mess you've gotten me into*, he thought, referring to a part of his anatomy that rarely got out these days.

"Why me?" he said, more irritated with himself than with her.

"Because they don't know you, and I've tried to find someone who could do this for weeks!"

He clenched his jaw. And now she had a sucker on the line.

"I can get you all the information I have on the homesteading parcels. Uncle Nick and I have been working with the UN mapping Antarctic geology and aquifers. I know the best areas; the ones with water and good soil."

With his mouth pinched, John glared at the caged Buddha mocking him from the open trunk.

Lowry stood and walked toward the door, pausing with a glance back at John. "This is a lot to dump on you. But time is tight—let me know by the end of tomorrow."

After Lowry left, John got up and wandered around the room, thinking on what she'd offered. He stopped in front of his tablet and saw Ginnie's lesson for the day still on the screen.

"Must the citizen ever for a moment, or in the least degree, resign his conscience to the legislator? Why has every man a conscience, then? I think that we should be men first, and subjects afterward. Let your life be a counter-friction to stop the machine. What I have to do is to see, at any rate, that I do not lend myself to the wrong which I condemn."

John pondered Thoreau's words as he prepared for bed. He thought about conscience, that moral issue of right or wrong. Should he sacrifice his life, and possibly the life of his daughter, for the future of Antarctica? For the greater good of humanity?

In his preparation for this trip, he'd read many of the reports written in the 1800s, which had warned of the tragedies of overpopulation and lack of fair water-rights legislation that became a problem in the American West.

The land promoters and railroad barons during the opening of the West had distorted the entire history of the States, and history might repeat itself on Antarctica. The same catalysts were in place and, if the authorities allowed it to happen, the land speculators and transporters would control Antarctica for decades, perhaps even centuries to come.

Stir into the mix the Russian mafia and a corrupt government. Without a counterforce, a disaster could unfold before their eyes. John was a private man, but he believed in public service; that brand of community aid where those who could help others, should. With a sigh, he crawled onto the couch. He was the type of person who stood by his beliefs. Now he was being called to serve, with no choice but to try and stop the speculators from corrupting Antarctica.

He jerked the blanket over him and gazed at the ceiling. Unable to sleep, his mind whirled. What if Lowry was wrong and all this was just a con-artist swindle that would ultimately fall apart? Or worse: if she was right, they could all be shark bait before they reached Antarctica.

He flipped onto his side and punched the pillow into a ball. In the dim light of the cabin, he saw Lowry's wine glass sitting in front of him. Gritting his teeth, he glared at the impression of her lips on the rim. *If only I hadn't met Lowry.*

CHAPTER 5

Early the next morning, John left the cabin and strolled onto the deserted deck. He leaned on the rail, staring out into the nothingness of the blue water stretching to the horizon. A wandering albatross appeared out of nowhere. Its long, dark wings and brilliant white body soared above the ship. John nodded to the bird as it flew out of sight. A good omen for sailors, and perhaps, for a lonely man.

The sound of the waves against the hull lured his mind into the past. This serene ocean had destroyed the coastlines of the Earth, drowning the historic seaports of civilization. Societal chaos had spread with the rising waters, and with it, religious comparisons to the Great Flood of the Bible. The economic turmoil created a haven for corruption and cronyism.

John had been firmly trapped in the metal teeth of a corporate giant, but in desperation, he had chewed through the proverbial leg to escape to a new life. A deep swell drifted into the ship, lifting the huge vessel up and then down after the swell passed. The undulation reminded John of his last day at work.

* * *

The monitor in the compu-table pulsed as Carl's fist slammed onto its surface, waves rippling across the gel screen. With his lip curled like a snarling dog, Carl leaned forward, salivating at the prospect of devouring his favorite meal: the soul of an employee.

John Barrous held his breath, his knuckles turning white as he gripped the edge of the table. He, and his co-worker, Miranda, had worked for months to complete the Hickston project, detailing the leakage from an abandoned refinery into the groundwater. Miranda remained frozen beside John as Carl's finger jabbed the screen repeatedly, marring the image with each blow.

"You two are supposed to be our best engineers," Carl sneered. "John, you're out of a top-ranked environmental program and you think this is right?"

John stared at Carl, his heart thumping as he weighed the consequences of leaping over the table and beating the other man senseless.

Carl sat back, pulling his thinning hair over his bald spot. His eyes darted from John to Miranda and back again. "Let's review this again after you and Miranda have corrected this crap."

Miranda flicked the screen off and the room became deathly quiet. In that silence, John heard his voice drift from his lips of its own accord. "I'm afraid that's not possible, Carl. This is my last day."

Carl's mouth dropped open and he gaped at John. "What did you say?"

Miranda stared at John as if he had gone mad.

John blinked. He inhaled the fresh air of freedom and smiled at the shock on Carl's face. "That's right, Carl, I quit." Woodenly, as if hearing a distant pied piper, John walked from the conference room.

Footsteps clattered in the hall behind him.

Miranda caught up and grabbed his arm. "John, don't do anything hasty. Even Carl knows the work is correct. He just loves being an asshole. Let's get out of here and have lunch at Josephine's."

They left the office, threading their way through the bums on the sidewalk, remnants of a society which had passed them by. As they turned the corner, a woman stepped out from a doorway. A shock went through his body. Was it . . . her?

She moved into the sunlight, revealing her face. A stranger—not his beautiful, sweet Helen. As if it could have been her.

He stumbled on the threshold and in a daze, followed Miranda into the restaurant. They sat and ordered the lunch special. After the meals came, John picked at his food, feeling Miranda's eyes on him.

He glanced at her with a shrug, and speared a slice of tomato. "Perhaps my quitting will save one of the other poor beasts waiting for slaughter. I've heard rumor of another round of layoffs."

John ate the slice of tomato and then laid down his fork, staring at the spaghetti on his plate as his stomach churned. He raised his eyes to Miranda's anxious stare, and with teeth bared, he clenched his hand in a fist. "Corporations are like spiders— we get trapped in their web and then paralyzed by a quick bite." A sick smile flashed onto his face. "They suck out our creative juices, and all the while, we have full knowledge of our host's feast." John plucked up his fork and stabbed a meatball, holding it up like a trophy. "All that remains are the leftovers, to be discarded with the next day's trash." His shoulders slumped as he dropped the meatball and let the fork clatter back onto the plate.

He stared at the plate. A bus-cart cleared a nearby table and the clink of dishes hurt his ears.

With a sigh, Miranda leaned forward and cleared her throat. "John, I know it's been a rough year." She reached across the table toward him. "What about your idea of homesteading on Antarctica?" Shrugging, she asked, "But perhaps your daughter doesn't want to go?"

John tilted his head. "Now that Helen is gone, it's certainly on my mind. Oddly enough, Ginnie wants to go, but maybe it's a reaction to her mother's death."

"Did they ever catch the guys who did it?"

His lips were pinched as he shoved his plate forward. "How do you catch a world gone mad?" He raked his hand through his hair, his fingers pushing into his scalp like tines. "All I know is that I don't want to wait for the last bus to the retirement home."

*   *   *

John clutched the railing of the ship. *And now, after escaping from the corporate insane asylum, I have a date with a criminal syndicate.* Scowling, he turned away from the peaceful ocean and climbed the stairs to deck three, annoyed at the irritating twist of fate that had gotten him sucked into this espionage.

Yesterday, John had found Buck and told him they wouldn't be homesteading after all, and that he needed the money. Buck remembered him and had been delighted to bring him into the fold. Buck was that "good ol' boy" sort, who would sell his mother with a smile.

John reached the room, took a deep breath, and knocked. Buck opened the door; he must have been waiting for him. With a grin, he dragged John toward the group gathered around a large conference table. "Come on in, come on in— Sergei wants to meet you."

With a sweeping glance, John perused the luxury suite, one of those huge cabins at the back of the ship that people like him never saw. Sleeping quarters flanked each side of the main room, with marble bathrooms off to the side. Beyond the table, a sunken lounge area faced a bank of windows stretching the width of the room, allowing an exquisite view to the occupants, but now completely shuttered with curtains. A sure sign of clandestine activities.

He set his jaw to keep his face impassive and exchanged looks with this band of merry men. He'd decided that the character he would play would be a reluctant Joe, a guy who wasn't quite sure he trusted anyone—a role he knew wasn't much of a stretch.

Surrounded by men of questionable background, a thin man with a short-cropped beard leaned on the edge of the conference table. John chewed the inside of his lip. This was the dude Buck had been working with at the conference, and who appeared to be the ringleader. He stared at John with a raised eyebrow.

Buck bobbed his head toward the thin man and waved toward John. "Sergei, this is John."

With a twitch of his lip, Sergei examined John from head to toe with eyes hardened with years of desperate living. "Buck tells me you want to join our little party?"

John swallowed hard and took a deep breath. "Yes. I quit my job and sold everything to make this trip. I need cash when I get back."

"Everybody did, so why are you really backing out?"

John's heart beat like a drum. The bastards weren't easily fooled. Blinking rapidly, he gestured with his hands, "The truth is that my daughter has become ill, so we have to go home."

Sergei's brow furrowed. "What's wrong with her?"

"She had a seizure a couple of days ago, but the doctor on the ship can't tell what's wrong. We have to return to the States to get her checked out."

Sergei turned to Buck and pursed his lips. "You vouch for this guy?"

Buck nodded. "Yep."

"OK, we do need another body for parcel fourteen." He looked hard at John. "You understand this is hush-hush."

Exhaling, John smiled at Sergei. "All I care about is the money and to get back home."

With a curt nod, Sergei turned away, and began to discuss strategy with one of the other men.

John interrupted him. "I hate to bring this up, but just how does this money thing work? Who pays me and when?"

Sergei shot a look to Buck and then narrowed his eyes at John. "You get a quarter of the money the day before the run. And the rest when you successfully make a claim." With a frown, he snarled, "After you sign it over to us, that is."

John shook his head with a puzzled look. "Odd that anyone would pay for free land. Who is this group?"

Sergei shot him a dead-fish look and turned his back. Buck shook his head with a scowl. John didn't press the question. He would have to work any more information out of Buck—alone.

As they walked out of the meeting, he called after Buck, "Want a beer? I'm buying."

"Sure!" Buck said, slapping him on the back.

They sat at the bar and punched in their choices on the screen. Two cold ones slid out.

"Service with a smile." John clinked glasses with Buck. "Thanks for your support in there. I need the money."

Buck shrugged. "No problem. Glad to do it."

John swallowed the crisp liquid and sat back with a grin. *Buck must get a nice bit of change for reeling me in.* After the first beer was history, John leaned in and asked Buck in a low voice, "Buck, you seem like you're in the know. What's the skinny with this group buying up parcels of undeveloped land?"

Buck tilted forward with a snort. "None of your damn business. Now shut up and let's get another round."

John wiped off the spittle that Buck had spewed his way. Old Buck wasn't as dumb as he'd thought—or hoped.

CHAPTER 6

Towering fjords threw shadows across the *Destiny* as she maneuvered through the passage into Prydz Bay. The contrast of dark and light played on craggy rock faces bearded with thin grasses. No one spoke as they waited to dock. John couldn't quite believe he was here.

Ginnie's face was bright with anticipation as she scanned the panorama. John still had nagging doubts about bringing her to this desolate land, but there was no going back now.

John clutched the railing. His need to escape sprang from more than his heartbreak over Helen's murder. He had hated the ruthless hierarchy of the "civilized" world. He shook his head to clear the specters of his past. Their entire social order had been left behind and they would have to build a new one from the ground up. This time, he had the chance to decide his future—his and Ginnie's—by the sweat of his brow, rather than trying to beat his way into an established system over which he had little control.

They eased toward the dock. He shivered against the cold wind biting his skin. Was he up to it? Was he the man he thought he was? Or would he crumple under the task?

Ginnie glanced up at him, cheeks pink and excitement in her eyes. Ah, to be so innocent again—to dive off that high dive without a thought. Her presence would spur him to reach deep within himself, no matter how difficult it would be. To bend this land to a plow would take every ounce of his strength. Only a fool would think homesteading a bleak land like Antarctica would be a walk in the park. Bodies would lie in that earth before this adventure was done.

The sky was a brilliant blue and the clean air intoxicating as he inhaled deeply to quiet his thumping heart. Tiny, windblown evergreens clung to the steep walls surrounding them. John perused the landscape of a continent virtually untouched by humans. During his environmental engineering career, he had witnessed the price of irresponsible pollution. Would humans defile this unspoiled land as they had the rest of the planet?

His thoughts drifted to Lowry, the woman who had dragged him into the last thing he wanted to get tangled with— politics. He knew it was inevitable on some level, but for God's sake, before he even reached the continent?

John had committed himself to derailing the land speculators while on board the ship, but he had told Lowry in no uncertain terms that his involvement ended the moment they hit land. He had to prepare for his run.

John heard his name and turned to find Lowry, the pale sun illuminating the beauty of her face. He waved and forced a smile. Whether it was good or bad, he had to admit that she was a force of nature.

Passing by him, she whispered in his ear, "Have you heard anything?"

He shrugged. "At the last session, I overheard Buck mention something about a meeting."

"What meeting?"

"Some guy named Durant and someone from Antarctica are meeting tomorrow morning."

Lowry's eyes grew wide. "This must be the big meeting! I knew they had to have someone on Antarctica giving them info." Nonchalantly, she gazed at the scenery, smiling like a tourist, then said out of the corner of her mouth, "John, you have to go to the meeting."

"I wasn't invited."

"Just say you overheard about a meeting and thought you were supposed to go. That's half-true. I have something for you to wear when you go." Then she disappeared in the crowd.

John stared at the approaching dock. *Great.*

An hour later, she knocked on the door of his cabin. With a sigh, he paused the maps he'd been studying of the Land Rush. He moved to the door, opened it, and Lowry slipped in.

John moved back to the monitor, blankly staring at the virtual terrain. Lowry glanced around the room.

"Ginnie's out with friends."

"Okay, good." She began pacing behind him. "Okay, this is the plan—you'll be in that meeting—with a hidden camera. All we need is a quick video of the principals at the meeting. Then you give it to us and you're done."

John bit the inside of his cheek.

She narrowed her eyes at him. "Is there something you need to tell me?"

Shrugging, he muttered, "I'm not a natural con."

"That's good news." She pointed to the monitor. "Remember, I already gave you information on the Land Rush tracts, even to the point of compromising the lands I want to claim."

John grimaced. She was right. "I said I'd do it, and I will. But after I turn over the video, I'm done. I have to finish planning my Land Rush tactics." He turned back to his maps. "You do remember our agreement—once on Antarctic dirt, I'm a free man."

Lowry pursed her lips. "Yes, and I will honor it." She dropped a bag onto the bed and pulled out a cap stitched with the Antarctic logo, the same one that all of the homesteaders had received in their welcome bag.

"I added a bonus to your cap. There's a camera in the middle A of Antarctica. You just flip this switch on the inside of the cap, and the camera is on."

"Fine!" he said, grabbing the cap. "But I need your assurance that after this my involvement ends." John faced her. "And what if you and your little troupe can't bring these thugs to justice? If I don't win their tract as agreed to, an unfortunate accident might be in my future."

"We have inside connections with the UN. My Uncle Nick and I have been consultants to them for years as a part of the Antarctic expedition. They've told us that if we can prove our allegations, they will shut down the scam before the Land Rush starts."

Lowry laid a hand on John's shoulder. "I know that you are also worried about Ginnie. I'll wait near your cabin and you can drop the cap in the hall, and then disappear, and they will never know how we found out."

After she left, John exhaled. *What have I gotten myself into?*

*   *   *

The next morning, John headed for Sergei's suite, his legs weak as his nerves flared. Before he turned the corner to the cabin, he stopped and pulled the cap off of his head. He leaned on the wall of the corridor, flipped it over, and stared at the tiny metallic camera. Exhaling, he switched the camera on and whispered, "God help me." He walked to the door of the suite, and paused, listening to the muffled voices in the room. With a deep breath, he knocked.

One of the underlings opened the door. John murmured, "Buck told me to come the meeting." Everyone turned their heads as he slipped into the room. The hush was palpable.

Nodding to Buck, John pasted a dumb smile on his face. He edged toward the large table surrounded by a group of men, several he knew, but there were a couple of new faces in the mix. "Buck mentioned something about a meeting?"

John moved his head slowly across the scene, videoing everyone in the room and a holomap of the Land Rush tracts on the table. The holomap imaged the desired tracts shaded in greens and unwanted in reds, with transport access, the proposed capital city of Amundsen, and the port overlain—a nefarious game of three-dimensional chess.

Setting his jaw, he fought to keep the stupid look on his face. This would put the group in control of the new city, the transport lines to the new farming areas, and the port. Lowry was right—they wanted it all.

Buck stepped toward him. "I didn't say shit to you about this meeting."

John made sure he videoed the two participants he didn't recognize. One was a distinguished-looking older man sitting in the corner. He appeared to be an outsider to the group; perhaps he was the Antarctic Connection.

A younger man, dressed casually, had been leaning over the holomap and appeared to be leading the meeting. He frowned at Buck, and then snapped at Sergei, "Get that son of a bitch out of here!"

Sergei strode over to John and grabbed him, shoving him toward the door. "Get the hell out. You weren't invited!"

John stammered, "I'm sorry. I thought I was supposed to come to a meeting and—"

With his lips taut, Sergei snarled, "Get out! NOW!"

"All right!" Turning, John shuffled out the door and down the corridor. He glanced back as he turned the corner, making sure no one was following him, and took off running.

Lowry was pacing the hall when John jogged to his cabin. Only her eyes betrayed her anticipation as he approached.

"Are they following you? Did you get the video?" She was shooting questions at him under her breath.

With a crestfallen looked, he shrugged. Her face fell. Then he doffed his cap with a grin to show her he had accomplished his mission.

"I don't know how to thank you, John. You've done a great service for Antarctica today." Her hands shook as she pulled the tiny disc out of the cap and clasped it in her hand. She handed back his cap. "Okay, you can disappear now."

John put the cap back on his head and leaned toward her. "You were right—they want total control. We would never be safe in a country run by those S.O.Bs." He waved her to follow him into the cabin. "Ginnie is having breakfast with friends. Come in and I'll show you."

With a smile, Lowry patted him on the shoulder. "Welcome to our troupe."

Once inside, he synced the disc to the monitor and hit play. He zoomed in on the holomap and Lowry's eyes grew wide at the damning evidence. All the key blocks were denoted with the acronym ANT.

She sucked in her breath. "That's our proof! It is ANT trying to monopolize the land grab. Those"—she tapped the screen—"are the plans for the proposed capital city, Amundsen. That man pointing to the center of the city is their head, Lorenzo Durant."

"ANT?" John asked.

"That's the syndicate that 'won' the transportation contract: Antarctic National Transport—ANT for short."

John pointed to the screen. "And the parcels in green— the city, transport routes, and tracts near the port—those are the ones our group is supposed to grab for them."

"Yeah. Bastards. They'd stand to make billions!" Staring at the screen, Lowry's face went white. She rewound and paused the video.

John glanced at her shocked face, then turned to the monitor with its frozen image of the meeting. "What's wrong?"

Lowry stuttered hoarsely, "Th-That man in the back."

"I figure he must be the Antarctic connection." John hit play. At the edge of the video, the older man slipped from behind the table when John focused on the holomap. "He slipped away just before the ANT guy told Sergei to throw me out. I didn't see him in the hall, so maybe he left the ship."

In a voice strangled with emotion, she whispered, "That man is my *father.*"

John's mouth dropped open. "Your father?"

Lowry shook her head as she stumbled away from the monitor. "My own father is in the middle of this."

John shook his head and gazed at the image on the screen. "Why would your father be involved?" He glanced around and realized Lowry was no longer in the room. "Lowry?" The door to the cabin was open, and he stepped out as she ran down the passageway. "Wait," he shouted. "Where are you going?"

He took off after her. She disappeared around the corner, but he caught sight of her on the long hallway. A housekeeper trundled a linen cart out of a cabin and he knocked a set of towels on the floor. "Sorry!" and kept running.

Lowry disappeared down the steps. She seemed to be headed to the cargo bay—and the ramp out of the ship. He followed the echo of her steps. A door opened and shut in front of him. He was gaining on her. He opened the door, blinded for an instant by sunlight spilling through the open doors of cargo bay. The dockworkers had connected the ramp to the ship and robo-lifts had begun the massive task of off-loading the crates and gear of the settlers.

Her long hair flowing behind her, Lowry zipped past the guards at the top of the ramp. Sprinting, he was right behind her. The guards screamed for them to stop, but they continued down the ramp, the shrill of whistles in their ears.

Lowry headed toward the city, racing through the covered passageway that connected the port to the center of the small mining town. He could hear her labored breath.

The tunnel split, and she took a right toward a domed building. Above the entrance, the Antarctic expedition emblem hung over the doors. She burst into the building, John steps behind her. She slowed to a walk as she strode through an empty reception area and into a large office. John entered just behind her, but remained at the door, leaning against the wall to catch his breath.

A hologram of Earth floated in the arched portion of the room, spinning on its axis, the weather patterns changing as the globe rotated. Behind the desk a monitor played a continuous loop of Antarctic scenery with the name DUFF WALKER floating in front of every photo.

Lowry stood in the middle of the room, breathing hard, staring at the man bent over a tablet at the desk. John recognized him as the older fellow in the infamous ANT video.

And as the photo montage behind the desk indicated, his name was Duff Walker.

She sprang at him like a lion tamer and shouted, "Why did you do it?"

Duff jerked up at the assault.

Lowry shook a finger at him. "You sold out Antarctica for what? What did they promise you?" She leaned over the desk. "I have video showing you at the meeting with the transport conspirators. I know it's ANT and I'm going to turn the video over to the UN authorities." With teeth bared, she yelled, "You son of a bitch!"

Several uniformed men burst through the door. The sergeant glared at John and motioned to another of the bodyguards, who pinned him to the wall. He turned to Lowry's father and asked, "Are you all right, Governor?"

Smiling, the man behind the desk waved the gorillas away, speaking with a soft brogue. "Yes—this is just a friendly father/daughter visit. You can go back to your duties. Shut the door behind you."

John's eyes grew wide. *Governor?*

The lead sergeant threw a warning look at John. He waved his arm and the trained goon released him from the wall. John exhaled and straightened his clothes.

With a cock of the sergeant's head, the guards left.

John studied the Governor. A handsome man, dressed in a fine wool suit, with a polished air of someone who takes pains with his appearance. But as he watched Duff, busy straightening his tie, he noticed something odd about his face—a suppressed current of hostility in the way his expression shifted from cold to hot in an instant. John had known men of that sort. Like a twisted rubber band, they could snap at any moment.

Lowry shook her head slowly. "This is serious business. You're allowing illegal acts to take place under your watch."

Duff snapped at her, "What am I to do? They have me in a box and there's no way out!"

Lowry touched the side of her face and blinked. "You owe Durant money, don't you? You swore your gambling was over!"

Her father's eyes became fixed to the top of the desk. She pointed at him with an accusatory finger. "You put yourself in a box. Now you're not only turning a blind eye to the corruption of this 'government,' you're helping the Russian mafia get a foothold into Antarctica!"

Duff met her gaze. "Lowry, even if they hadn't bought my gambling debts and held them over my head, they would have found someone else to blackmail." He shook his head. "These men are not to be trifled with. I know I'm not a perfect man, but let this go, not for my sake, but for yours."

Lowry's face softened, and then she leaned toward him. "You can be a better man. Take the high road. *Resign*. Let Antarctica have elections to start a new government."

Duff crossed his arms and tilted back in his chair. "You can have your elections, but Durant will win, either with him as president or as the puppet master of some fool." He exhaled. "I love you, Lowry, but my hands are tied; there's nothing I can do." He pointed at her. "I'm not kidding about these thugs. Watch your back." He nodded toward John. "I hope he's your bodyguard."

Lowry stared at Duff. Her shoulders sagged, and her hand touched her stomach as if she was nauseous. The tense silence between them was deafening. With a grimace, she pivoted, and stalked toward the exit. She glanced at John and cocked her head toward the door. "Let's go."

As she turned away, Duff glanced up, and the initial charm which had been present on his face was gone, replaced with a deep rage. Swallowing hard, John followed her out, with a bad feeling in his gut. This game had just begun.

CHAPTER 7

Anger and disappointment dogged Lowry's steps back to the ship. "Why can't Dad change?"

It was wishful thinking that somehow all the barriers would drop between them, that some epiphany would occur and that she and her father would have a loving relationship. It would never happen. He was a little man—not in height, but in character. His spirit had not survived a violent past. It had been broken long ago by his drunkard father.

She pressed her fingers to her temples, trying to skirt around her bad memories, the way one avoids a dead animal in the road.

John caught up with her and touched her arm. "What's going on?"

With a slow shake of her head, she gazed at John. "Sure you want to know?"

John grimaced. "No, I'm not sure, but I need to understand the situation."

She sighed. "Okay, but it's not pretty." They walked up the ramp of the ship. "My father is a 'functioning' alcoholic and gambler, who drowned any hope for adulthood in a bottle of booze. He's one of those people with a varied career path. In other words, he couldn't keep a job for long."

"How did he get down *here?*"

"Remember my Uncle Nick? My dad's brother. He had taken a job in Antarctica as a geologist with the first UN expedition, and my father followed him after he lost a job in the States. Uncle Nick got him on a short-term project, and then Dad snagged a minor position in the temporary government created for Antarctica. Within a few years, he'd charmed his way—or snaked, depending on your point of view—into the provisional Governor's post. Not that it's an esteemed role. It mainly deals with such high-powered issues as backed-up septic systems and black-fly invasions. But in his shallowness, he's pleased to make a speech every year at the annual New Year festivities."

"Everyone has skeletons in their closets, but that one's a beauty." John looked at Lowry with a furrowed brow. "I wish you'd mentioned that your father was the Governor."

Lowry shrugged. "It never came up in conversation. Does it really matter? I didn't know he was involved with the scam, apparently sucked into it by gambling debts. Durant bought the debts and leveraged them to his advantage." With a wag of her head, she continued. "If Uncle Nick and I have any sway, he won't survive in a leadership role after the new government is formed.

"That's it in a rather large nutshell." Lowry squeezed John's arm. "I know it's been a lot to throw on you, but I want you to know that I appreciate all you've done."

"I'm not sure the game is over." At a buzz, John looked at a message on his phone. "Ginnie forgot to unpack her coat and wants me to meet her in the hold to get it out of the crate. She's heading that way and I don't want her down there by herself."

"I need to get the video from your room."

He pulled a small card out of his pocket and handed it to her. "You can borrow my back-up keycard. I'll swing by your cabin later and pick it up. Does that suit?"

"Sure."

Lowry walked along the hall to John's cabin, her stomach queasy. The screaming match with her father brought back memories from the past—ones that she preferred to keep locked away.

A decade past, she'd been a grad student on the International Space Station, freshly divorced. After a terrorist attack on the ISS, she had become an inconvenient witness, caught in a web of political corruption spun by the Attorney General of Amerada, Elliot Halder.

She closed her eyes. The face of Halder—a man with no morality—flashed into her head. Her youthful innocence of the world had been burned to a crisp by that conniving bastard. She had been the mouse, and he, the cat. She inwardly shivered. *I never want to feel that helpless terror again.*

Her father's role as a bit player in the tragedy had led to their huge fight, but it was Duff's willingness to be bought and sold that had revealed his failings as a man. And now Duff's flaws had resurfaced to be manipulated by a new puppet master pulling the strings.

Her fingers trembling, she swept her hair back. Whatever it took, it was imperative that Antarctica did not fall under the same shadow of immoral leadership. Durant and his ilk must not get their claws into her.

*   *   *

Emotionally drained, Lowry meandered along the corridor to the cabins. She stopped at a housekeeper's cart with a tub of small water bottles marked with CLEAN ANTARCTIC SPRING WATER on the front. She took one, opened it and guzzled the water. Exhaling, she put the bottle into the recycling bin and continued toward John's hallway.

She pulled out John's keycard just before she turned onto his hall, but stopped in mid-stride at the sound of muffled voices in the adjoining hall. Gasping, she recognized one of the voices—Sergei's. Lowry flattened herself against the wall and hid behind the corner, listening to their hushed conversation.

"Is this John's cabin?" Sergei asked.

With a snap of his fingers, Buck said, "Yep. Boy, that Pee-Wee hacked into the ship's computer like that—"

"Shut up, Buck."

Lowry heard the sound of the door latch opening and peeked around the corner as they disappeared into the room. Silently, she leapt toward the closing door, catching a glimpse of the two hoodlums gazing around the cabin. She slipped John's keycard at the edge of the jamb and the door slowly closed until it met the card, keeping a narrow slit open.

She squinted through the slit with only a thin sliver of the room visible. But she could hear their conversation.

Buck mumbled, "Nobody home."

"Look around," Sergei growled. "Something's rotten with that John guy—I smell it."

Amidst the sound of drawers and cabinets opening, Sergei passed the monitor, with the video frozen at the image of the ANT holomap and the ringleaders of the meeting. His head jerked up and his mouth tightened. "That asshole—he videoed the meeting!"

Lowry covered her mouth with her hand. *Shit.*

"We have to find the camera disc. It's gotta be close." He knelt and searched the desk area under the monitor.

Buck walked into her narrow line of vision, staring with his mouth open at the captured scene of the meeting on the screen. "Son of a bitch."

Sergei straightened up and backhanded Buck across the face, knocking him to his knees. "As I remember correctly, you vouched for him."

With his hand to his cheek, Buck staggered up. "Shit, Sergei. You know as well as I there was nothing connecting him to anybody gunning for us."

Ignoring him, Sergei found the tiny disc in the corner of the desktop. He lifted it to the light and studied it with narrowed eyes. Then he synced it to his watch. Watching the screen, he shook his head, and then clasped the disc in his fist. "Bastard." He snarled to Buck, "I've got it—I doubt he had time to make a copy. Let's get out of here."

A chill went down her spine. Lowry's mind whirled as the two approached the door. She pressed herself flat against the wall outside of the cabin. *What should I do?* Buck and Sergei were stealing the evidence they needed to stop ANT, and with the Land Rush only days away, it was too late for another chance.

With her jaw set, Lowry braced herself for a fight. The door eased inward and the small keycard fell onto the ground as Sergei stepped through the opening. With a puzzled look, he dropped his gaze downward at the motion of the card. His clenched left hand, still holding the disc, was fair game.

Lowry kicked his fist like driving a soccer ball into a net.

"God-dammit!" He screamed, clasping his hand. Like a coin, the disc flew across the hallway, hit the opposite wall, bounced, and then rolled across the carpet.

Lowry bounded to the tiny disc, swept it into her hand, and bolted down the hall.

"What the hell?" Sergei yelled. "Buck! She grabbed the disc! Get her!"

Lowry spotted a crew maintenance area, and skidded into the tiny room. She slid into a small, dark cabinet and shut the door. The sound of their footsteps thundered past, matching the beat of her heart.

She breathed shallowly, her mind whirling. *Where to go— where to hide?* The cargo bay. In the stalls with her mares. *Who would think to look there?*

Lowry gazed at the small disc in the palm of her hand. Was it worth losing her life? She stuffed it deep into her pocket, opened the cabinet door and slithered out. Her heart pounded as she crawled out of the crew service room and stuck her head into the corridor to see if they were gone or just waiting for her. *No one in sight.* With a sigh of relief, she stood, tiptoeing toward the stairway that led to the lower decks.

"There she is!" Buck's voice echoed in the hallway. "I knew that bitch was still around. Catch her!"

Lowry opened the door and flew down the stairs. Her skin prickled as she heard the door slam again and their footsteps— and labored breath—close behind. She burst into the cargo hold with them on her heels. She darted around a robo-lift and sprinted to the stalls, knowing there was no chance to hide.

Sensing something was wrong, Sparky leapt up, barking like mad.

Hadeel shied as Lowry threw open the door to the mare's stall. Lowry grabbed a handful of her mane and swung up onto her back. The mare reared, but Lowry hung on.

Sergei blocked the exit of the stall. The veins in his skinny neck throbbed. "Going for a ride?"

Lowry dug her heels into the mare's flanks, and Hadeel reared again, then bolted forward. Sergei dodged the horse but caught Lowry by an ankle, twisting her halfway off the horse. She clung to Hadeel's mane.

With the hair raised on his back, Sparky leapt between Sergei and Lowry.

Sergei yelled, "Get back, you mutt."

Sparky rushed him with a growl. He locked his teeth onto one of Sergei's legs. With a scream, Sergei lost his grip on Lowry's ankle. Swearing in Russian, he kicked the dog off with his boot.

Lowry righted herself and wrapped her arms around Hadeel's neck, fighting to stay on as the horse bounded sideways. Buck jumped in front of them, but the mare had had enough. With her ears pinned back, she forged ahead, slamming him to the ground with her passing shoulder.

The mare slid on the metal floor of the ship's hold, careening out of control across the deck. They headed for a patch of light—the open cargo doors. Lowry cringed as robo-lift moved a crate out, directly in front of them. The horse barreled toward the robo-lift as it beeped and scurried out of their way.

With crates piled to the ceiling, the only clear path was where the robo-lift was maneuvering. Hadeel's ears pricked forward and she headed straight for it.

The deckhands shouted for them to stop. One pointed at her.

Lowry glanced at him. *Yep, it's that crazy bitch again.*

Hadeel cleanly jumped the robo-lift and crate. Lowry slipped to the side as they landed, but pulled herself back into place as the horse raced out of hold of the ship. She squinted against the blinding sun as they thundered across the planks of the dock. Lowry felt rather than saw the mare leave the dock and find solid ground.

The mare raced away from the dock. She flew across gray limestone gravel and between monolithic boulders littering the ground—geologic leftovers from the massive ice sheets as they melted away. Her white coat sparkled in the sunlight and the reverberation of the mare's hooves echoed off the stark fjord cliffs. A dry, cold wind sucked the moisture out of Lowry's mouth. What a homecoming.

Hadeel stumbled over the rocks. To their left, the shimmering domed buildings of the mining town beckoned, and Lowry tried to twist the mare's neck toward them, but to no avail. The mare galloped toward the mountains in the distance. Lowry's eyes watered from the icy wind whipping her face.

Lowry finger's cramped as they gripped the mare's mane and her legs ached with the strain of clinging to her back. The chill penetrated her thin clothes, and she leaned over Hadeel's withers, clasping her arms around the warm muscles of the mare's neck.

Hadeel ran deep into one of the valleys near the port. Rocky walls towered above them, narrowing as they traveled farther into the gorge. At last, the horse broke into a trot, and then skidded to a halt, nearly hurling Lowry off.

The steep valley walls corralled the horse and she pawed the ground, trembling with fatigue. One hand at a time, Lowry stretched her cramped fingers. If she dismounted, Hadeel might take off again, leaving her far from the ship. Panting, Sparky caught up with them, and then collapsed on the ground.

Lowry heard shouts in the distance and looked back in panic, afraid to see Sergei and Buck chasing her. But it was John and Ginnie, hovering over the plain in a small hovercar, waving their arms. Crying with relief, she waved and slipped off the mare's back. She knelt and patted Sparky's head. *Saved by a dog and a bottle of Antarctic spring water.*

CHAPTER 8

John jumped off of the hover and ran to Lowry. "What happened?"

"When I got to your cabin, Buck and Sergei were inside, stealing the video. I snatched it from them and ran like hell." Lowry swayed and he reached out to steady her. Smiling, she held up the disc to show him. "And I have it!"

John stared at Lowry's tangled hair and dirty shirt. *She could have been killed.* He wrapped his arm around her. "Jesus! Are you all right? Are you hurt?"

She shook her head. "No, I'm fine! Tired, but okay."

They stepped back from each other, and John cleared his throat, self-conscious at his overt show of emotion. Ginnie stood beside Hadeel, petting the exhausted mare. "She was gorgeous jumping that robo-lift."

Lowry chuckled. "You saw the whole thing?"

John shrugged. "Ginnie and I had just gotten to our crate when we saw you riding bareback on a half-crazed horse with Buck and Sergei running after you. We grabbed a hover and followed you."

Lowry touched his arm. "Thank you, my friend."

Ginnie knelt and petted Sparky. "Poor Sparky looks exhausted."

Pricking her ears, Hadeel looked toward the city. With a puzzled look, Ginnie said, "Dad, what's that sound?"

A strange whirring noise echoed in the valley, and a great dust cloud rose from the direction of the port.

"Ginnie, can you hold Hadeel's mane?" While Ginnie held the mare, Lowry yanked off her belt, improvising a halter to hold the mare still.

The cloud billowed like a storm skimming across the land. John shaded his eyes from the sun and his heart beat in staccato. Four hoverbikes raced across the wasteland of glacial till, like horsemen from hell.

John had a bad feeling in his gut. These weren't tourists out on a joy ride, but thugs wanting to kill them. And they were sitting ducks, with no weapons to protect themselves, and no one else aboard the ship knew, or cared, that they had left.

Terrified, Hadeel reared, lifting Lowry off the ground.

"Whoa!" She pulled on the makeshift halter.

Ginnie held her ears as the deafening roar of the engines reverberated off the rock walls. Riders wearing black jackets and helmets drove into the small valley. They slowed to a stop in front of them, killing the engines. A hush dropped over the canyon as the dust enveloped the four riders, hiding them for an instant.

A breeze lifted the dust like a curtain on a stage. A man strolled toward them with an air of confidence and boyish charm. John recognized him as the head of ANT: Lorenzo Durant, the mastermind of the Land Rush scam.

Sparky trotted over to Lowry's side and sat, carefully watching Durant as he approached.

John had only briefly glanced at Durant during the meeting he had videoed. Now he studied the man. He looked to be in his mid-thirties, with short dirty blond hair, but his eyes had the icy luster of steel. John swallowed hard; he was in for a fight with this one.

Durant held out both of his hands to greet Lowry. With a charming smile and smooth European accent, he said, "Lowry! I do hope you'll forgive my being so familiar." Durant laughed. "I've heard so much about you, that I feel I've known you for years!"

Sparky growled.

Sergei called out, "Watch that dog—he's a biter."

Lowry said, "Yeah, he has a taste for Russian jerky."

John glanced at Lowry, and bit his lip to keep from smiling at the disdain on her face. She wasn't taking Durant's hook. She knew exactly who he was and why he was there.

Lowry crossed her arms as he approached. "Durant—"

He held his hand. "Please, call me Lorenzo."

She continued flatly. "Durant, I'll be honest with you. I don't like you, or what you are doing on Antarctica, and I'll do everything in my power to stop you."

His smile hardened. "How charmingly honest."

Durant pivoted to John and Ginnie. "I believe it's John, isn't it?" His smile broadened as he turned to Ginnie. "And who is this lovely young woman?"

John stepped between Durant and his daughter, and then nodded. "Yes, we had a brief encounter earlier. John Barrous, and this is my daughter."

Durant bowed slightly. "That 'encounter' is precisely why I'm here." He turned on his heel and began pacing in front of them. "We have a bit of a situation. I believe you have something that might prove awkward for me if it got farther than our little circle." He stopped and held out his hand. "I want it, now, if you don't mind?"

Sergei lifted a rifle from a scabbard on his hoverbike. Ginnie jumped behind John. Durant waved Sergei off. "No need for that, just yet. I'm sure these people are intelligent enough to understand it's in their best interest to hand over the video."

John tilted his head. "And how, may I ask, is it in our best interest?"

Like a carny running a crooked game, Durant smiled, lifting his index finger into the air. "I checked your background, John, and with the depth of your knowledge of science and art, you are a man I could use. You see, I want to create a cultural utopia in Antarctica."

John's eyebrow twitched. What was this guy selling?

Durant faced John and held out his hand. "I would offer you an opportunity of a lifetime. I can help you win your land

and satisfy your need for art and literature. I need someone to fill that void on my team."

He paused, staring at John. "The Land Rush is only the beginning. The vote will soon be coming to Antarctica, and I plan to be the first elected president."

"A rather lofty goal," Lowry sneered, "for a two-bit hustler."

Durant's lips thinned as the cloak of charm disappeared. He stepped toward John and in a cold voice, snapped, "Just give me the video."

Silence filled the valley as the adversaries faced each other, waiting for a break point.

A voice with a hint of a Scottish brogue echoed through the valley. "Heard you were back in town, Lowry girl."

They snapped their heads up in unison. Heavily armed men ringed the valley walls, rifles aimed at the gang.

Laughing, Lowry waved. "Uncle Nick!"

Durant's men edged backwards toward the bikes, with their rifles pointing at the men above them. Nick gestured with his rifle. "Maybe these men should move on back to the ship, so we can have a visit?"

Durant's scowl broke into a laugh. He made a slight bow toward to John and Lowry. "You may have won this battle, but you won't win the war." They returned to the hoverbikes and mounted, then Durant circled back toward them. "And trust me, I *will* win." He sped off, and Hadeel skittered sideways from the pebbles and dust sprayed over them.

Lowry stroked Hadeel's neck, calming her. She turned to John. "Lucky for us that Uncle Nick was at his retreat. He must have seen the ship in port, and then me and good old Hadeel, racing away from it like mad."

Nick and a few others descended into the valley. He gave Lowry a bear hug, then stepped back with a grin, tugging a strand of her hair. "It's good to see you, girl." He gestured with his thumb at the retreating hoverbikes. "Too bad Durant arranged your welcome-home party."

Lowry nodded. "I've got a lot to tell you." She turned and gestured to John and Ginnie. "Uncle Nick, this is John Barrous and his daughter, Ginnie. I met them on the ship."

John stepped toward Nick. Tall and lanky, his penetrating green eyes scrutinized John as they shook hands. The roughness of Nick's hands spoke of an outdoorsman, and John inwardly winced at the strength of his grip. He was exactly the type of man John had hoped to find in this wilderness.

John returned the frank look with a smile. "Pleasure to meet you, sir. And thank you for arriving just in time."

Nick shook his head with a grimace. "Believe me, it's my pleasure to be able to poke Mr. Durant. That scoundrel shouldn't be allowed on Antarctica." He cocked his head toward the hillside. "It may not be safe to go back to the ship just yet. Let's go to my place."

Lowry looked back at the mare. "What am I going to do with Hadeel?"

"Armando can lead her back to the ship using the hovercar." He glanced at John. "As long as John doesn't mind if he borrows it? Then I'll take you back to the ship in my vehicle."

"Armando is welcome to the hover. We appropriated it ourselves—the crew is probably wondering where it is."

Panting, Sparky hobbled over to Nick. He knelt and ruffled the fur on Sparky's head, and asked Lowry, "Is he okay?"

"He's just tired. Two of Durant's men attacked me on the ship which is why I jumped on Hadeel." Lowry dropped to her knees and hugged him. "Sparky bit one of them and probably saved my life."

Nick patted the dog's head. "Good boy. Thank you for saving my Lowry." He pulled a canteen from his knapsack and poured water into his hand. He offered Sparky a drink and the dog lapped up the water. Nick stood. "Come on, Sparky. You can go a little more, can't you, boy?"

Sparky stood and wagged his tail.

The group climbed the narrow path out of the valley and reached the ridge line. Nick pointed toward the port where *Destiny* was docked. "I watched her cruise in last night."

Nick led them along a narrow path, edged with tufted grasses and lingering snow. They rounded the next curve and before them was a small door set directly into the side of the hill.

Nick stopped in front of the door. "We're here." He turned and waved to the rest of the escort. "Thanks, boys, and watch yourselves."

With a big smile, Nick opened the door. "Welcome to my hideaway from the mining camp."

Like elves, John, Lowry, and Ginnie stooped through the doorway and entered the side of the hill. Lights brightened as they moved inside.

John and Ginnie gasped at the wondrous sight in front of them.

Nick had created a sanctuary inside of a mountain cave, with exotic, natural formations of stalactites and stalagmites. They walked farther in, and the lights automatically turned on in front of their steps, leading them deeper into the cavern. Ginnie oohed at the sight of delicate columns formed by calcium carbonate deposited over millions of years. Opalescent nodules dotted the ceiling, shimmering as they moved through the room.

Nick slipped around them, gesturing for them to follow him into the living area. Sunlight streamed through large windows set in the exterior rock wall with a line of vents along the top. He pointed to the windows. "I blasted away the rock and put in glass windows and ventilation ducts." With a smile, Nick tilted his head to the panorama below. "You can see the entire valley from here. I had a front-row seat to the showdown with Durant. And luckily, a few of my buddies were nearby."

John stepped up to the bank of glass. "Lucky for us." Shaking his head, he said, "This place is incredible! I assume this is now a dead cave? You don't appear to have any moisture seeping through the walls. Do you think the warming is going to change that?"

"I certainly hope not, but I'll admit it is something I worry about. I cross my fingers that it will stay dry, at least for my lifetime." With a grin, he winked. "But, I do have running water." He motioned for them to follow him. "I don't have many guests. Let me give you the grand tour."

The incredible cave formations continued into the kitchen. In the corner of the room, a dripping sound drew their attention to a bowl carved out of the rock, brimming with water. "Without the spring, I couldn't live here." He waved his hand to the wall. "On the back side of this wall is the bathroom with basic facilities, including a crude shower."

In a small alcove next to the kitchen, John pointed to a light fixture emitting a glorious luminescence. "What is this light?"

"Natural light, my boy, during the summers, I use fiber optics to pipe in the sun."

They moved into the bedroom, and delicate white minerals hung from the ceiling. "Here, I added fiber optic lights between the crystals, making a chandelier of the entire ceiling."

After the tour, they returned to the large living room, and sat in a circle of chairs.

Nick gazed at Lowry. "A lot has happened since you left Antarctica. That lovely gentleman you were having the conversation with is determined to be Antarctica's first president."

Lowry grimaced. "Yeah, that's what his majesty told us."

With a furrowed brow, John asked Nick, "We know he's a shyster, but what do we know about his background?"

Nick leaned forward in his chair with a scowl. "He's one of the vultures who sprung up in Europe after the years of post-Melt depression. He's smart and has powerful friends in key positions—especially in Moscow." He spread his hands. "Some say he's bribed half the politicians in the U.S. and Europe and blackmailed the other half! He's made millions, selling stock in this ANT company, which is supposed to set up the transport system. He has hooks into the UN, but they voted down the land grants he wanted by a narrow margin. The man has balls!"

John asked, "But why Antarctica? It's just a wilderness."

With a nod, Nick replied, "That is a good question. I'm not sure if it's the natural resources or a power play. Regardless, it's a land ripe for dominating."

Lowry said, "I've done a little research on him, but his family's names shifted with the wind, so his early life is pretty murky. But all evidence shows him growing up in the Ukraine, with his family always on the move. Not surprising, as there were rumors they headed a trafficking cartel—drugs, slaves, even illegal VR paraphernalia."

John blinked. "I hate to ask, but what's VR paraphernalia?"

"Virtual Reality suits and headgear, but the illegal part is the 'quality' of software they peddled—sex and violence, as addicting to some people as drugs."

Shrugging, Lowry continued. "The family had a few scrapes with the authorities, but deep connections to the Russian mafia and backdoor relations with the Kremlin. Anytime they crossed the line too far, they spread enough bribes to keep out of jail.

"As far as his early life, I doubt he was ever hungry; money never seemed to be an issue. When Interpol got serious, the family scattered, and the trail went dark. Around twenty-five years old, he re-emerged as a new man, literally creating Lorenzo Durant, a man of money and power, or a monster, depending on your point of view."

Lowry leaned forward. "But, we may have the ticket to his downfall." She cocked her head toward John. "John infiltrated their Land Rush scam, posing as a dupe—"

John grinned. "I was a natural."

Lowry rolled her eyes. "He took a video of the meeting that shows Durant pointing to the tracts ANT wants to grab."

Lowry dug the tiny disc out of her pocket and handed it to Nick.

Nick held the silver disc up, turning it in the light. "This ought to play well with my connections at the UN who hate Durant."

Lowry pursed her lips. "That's the good news." She shot a look at Ginnie, gazing out of the window. In a low voice, she continued. "The bad news is that Dad is also on the video. Durant has him in his pocket with called-in gambling debts."

Nick's eyes grew wide. "Damn it, Duff." Then he shook his head. "My own brother is up to his eyeballs in this mess."

Lowry touched his arm. "We've got to get that video to the authorities, no matter what it does to Dad."

"Yes, there's no question of that. The man will have to live with his own devils." Nick rubbed his mouth, and leaned forward, staring first at Lowry, then at John. "It'll be hell if this Durant cock gets his talons into Antarctica. They'll rename it Durantland before he gets through."

"Or New Russia," Lowry murmured.

Nick hit the arm of the chair with his fist. "Over my dead body, by God!"

John watched Nick's face flush as he sat quivering in fury. Perhaps to Nick, killing a dangerous man might not be any worse than eliminating a poisonous snake. John raised an eyebrow. *Maybe the brothers weren't so different after all.*

Exhaling, Nick rubbed the stubble on his chin. "Let's not dwell on this. Ginnie girl, help me get drinks and a snack for everyone, and I'll tell you a few stories of the opening of Antarctica, back in the good old days."

The two left the room, and John stared at Lowry. He scooted his chair nearer to her and whispered, "Tell me about your Uncle Nick. You keep pulling these rabbits out of hats. What's next?"

Lowry shrugged. "I told you. My uncle came here as a geologist on the first survey expedition."

"And he stayed? He must have been a young man. No wife, kids, nada?"

"There was a woman." Lowry glanced at him sideways. "Really like digging through the skeletons, don't you?"

"I'm not trying to pry, but it *is* getting juicy."

With a sigh, Lowry faced him. "It's a long, irritating story. My grandfather was a vicious bastard who beat my father and Nick, though the way my dad tells it, Nick was protected by my grandmother." She shrugged. "Regardless, the scars have never healed, and a deep hatred grew between them. Classic Cain and Abel."

Lowry ran her fingers through her hair. "While Nick was away at college, my father married my mother, Margaret. After Nick graduated, he returned home. Rumor was he fell in love with her. As the family story goes, Nick signed up for the Antarctica trip because of an 'incident' with my mother. You can imagine my father's anger."

John raised an eyebrow. *Rage seems to be a family trait.*

"To tell you the truth, I don't know what happened between my mother and Nick, but I do know one thing: he's a great man and a natural leader. He led the miner rebellion over the mining company's use of convict labor." She glanced around the room. "That's why he has this cave. He was under death threats for months and made this his home for his protection. He wound up liking it so much, he stays here whenever he can."

"Perhaps he should run for president once they set up elections."

She smiled. "He'd make a great first elected president. He feels that a government should perform certain tasks: protect the borders, keep transport and communication lines open, and limit the power of economic vultures like Durant. Beyond those functions, he's as near an anarchist as is possible. 'Keep the government off the backs of the workers,' is what he always says. He believes that a true democracy requires a strong free-enterprise system."

Lowry's mouth tightened. "I know folks at the UN, and I'll make sure that Nick's name is on the ballot for president. He has grass-roots support from the miners, and I'm sure the homesteaders will love him. He's what Antarctica needs in its infancy. He would be like George Washington at the birth of the United States." She put one hand out and then the other. "We have Nick on one hand and Durant on the other—what a choice!" Lowry shook her head. "Washington or Stalin as the first elected leader of Antarctica."

CHAPTER 9

The beeping of robo-dollies intermingled with the din of the crowd as the settlers descended from the ship.

"What a madhouse," John muttered as he and Ginnie watched their crates moving smoothly into a temporary warehouse near the dock where they would be stored until after the Land Rush.

The campsite in the distance bloomed with tents, and excitement snapped as loudly as the pennants bordering the camp. With the Land Rush two days away, final preparations were in high gear, and crews hurriedly erected water and food stations near the campground.

John looked over his shoulder. Supposedly the ANT scandal was over, at least for the time being. Once the video of the meeting got to the UN, Durant's contract for ANT had been suspended, but Durant himself had vanished. John crossed his fingers. *No news was good news?*

When the solar-electric dune buggy came off the ship, John drove it to their campsite and unfurled the solar panel to charge the battery. It was rugged, built to withstand the rough terrain of the Land Rush and fly like the wind. John checked over the vehicle for any problems that might have cropped up during the voyage. After the campsite was set up, Ginnie sat cross-legged on a blanket, sipping lemonade like a kid at summer camp.

Once the dune buggy's battery was fully charged, John climbed into the driver's seat and gestured to Ginnie. "Come on, Sunshine, let's take a shore excursion."

With a grin, Ginnie jumped in and they headed away from the base camp, past the crew erecting the framework for the Land Rush banners.

Ginnie pointed to the crew's hovercar. "Why aren't we using a hover for the Land Rush?"

"Speed mainly. Hovers aren't fast—at least as yet."

"I think the air cushion needs to push against a fairly level surface?" Ginnie held her hand out flat.

"Exactly. They're great for a continent with no roads, but they don't do well over extreme inclines like we'll experience during the Rush."

They drove onto a flat plain of land covered with hardy grasslands. He took the buggy through its paces, speeding over ridges of dirt and around piles of stones deposited by glaciers on their way to the sea. The buggy performed like a dream and seemed well worth the money he had spent to have it modified for the race.

John slowed as they dropped into a valley and crossed a patch of muddy tundra. At a large river, he parked the buggy on the high edge of the bank. Overhead, birds flitted across the flowing water, searching for dinner. They crawled out of the buggy and hiked toward the river bank across a field of tussock and Antarctic hair grass. It was deathly still; the only sound was the soil crunching under foot.

He shivered in the chill air and smiled to himself. They had made it to Antarctica. The beauty of the valley took his breath away. The river flowed around boulders sculpted by the melting ice sheets. Patches of buttercups clung to the river's bank, growing in soil littered with fossils of creatures that had preceded the ice caps.

He winked at Ginnie. "Do you think any ghosts were left behind?"

Ginnie raised an eyebrow. "Yeah, and maybe we'll finally find Bigfoot," she teased, sticking her tongue out at him.

Shrugging, John said, "It would be interesting if there were humans here before the ice sheet formed."

They hiked down toward the river's edge. Ginnie laughed as she slipped on the loose gravel along the bank.

"Are you okay?"

"I'm fine." She picked her way to the water's edge.

"We need to be careful. I'm not sure if this is a permafrost area or not." He grinned. "We don't want to be swallowed by Antarctica the first day."

The river was high, filled to capacity from melting snow in the mountains, rushing its way to the nearby ocean. The water glistened in the sunlight, rolling like a festive Chinese dragon, roaring with power.

John wanted to pinch himself. Was he really here? Was he, John Barrous, actually standing on the continent of Antarctica, contemplating the view, like a tourist on vacation? A few short months ago, he was in an office, trudging to work every day. Now his dream of freedom from a stagnant Old World unfolded before his eyes.

Other creatures of the Earth had already moved to Antarctica. Birds were abundant; dogs, cats, and livestock came with the miners, and the lowly mouse had made itself at home in the mining station. He wondered if they thought it strange to now live on another continent. He shook his head. Of course not. Only humans think living is strange. Other creatures just live; they fight, they eat, they procreate.

John knelt and picked up a handful of loose soil. He sifted it through his fingers, letting it fall back to the ground. Not a sliver of plastic or trash—not yet, anyway. He stood and brushed the dust from his hands, feeling like an intruder to this pristine land.

The slanting rays of the sun signaled it was time to return to camp, and John waved to Ginnie. She sauntered back, showing him the freshwater shells she had found along the shore. They jumped back in the buggy, and John punched the accelerator, pressing their heads into the seats. Ginnie screamed in joy as he maxed out the speed of the buggy, bouncing along the rocky shore and laughing as they zoomed back to camp.

That evening, the camp was boisterous with the adventurers enjoying dinner, drinks, and music provided by the UN staff. Children and adults danced in the firelight, parents as excited as their children to be so close to their dreams of free land.

John saw Lowry near the edge of the bonfire and he sidled over to her with two glasses of wine. They toasted to the night, and then John asked, "How's Durant and the boys?" With a grin, he winked. "I don't see them here tonight."

Lowry shrugged. "I heard they were in 'discussions' with the authorities on alleged improprieties with their charter."

"Good. It sounds like the Land Rush scam has been sidelined."

Lowry raised her wine and clinked his glass. "Here's to the hero of the hour."

John smiled. "You are the real hero in this story, so I'll drink to you."

She tilted her head toward him, and they drained their glasses. "John, I'm taking the mares out for some exercise tomorrow. Do you and Ginnie want to join me? We'll be riding out to a picnic spot I know about an hour from here."

"Ginnie's going to a *Youth Orientation to Antarctica* program tomorrow." Swallowing hard, he silently waited for her reply.

"I'd be happy if you came with me. It's a beautiful spot." She gestured with a hand. "The mares are dead broke. They're very easy to ride."

"Okay. What time?" His insides squirmed at the thought of being alone for the day with Lowry. Scary on several levels.

"I'll pony one over and pick you up near the starting line at eight tomorrow morning."

John coughed. "Okay, see you in the morning."

*　　*　　*

Up at dawn, John grabbed coffee and breakfast, and took Ginnie to the meeting point for the youth program.

With his second cup of Joe, he waited beside the tall metal support set last night at the starting line, ready for the banner of the Land Rush to be placed. Lowry cantered across the field, riding Hadeel and leading another gray mare, already saddled.

"Good morning!" she called out, dismounting in front of him.

"Top o' the morning to you, too," he replied, not knowing why he'd used that hackneyed phrase. The beautiful horses sported Australian-style saddles. He exhaled a nervous breath. *Here goes nothing.*

He tied his water bottle on the back of the saddle and mounted. Lowry adjusted his stirrups, remounted, and they turned away from the camp area.

"It looks like you've ridden before," she said, nodding.

"When I was a kid, I rode at summer camps in Colorado."

"It's like riding a bike, you never really forget how."

The air was cold and dry as they trotted toward the hills. A breeze kicked up and the mare skittered under him as a dust devil spun across the glacial till. They slowed to a walk as the terrain got rougher and entered a narrow canyon. John jumped as a cold splash of water dripped onto his shoulder from a high ledge. The canyon narrowed further and sandwiched the horses and riders into single file.

John's brow furrowed; if he stretched his hands out, he could touch both sides at once. Rocky knobs jutted from the walls, like stone fists threatening to strike his legs. He hoped the nag wouldn't panic.

They turned a corner. Lowry stopped her mare and glanced back. "Just ahead, it gets really narrow for about ten feet, so hold your legs close to the horse."

John muttered, "Much narrower and I'll need a skinnier horse."

The sheer rock walls rose above them. The wind whistled eerily as they threaded their way into the crevice. Ears pricked forward, the mare snorted at the fluttering sounds of birds nesting in the deep cracks of the sheer walls.

The rock walls widened and John gasped as they entered a luscious, emerald oasis. The air was humid and warm in this isolated valley. John turned to the sound of falling water, cascading into a small pool near the center of the meadow. A warm haze hugged the surface of the pond, glowing from a narrow shaft of sunlight. Delicate dragonflies hovered above the surface of the clear water.

Pale green tufts of grass grew between the marble stones on the bank of the pool, and ancient blue-green algae covered the rocks beneath the surface of the water. Small, exotic trees with branches like palm fronds leaned over the warm water. He breathed in a voluptuous scent, emanating from the orchid-like blossoms hanging from the rocks on either side of the waterfall.

They halted the horses near the pond and dismounted. John shook his head at the wonder of this Shangri-La, he asked Lowry, "How did you find this place? What *is* this?"

"Uncle Nick and I stumbled onto it years ago on one of our expedition trail rides. This is a thermally active area, and the meadow exists because there must have been a warm pocket in the ice surrounding it, with just enough light through the thin ice above to keep the plants alive—like a greenhouse." She pointed at a waterfall streaming down the rock face and then gurgling its way into the pool. "That cold water mixes with the boiling water percolating up from fissures below. The blend creates a pool of water as warm as a hot tub. Because of the thermal activity and protected location, the air temperatures have remained much warmer than the rest of the area. It's hard to believe, but the natural fauna pre-existing the ice caps survived."

"It's stunning. Does anyone else know about this place?"

"No, just Uncle Nick and myself." She wagged her finger at him. "Don't tell anyone—I know it will be discovered soon enough, and then, so long to my retreat!"

"Maybe you should claim it?"

"Unfortunately, it's not within the designated Land Rush tracts. I'm trying to establish a preserve area, which would include the oasis."

Lowry untacked the horses and hobbled them in a patch of grass, while John spread out a blanket near the edge of the pond. She untied the saddlebags and dropped them beside the blanket. She knelt, pulled out a thin wooden board and laid out a lunch of cheese, dried sausage, and bread.

John rubbed his rear end, and with a sigh, gingerly sat on the blanket. "My butt needed a little rest after that ride." He removed his boots and socks and splashed his feet in the warm water.

Lowry pulled a bottle of red wine and two camp cups from the saddlebag. She opened the wine and filled the cups. "Come and get it before I throw it out," she said.

John pulled his feet back onto the blanket and scooted closer to her.

They clinked cups. "Cheers."

"Cheers." He gulped the red wine and held out his cup for more. He pointed to his rear with a grin. "For medicinal purposes."

She laughed and refilled his glass, then nodded toward the lunch. "You'd better eat, or you'll get sloshed." Lowry raised an eyebrow. "I don't want you falling off the horse and scaring her."

John stuck his tongue at her. "Since I'm starving, your words are my command."

They layered the cheese and sausage onto the chunks of bread and devoured the meal. After lunch, they relaxed in the warm air. A tiny iridescent hummingbird buzzed past them, thrusting its beak into the pale pink orchid over Lowry's head, before disappearing into the palm fronds hanging over the water.

"What a little beauty!" John said. He picked up the wine bottle and refilled their glasses.

With a smile, Lowry looked into the branches, trying to catch sight of the bird again. "I've only seen the one species of bird in the oasis, but I'm not sure what it's called."

John gazed at Lowry's profile. "Lowry's Hummingbird," and raised his wine glass to her. "Let's have a toast to The Oasis."

Clinking glasses, they killed the bottle of wine, and then Lowry brought out chocolate squares for dessert.

After lunch, John peeled off his sweater and wadded it up into a pillow. He lay back on the blanket, breathing in the scent of the fragrant blossoms.

Lowry finished her glass of wine and stood. "I'm getting hot." She glanced at him. "I hope you don't mind if I take off some layers." She slipped off her riding pants, down to her underwear. She sat back and splashed her bare legs into the pool.

He bit the inside of his mouth and swallowed hard. "Great idea." He stripped off his pants and joined her by the edge of the pond. The steam twisted in slow spirals as they dangled their feet in the warm water.

Emboldened by the wine, John tapped her leg, letting his hand linger for a moment. "You know, you've been driving me crazy. I think about you all the time."

Lowry laughed. "Maybe you need to take the waters to cure your state of mind." She shoved him into the pool.

John plunged into the clear blue water. He opened his eyes and swam through the hot and cold currents swirling around the small pool. Turning back to where Lowry was sitting, he broke through the surface of the pond, with a broad grin. Then, he reached up and yanked her into the water.

Lowry screamed. For a moment, she sank beneath the surface, then kicked off the rocks and came up behind him. Laughing, she dunked his head under the water.

He twisted in the water and found his footing on a rock near the edge. John pulled her to him and they locked eyes. He ran his fingers through her hair and with a gentle touch, caressed her cheek. Uncertain, John hesitated, but she looked at him, lips open. He pulled her into a kiss, her lips soft and warm. With a moan, he kissed her hard and her body molded to his.

John gently lifted her from the water and onto the blanket. He crawled out of the pool and nuzzled her neck, then moved to her ear, her scent roiling over him. For a second, they broke apart and he stared at her. Breathless, she pulled him down into a deep kiss. His hands shook with pent-up desire as he stroked her body, slowly peeling off the rest of her clothes, while Lowry pulled off his. He laid a trail of kisses down her body and satisfied her desires. Then he found his way back to her mouth. He clutched her hair, pulled back her head and kissed her hard. Lowry wrapped herself around him, and they made love.

Afterwards, they laid near the pond, the water and sweat drying on their skin. John's breathing calmed and he kissed her cheek, then shifted onto his back, with Lowry's head on his shoulder. He smoothed back her wet hair as her breath slowed, and with a little twitch, she fell asleep in his arms. Lowry's warm body lay next to him, and he sighed, staring up at the small patch of sky above him.

A shadow fell over the oasis as a cloud drifted past. In the dim light, a wave of guilt washed over him. The ache for love and his passion for Lowry had blinded him. In this beautiful Eden, he lay with Lowry, her skin soft and warm against his. A woman he barely knew.

Helen had been a wonderful wife and mother; witty and loving. Emotionally, he had withered and died with her passing. *Hadn't she had been the love of his life?* He clenched and unclenched his fist. *How many true loves can one have?*

But he knew that Helen, a woman of grace and gentleness, would never want to immigrate to the wilderness of Antarctica.

His insides felt like butterflies, but was this a sensation of love? His heart had been numb since Helen's death, but the pain—and panic—of its resurgence was overwhelming. With one door closed, had another opened? He exhaled. *Or was it a trapdoor beneath him?*

What would Ginnie's reaction be to a blossoming relationship with another woman so soon after her mother had died? And his daughter meant everything to him.

Ah, these consequences of desire.

Lowry sighed in her sleep, and he swallowed hard as her breath touched his skin. He glanced at her lovely face and bit his lip. He felt an animal magnetism with Lowry that he had never felt with Helen. Adventurous and brave, Lowry regarded the world with a quiet confidence, and yet there was an innocence about her that he found beguiling. John knew if he were younger he would feel intimidated by her.

Lowry awoke with a start. She murmured, "How long did I sleep?"

Shifting under her, John blinked at her, and then coughed and averted his gaze. "Not long."

Out of the corner of his eye, he caught the puzzled expression on her face.

She propped herself onto her elbow, staring at him. "What's wrong?"

He turned his face away. "I'm sorry, but I've been feeling a bit—my wife's death—"

She put her hand on his arm and squeezed lightly. "I see. Don't worry, John, I understand."

Startled by the intimacy, John sat up. "I think Ginnie will be getting back soon." He slipped away from her, instantly missing her warm body. He grabbed his clothes and got dressed. "A little chill in the air," he mumbled.

Lowry replied in a thin voice, "Yeah, I noticed it, too." Her face was pensive as she sat up, gathered her clothes and pulled them on. "We'd better start back. It's getting late."

Silently, they packed everything, and as they mounted the horses, John kicked himself for ruining a lovely day. But what could he do? It was too soon. The remnants of Helen still haunted him. He swallowed hard—dearest Helen—and became lost in his thoughts as if Lowry wasn't there.

They reached the camp, and he dismounted, handing the reins of his horse to her. He cleared his throat and said, "Good luck during the Land Rush."

"Yeah. Thanks." Lowry said, clipping a rope on his mount's halter. She nudged her horse into a canter, and they disappeared behind the tents.

CHAPTER 10

A chill wind buffeted the tent, and shivering at a rickety camp table, John pulled a blanket over his shoulders. He closed his eyes and took deep breaths, trying to calm his pounding heart. Tomorrow was the Land Rush. Would all of his planning pay off? His papa always said it was better to be lucky than good. And luck he would need.

He glanced at Ginnie, who lay sleeping on her cot. He not only had to worry about his hide, he had to think about Ginnie's too. They could both die tomorrow. Or worse, something could happen to her and he would be left to confront unimaginable pain and guilt. He pushed the thoughts from his head. *Why ruminate on the what-ifs?*

John studied the holomaps one last time, then took a swig of coffee and made a face. Cold as ice. *I guess I've been sitting here longer than I thought.* He needed to rest his body even if he couldn't rest his mind. He turned out the lights, then lay on the cot and tucked the blanket around him.

To his irritation, thoughts of Lowry and their afternoon interlude surfaced. A surge of remorse swept over him. He closed his eyes and sent a question up to Helen. *What am I supposed to do?*

Their marriage had faced many ups and downs. After the twin boys died, they had nearly divorced. Ginnie's birth had healed their marriage. And now, Ginnie was all he had left. It was hard to look at his daughter and not think of Helen, making his guilt more difficult.

There were empty rooms in his heart where the echoes of their love still existed. He remembered the words she had once said to him: "Life is God's breath into a body. At some point, He has to inhale."

"Goodbye, Helen," he whispered. A tear crept into his eye, and he wiped it away on the pillow case. He sighed, knowing in his heart, that Helen wouldn't want him to grieve forever. It was time to move on.

Still unable to sleep, John sat up in bed, reaching out to caress the small disc by his bed. He carried it everywhere, this holovideo of the graves of his wife and boys. He knew he might never return home and knew of no other way to visit them.

John lay down again and rotated the disc in his hand. The light from the charger glinted on the smooth surface, and he finally faced his dilemma of conscience. An epiphany had hit him as he lay with Lowry.

Helen's death had freed him.

Groaning, he clutched the disc in his fist, pressing it onto his forehead. If she hadn't died, he would still be commuting every day to a job he hated. This was his true guilt: not wild sex with another woman, but the realization that his wife's murder had allowed him to pursue his dream of a new life.

Like a kick to the solar plexus, his insides twisted in pain and he curled into a fetal position on the cot. He had been a good husband and father, but Helen had known that he hated the chains of corporate life. They had spent weekends traveling to the countryside, but both knew it was only a dream to be fulfilled after retirement.

John replaced the disc in his satchel beside the bed and stared up at the roof of the tent as it breathed in and out with the wind. He cocked his head, listening to a child crying in the darkness of the camp.

After the child quieted, John lay in the darkness examining the arc of his life. At birth you're king of the hill, but honesty displaces ego, grain by grain. Life is a humbling experience.

He was a stubborn and independent soul, desiring to live fully and without equivocation. He thought about his childhood; he hadn't had many friends. Occasional overnight camping trips with a few good buddies and some painful first dates—life lessons learned and earned. Through it all he refused to be conventional. He had been an athlete, yet he studied science, wrote poetry, made love to a few girls. He grinned. *Fewer than I want to admit.* He imagined their faces: his first crush, Clarita, with curly dark hair, followed by wild, funny Stephanie in college, and lastly, his sweet, lovely Helen.

He had stampeded through his twenties with the herd of society, and now he wondered why he'd been running. The momentum of a lifetime wasn't easy to overcome. Like a hooker who needed the money, but hated the work, he hadn't known how to get out of the corporate rat race.

John touched the chain around his neck and felt for the Land Rush key. Despite everything, he hoped Helen would be proud of him for taking this last chance to fulfill his destiny. If only for an instant, he had unchained himself from the stifling culture in which he had been a square peg in a round hole.

A gust popped the flap of the tent and his thoughts returned to the next day's event. He clenched his fist. There was no second chance. He had to win his tract.

He fell asleep, dreaming of a footrace along the shore of the ocean, with a devilish Durant on his left, flanked by a White Rabbit Buck and Mad Hatter Sergei. A throng of desperate souls threatened to overtake them no matter how fast they ran. When the shoreline turned, and the end was in sight, the racers were neck and neck. John laughed as he burst over the finish line, but just as he stopped to rest, the sunlight broke through the clouds. Shielding his eyes, he saw Lowry, her long hair draped around her nude shoulders, standing on the rocks above him.

CHAPTER 11

The thin, crisp air stung John's throat, and he squinted in the bright sun at the odd assemblage of humanity and vehicles sprawled around him. The Great Antarctic Land Rush banner hung between the temporary metal frame, the sides lined with neat rows of UN flags. News crews from across the globe staked out the territory beyond the starting gate, aiming their cameras toward the homesteaders to capture the onset of the race.

Everywhere, people waited; they played cards, talked, anything to pass the time. A group of miners from Antarctica huddled together, casting dubious looks at the invading cast of characters. He recognized a couple of competitors from the ship: the young Japanese man with an acne-scarred face and the tall, middle-aged Nigerian sporting a leather jacket.

Misfits from around the world, willing to fight for a new life. Faces around him had a hungry look as they sized up the competition. They had waited a lifetime for this chance, and no one wanted to be too friendly with someone they might end up killing later in the day.

John flinched as a flag snapped in the wind, and then bent down by the buggy, clutching a handful of soil. He wondered if the authorities had fully thought out what they were doing. They'd decided to open the Antarctic territories with an Oklahoma-style race for land. A great PR event to show back home, but a big risk as well. Who knew how much blood would soak into the dirt today? Of course, the media would edit out anything too gory from the footage, with just enough blood to start the good folks back home salivating. The stakes were high—some land had good soil and water and some didn't. There was no doubt on the viciousness of this race.

Everyone here had an agenda. Most folks wanted to farm; there were government subsidies for those who chose that route. Farming would stabilize the fragile Antarctic ecosystem and was vital to the longevity of the continent's habitation. Others were bent on setting up towns to supply all these madcap homesteaders. Towns, which didn't exist one day, would be bustling the next. People had to eat, buy clothes, and do laundry. Humans never stop being human.

John heard the snort of an animal and blinked in disbelief at the silhouette of a woman dismounting from a horse. "Lowry, you're using a horse to win your homestead?" He momentarily forgot the barrier that had risen between them, due to his inept handling of his feelings.

With a deadpan face, Lowry glanced at him. "Just wait until the gun goes off and when the terrain gets rough, you'll wish you had one too." She turned away and checked the girth of the saddle.

He felt a thorn of disappointment in her look and heat rushed to his face. He clenched his teeth and looked down, pretending to check his tires. If she couldn't understand his feelings, perhaps he'd made a mistake all the way around. Maybe she was a bitch. At least thinking so made it easier for him to not get involved with her. The last thing he needed was to get romantically entangled with someone the second he landed—especially with the emotional baggage he needed to sort through.

John gazed again upon the scene, trying to cement it in his memory. People so desperate for a new life, they would leave their homes and families far away to try conquering a new world. The immigrants were already calling their homelands the Old World, psychologically breaking with what they once knew.

"And here I am, a regular Davy Crockett," he mumbled.

The organizer of this party bellowed for everyone to line up at the starting line. The crowd burst into cheering and applause. Lowry fastened her helmet and vaulted onto the mare. John jumped into the buggy and then looked around for Ginnie. *Where the hell had she gone?*

She squeezed through the crowd, yelling, "I'm coming!" and leapt into the passenger's seat.

"Buckle up, this ain't no kiddie ride."

John inched the buggy closer to the starting line, toward the freedom he had left everything for. The band played a march, his heart thumping to the beat of the base drum.

The announcer reviewed all the rules and regulations of the event. Referees lined up in front of the contestants to control them. John muttered, "Fat chance."

The droning voice wore on John's nerves. His knuckles whitened as he gripped the steering wheel of the buggy. "Come on!" he said under his breath.

The gun went off. John slammed the accelerator to the floorboard. The tires spun, then caught, and the buggy jumped forward. Lowry sprang by them on her horse, and he grunted an expletive.

Ginnie rode shotgun, her duty to watch for interlopers and obstacles. They headed for their top choice, and by the looks of it, they had competition. Four groups all headed in the same direction—a contest to be the first to punch the locking key into the stake at the northwest corner of the tract.

They barreled forward, bouncing over dry channels flanked by boulders. Even the hologram sessions hadn't prepared him for the roughness of the land, but they continued at top speed. Racing into a narrow pass, the competitors squeezed closer as the walls narrowed.

"Watch your left!" Ginnie shouted to him as the miners' vehicle swerved toward them, challenging to be the frontrunners into the valley below the ridgeline. John had the pedal to the floor, but the miners had more juice and shot into the lead, their wheels throwing dust into John and Ginnie's faces.

"Dammit!" He gritted his teeth and followed them through the gap, the rest of the pack on their tail.

The buggy jolted over a rough set of rocks, but they picked up speed down the slope.

At the bottom of the valley, a sinuous river cut through marshy lowlands. Their route would take them away from the marsh. Getting stuck in the mud was not on his to-do list. As they reached the base of the hill, a three-wheeler painted with a Brazilian flag bore down upon them.

John shouted, "Watch the three-wheeler on your right, Ginnie!"

Over the din of racing vehicles, John heard a deep cracking sound, and gasped as the ground fractured under the weight of the three-wheeler, and like a trap door opening on a stage, the Brazilians disappeared as if they had never existed.

"Permafrost!" John shouted. The expanding fissure zipped toward John and Ginnie's buggy. John held the wheel tight, keeping the accelerator smashed to the floor. With speed and luck, perhaps they might dodge the cavern.

With a shriek, Ginnie pointed. The ground was collapsing ahead of the buggy. The front wheels bounced over, but the rear tire slid off, dragging on the edge of the crack. They slammed forward into the shoulder harnesses.

"No, no, no!" John yelled, as they spun to the side, pitching the buggy toward the deepening crevasse.

A second more and the other three tires caught traction, popping the rear tire free, and the buggy careened ahead, shoving them back into the seats.

Every cell in John's body burned. He had never felt such exhilaration. Adrenaline shot through his limbs and he reverted to his animal instincts, thriving on power and speed. He blocked the Australian truck through a curve. At the crest of the next ridgeline, he flattened the pedal to the floor. John and Ginnie swept alongside the miners' modified Jeep to their right.

A wall of dust in the distance caught his eye. Perfect—a dust storm to make the race more interesting.

"Tighten your goggles, Ginnie. Look at the horizon."

As the storm approached, he recalled a narrow pass into the next valley, which might shield them from the brunt of the storm. He chewed his lip. *That would bring us to the southwest corner of the property . . . and then we'd cross the tract to reach the stake.* The decision would make or break them.

"We're taking the scenic route, Ginnie." He cut toward the alternate pass. They were committed. A team of rough women—in a rougher jalopy—made the break to the pass as well and had a slight jump on their buggy. Both vehicles raced toward the narrow opening—first in, first out. John closed the gap with the women, but then a pop came from the jalopy's engine, with a blue flame shooting out the back of the vehicle.

"Jesus Christ!" John yelled, swerving away, narrowly missing the smoking vehicle as they passed.

The jalopy burst into a fireball. The face of the driver melted against the glass, in mid-scream.

With a shriek, Ginnie clutched John's shoulder. The women's jalopy crashed into a boulder and a second explosion finished the job. John clenched his jaw. If they had been any closer, they would have been in the roast as well.

Ginnie was crying, but there was no time to console her. If there was any silver lining to the madness, at least they were first into the gap.

The sandstorm struck with a vengeance. Like shards of glass, blowing sand pummeled his face. "Get your head down, Ginnie."

Ginnie crouched in the buggy, holding her hands over her ears as the rat-tat-tat of the pellets beat the fiberglass body. Dust swirled in front of them, and he wiped the dirt from his goggles with his sleeve, then aimed for the pass.

The effect of the storm died as the walls rose on either side of them. The buggy bounced from side to side over piles of loose rocks, every jolt threatening to crash them into the side of the gorge.

The passage widened as they left the pass.

He smiled. "I smell water!"

Ginnie pointed to a stream of water gushing from a crevice in the rocks.

Shouting, he punched the air with his fist. This was on the land he wanted to claim.

John and Ginnie burst onto the valley floor. No one in sight. They flew across the ground as he searched for the stake.

A small object moved vertically down the ridge in front of them. As they came nearer, the horse and rider reached the valley floor, galloping across the flat surface toward the west. *Lowry and her blasted horse.*

"Bloody hell! If she claims our fucking parcel, I'll shoot that nag of hers," he mumbled under his breath.

He stomped the pedal flat and the buggy flew, bouncing across uneven ground and skirting clumps of low brush.

Lowry's horse sprinted past and kept going west. John let out a sigh of relief.

Ginnie pointed to the east. "Dad, on our right."

He squinted. Dust rose from a vehicle clipping along toward the northwest corner—of their land. John maxed out the buggy. "Hold on, Ginnie!"

The key around his neck bounced against his chest as they catapulted over rocks. A hundred meters to go, and a Jeep was closing in. A reflection hit his eye. A gun pointing directly at them.

"Get down on the floorboards!" he shouted to Ginnie. She crouched, then edged up with a small pistol.

John's eyebrows shot up. "Where the hell did you get that?"

"Mother gave it to me for my protection, before she died. She didn't want to tell you. She knew you'd worry." Her face was determined, her pistol cocked. "I'm not letting those bastards get our land, Dad."

John saw the stake, then a bullet whistled overhead. The Jeep barreled toward them. Sergei was bent over the wheel and Buck was pointing the gun.

"I thought those son of a bitches were on their way back to the U.S." John said under his breath. He turned to Ginnie. "It looks like some old friends are calling on us."

A pop-pop-pop of gunfire ripped across the side of the buggy.

"Get down!" he screamed to Ginnie.

John jerked the wheel to dodge the line of fire, but the buggy lost traction and slid across the glacial till. Ginnie screamed as they careened sideways into a berm of rocks. The buggy flipped, rolling over the berm and down a slope, the fiberglass fender tearing off with a ripping sound.

Showered in dust, they came to a stop, swaying upside down in the harnesses. John snarled at the sound of Buck's laughter. He released his harness and crashed against the seats. Then he unbuckled Ginnie's harness and caught her in his arms.

They crawled out and John yelled to Ginnie, "Stay behind the buggy." He ran toward the stake, fumbling to get his key ready. A bullet burrowed into the sand in front of him.

Sergei jumped out of the Jeep. John saw the flash of the metal key clenched in his hand as he raced toward the stake.

John's heart thundered in his ears. This was it—the moment he had envisioned for so long. And it all boiled down to a simple footrace. John sprinted up the hill, his heart pumping and his lungs ready to explode. Everything seemed to be in slow motion.

Sergei cut toward John and tackled him to the ground. John's key flew into the rocks. Sergei jumped up, kicked John in the stomach, then scrambled toward the stake. John lunged, caught Sergei by the ankle and dragged him to the ground. They rolled back down the hill.

Sergei yelled at Buck, "Take the key!" and tossed it toward him.

Buck grabbed the key in mid-air, shoved the pistol in his pants, and started toward the stake at a full run. Almost to the stake, he halted in his tracks.

"Why are you stopping?" Sergei screamed.

They all heard the click of the key as Ginnie locked it in place, pistol aimed at Buck with the other hand. "The land is ours. Back off!"

Staggering up, John shouted, "That's my girl!"

Sergei punched John in the mouth and started toward Ginnie.

John reeled backward, then grabbed Sergei by the back of his collar, and jerked him around to face him. He slugged him in the stomach, followed by an upward punch to the face. It felt so good to beat this man. The anger of all that John hated in the world surfaced. Every punch was a catharsis as he battered Sergei into unconsciousness. His knuckles ached when he finally let the thug's body sink into the dirt.

John bolted upright at the crack of a shot. Ginnie stood by the stake, her hands trembling as she aimed the pistol at Buck.

Buck knelt on the ground, clutching his arm. Blood streamed down his useless limb.

"The little bitch shot me!"

"You pointed your gun at Dad," Ginnie retorted. "I couldn't let you do that."

John ran to Ginnie and eased the pistol from her. He stood over Buck, shoving the barrel into his face. "I'll finish the job, if you don't get your ass—and your little lump over there—off our land." He waved the gun. "Pronto!"

Buck clambered over to Sergei. With his good arm, he dragged him to the Jeep and grunting, shoved him into the back seat. He jumped in the front and sped off, showering them with dust.

John coughed, waving the cloud of dust away as he joined his daughter beside the stake.

He sat with a huff and wrapped his arm around her. Plumes of dust rose around them as a crazy circus of cars, hovers, jalopies, and miscellany passed by, all still racing toward their dreams. Distant sounds of gunfire intermingled with the beeping horns and shouting warriors, battling for their land.

He quoted Shakespeare in a tired voice:

"O brave new world,
That has such people in't!"

*   *   *

A trail of dust came closer from the same direction that Buck and Sergei had left. John stood shielding his eyes—a small 4x4 truck approached them.

Ginnie waved. "It's Debora and her family!"

"Who?"

"Don't you remember the Ramos family from Argentina? We ate dinner with them a couple of times? Debora did the Orientation Day with me."

The dust covered truck came closer, with Ginnie's friend and her family. "Sure, I remember. A nice family."

"Yeah, she's really fun."

They stopped and John noticed the dents in the truck. "Did you get a tract?"

Debora's father grinned. "Si!" Shrugging, he said. "If we hadn't gotten into the dust storm, we might have gotten our first choice, but we won our second choice, by the width of the truck." He waved to the large dent in the side bed. "We drove up just in time to block a hoverbike, who slammed into our truck. I jumped out and locked my key in before he did." He chuckled. "He shot us the finger and then took off for another tract."

The younger boy in the backseat pointed at a glittering black object on the top of the ridge. "What's that, Papa?"

With systematic precision, the horse and rider descended the steep slope.

"Now what?" John said. There was something odd about the way the horse moved. As it came closer, he saw the sun glint on the face of the "animal." It was a robotic horse.

The robo-horse and rider reached the bottom of the hillside and cut across the flat of the valley, the horse's stride even and fast. The entire "skin" of the horse had a black, iridescent sheen to it. *A type of flexible solar panel?* The horse had no mane, but the tail had long bristles, perhaps some type of telecommunication link. A robotic horse was the perfect conveyance for a continent with only one road.

His blood ran cold as he recognized the rider's profile—Durant. "God help us."

"What's wrong?" Ginnie asked.

"I guess this is garbage day." His hand went to the pistol. John breathed easier as they faded into the distance. Then he swallowed hard. Durant was following Lowry's track. "Damn."

John turned to Ginnie. "Durant may be after Lowry." He looked at the family, crammed together in the truck. "Would you mind if Ginnie rides back to camp with you?"

Mr. Ramos nodded. "Si, Si."

Ginnie reached up and hugged her father, whispering, "You keep the pistol."

"Okay. I'll try not to shoot myself." He looked at Ginnie's dirty face. "I love you, Ginnie, and I'm very proud of you."

"Back 'atcha." She ruffled his hair. "Be careful, Dad. I love you very much." She poked him in the chest. "Don't stub your toe." She climbed in, squeezed between the two kids in the backseat, and they drove away.

John shoved the pistol into his belt and ran to the front of the overturned buggy. He reeled out the winch on the front bumper, wrapped the cable around a craggy boulder nearby, and hooked it into place. He leapt back to the front of the buggy and started the winch. Humming, the motor pulled the cable taut, then with a creaking sound, the buggy slowly rotated, and flipped upright, bouncing on the tires. John unhooked the cable and reeled it back into the winch.

He jumped in and started the engine. "I promise, after this, you can rest. Just keep it together a little longer, please?" He jammed the buggy into gear and headed toward the west, accelerating the vehicle as fast as it would go. "Go, you piece of crap!"

John followed the two sets of tracks across the valley and started up the next ridge. The buggy protested the ascent, grinding and lurching up the slope as it snaked toward the ridge where Durant had disappeared. The muscles in his arms burned from holding the wheels in line.

He reached the crest at last and got out, shading his eyes from the sun, and surveyed the valley below. His heart went to his throat at the crack of a gunshot.

He searched the landscape for any sign of Lowry and her horse. *Where was she?*

There! Lowry was on her mare, at a dead run across the valley floor, with Durant right behind her, the robot gaining on his living cousin. His arm raised and a glint of metal reflected in the sunlight—Durant's pistol, aimed straight at Lowry.

John leapt back into the buggy, and with a Hail Mary, descended into the valley. His teeth rattled as his speed increased. Like a deer, the buggy jumped down the face of the incline. *No stopping now.* He held the bucking demon in line, every rock ahead presenting an opportunity to turn them over. His arms and shoulders cramped as the jarring pace quickened. With the valley floor fast approaching, he struggled to keep the wheels straight ahead.

Another crack from Durant's pistol and Lowry's mare faltered. She fell to her knees as the bullet hit her body. With a shriek, Lowry sailed over her head, then hit the ground with a thud, and tumbled into a boulder. Her body went limp.

John screamed as he hit the bottom of the slope, turned the wheel, and accelerated straight for Durant. As he caught up to the robotic horse, Durant's shocked face jerked around, and then with a snarl, he aimed the pistol at him. John whipped the buggy in front of the robo-horse's front legs.

The robo-horse slammed into the hood with a crunch. John flinched as Durant's pistol hit the windshield of the buggy, then bounced over his head. The robo-horse somersaulted into a tangled pile. Durant flew through the air and landed hard on the rocky ground. He lurched forward for a second, then collapsed in the dirt and lay still.

John killed the engine, and with Ginnie's pistol in hand, ran toward Lowry's inert body.

Half-way to Lowry, he felt someone upon him. His face smacked the hard-packed earth and dust filled his mouth. Durant was on top of him, knocking the pistol out of his hand and behind the rocks.

John twisted beneath him, jerking his head to the side as Durant hurled a large rock past his ear. John slugged him in the mouth and Durant's blood splattered into his face. John pivoted his body and with a hard kick in the chest, knocked Durant onto his back.

Gasping for breath, Durant scrambled up onto one knee.

John staggered to his feet and faced him. With a grin, Durant pitched sand into John's face.

Blinded for a second, John stumbled backwards, his hands frantically clearing the sand from his eyes. Durant leapt forward and punched John in the mouth. John's head snapped back with the blow, but he pivoted around, and clipped Durant full in the face with his elbow. Durant grunted and backed up, blood flowing down his face.

The two faced each other. John licked his lips, the metallic taste of blood in his mouth.

Durant spit onto the ground, and with red-streaked teeth, he sneered. "You picked the wrong answer the other day, my friend. I can give you everything you want. You're not one of the fool homesteaders, scratching out a living like pigs, half of them going back after they've failed." He spread his hands wide. "They're too witless to lead themselves. They need a strong leader. They don't understand the game that's about to be played here."

John grimaced. "And you've decided that great leader is you. What about the novel concept of democracy?"

Durant's smile faded. "There hasn't been an opportunity like this since the opening of the American West, and it may be centuries before there's another." Durant tilted his head, his face softening as he changed tactics. "If you pick the right side, you'll have the power, influence, and riches that you were denied in the Old World."

John sighed. He had spent his life turning over the stones that made him who he was. He'd felt every rough spot, every hidden crevice. Durant knew how to tempt him, knew the words to say, like all great con men. But John knew that nothing was worth the collar Durant would give him.

John shook his head. "It wasn't the wrong answer. You asked the wrong man. Men like you raped the American West. I won't be a part of that sacrilege. You want to set yourself up as dictator of an entire continent."

Durant opened his mouth, but John lifted his hand, stopping any further appeal. "I've fought too hard and too long to throw my soul away." With a sigh, he shook his head. In an odd way, he pitied Durant. "The truth is, you're just chasing the wind."

Durant snapped. "You're wrong—I *am* the wind."

Lowry's voice rose behind them. "Or an arrogant blowhard who wants to be the self-anointed King of Antarctica." She stood beside the property stake, her key glinting in the lock box.

She pointed Ginnie's pistol at Durant's chest. "No matter what you try, Durant, we won't let you and your Kremlin cronies take over Antarctica."

His lip curled. "And you think your Uncle Nick is going to lead this new nation?"

"Yes."

Durant threw back his head with a laugh. "He couldn't lead a hog to its trough."

Gesturing with the pistol, Lowry snapped, "Durant, I want you off my property, or you're as dead as my horse."

Durant smiled, then whistled. The robo-horse struggled up and straightened its legs. Durant stepped behind John as a shield, keeping him between Lowry and himself. Creaking like an old jalopy, the robo-horse raced toward Durant. He sprang to its back, and they lurched away.

Lowry lowered the pistol. "Good riddance." She turned to John. "Are you all right?"

John wiped the blood from his mouth and nodded. "Yeah, I'm fine." He looked at her. "You took a hard fall—are you okay?"

With a sigh, she rubbed her head. "I've been better, but I'll live." Lowry turned and walked to Hadeel. The beautiful mare lay in the dirt, her white coat streaked with dried blood. Lowry collapsed by her side and stroked the neck of the animal, tears rolling down her face.

John stumbled over and stood next to Lowry. "I'm sorry about Hadeel."

Lowry arranged Hadeel's mane. "She was my best mare." Her mouth trembled as she glanced towards Durant's trail. "Someday, I'll kill that son of a bitch!"

He squeezed her shoulder and said, "I have a feeling you'll get another chance. I can almost guarantee we'll see Mr. Durant again."

Lowry blinked through her tears. "John, you saved my life."

He held out his hand and helped her up. A gust blew strands of her hair across her face and John gently smoothed them back into place. They held onto each other, ragged and dirty, so tired they could hardly stand. With a weary smile, he wiped the tears from her grimy face.

CHAPTER 12

Laughter rang out behind him. John glanced over his shoulder at the happy group surrounding a campfire. He raised a glass of beer to them and they shouted, "Cheers!" Not everyone had captured their top choices, but the land was theirs.

Officially over, the Land Rush settlers had gathered at the starting line to celebrate their victories. Unofficially, the rumble of vehicles echoed across the plains as the race for land continued under the setting sun.

He scanned the crowd, shaking his head at the numerous white bandages, similar to his, of the walking wounded around the campfires. The list of injuries from brawls and vehicle run-ins reminded one of an ER ward after a riot: gunshot and knife wounds, broken bones, lacerations, and contusions. Luckily, the Brazilians, whose three-wheeler had fallen into a sinkhole, had only incurred a few broken bones. With a grin, John looked at his bandaged knuckles. The last time he'd been in a fistfight was in middle school.

Gingerly, John slipped on his jacket and sauntered to the beer keg to refill his cup. Someone had placed a makeshift memorial next to the drink stand. With a sigh, he perused the images of the dead, wishing peace to all those who had not survived the ordeal. Memorials had been held earlier that afternoon, marking this day one of sadness as well as joy.

Five people had perished during the Rush. A couple and their two-year-old boy had been lost in a deep permafrost sinkhole. Eyewitnesses said they simply disappeared from sight, dropping into a yawning cavern under their vehicle. When rescuers reached them, they found the broken bodies of the man, woman, and the little boy, still in his mother's arms. The husband and wife were only in their twenties. One rescuer had broken down sobbing at the sight of the traces the husband had left in the dust, crawling to his wife. And the women who had been roasted alive—John shuddered at the memory of the woman's face melting on the window.

A cool breeze slithered through the valley and he draped a blanket over Ginnie's shoulders, and with a groan, sat on the ground. John gazed at the scarlet tinted ridges above them, and breathed in the fresh, crisp air. He raised his cup in a toast to the rising moon and took a sip. John Barrous: now a homesteader on the continent of Antarctica. Despite his pain or perhaps because of it, he felt truly alive. All his adult life, he had been a corporate stooge, trapped in an office without clean air to breath or the touch of the sun on his face.

John turned as Nick's voice called him to the front of the crowd. With a wave to Nick, he staggered up and threaded his way through the celebratory bonfires built from discarded shipping crates. John looked for Lowry, but she was nowhere to be seen. Understandable with the grief of losing her favorite horse.

Nick glanced at the bandages on his hands, grabbed John in a wristlock and pulled him up onto one of the open jeeps. He clapped him on the back. "Thanks, my boy, for saving Lowry today. I'll never forget it."

Shrugging, John looked away with a smile. "I did what anyone would have done."

With a grimace, Nick snorted. "You must have a higher opinion of 'anyone' than I do." He squeezed John's shoulder. "A man's actions say more than his words."

Nick turned to the crowd. "Fellow Antarcticans." He held his hand up to the raucous group. With aid from the less intoxicated settlers hushing the drunks, he finally silenced the boisterous homesteaders.

With a raised glass, Nick smiled to the gathering. "Fellow Antarcticans, welcome to the land of milk and honey, where insects abound and only goats can survive." After the laughter quieted, he continued in a more serious tone, holding his hand out to the crowd. "We also pray for those who lost their lives today—not lost in vain, but in a glorious quest." Murmurs of condolences sprang from the assembled settlers.

Nick gazed across the crowd, his arms spread. "The Great Antarctic Land Rush will go down as one of the greatest events in the history of the world—humans once again colonizing a New World." He pointed a finger into the air and shouted, "In Antarctica, this day will be celebrated every year as the anniversary day of her first immigrants."

A roar from the crowd rang out in the night air. Celebrating their triumph, new friends bonded with handshakes and hugs, amid the confetti of hats, plates, and various articles of clothing flying through the air.

As the melee calmed, Nick turned his glass toward John, and spoke, "Though there were many heroic and some not so heroic acts today"—laughter sprinkled from the group, and Nick grinned—"I want to propose a toast to one of the heroes of the day, John Barrous, who saved my niece, Lowry Walker."

Whistles, yells and claps rose from the crowd.

"Speech, speech!" someone yelled, and the chant started amongst the more inebriated ones.

Nick gestured for John to address the crowd. John scanned the tired, but relaxed faces—faces that, earlier in the day, had been tense and furtive, but now were alight with hope and joy. Men clapped each other on the back and laughing women danced with their children in their arms. The homesteaders had won the right to be masters of their own fate, with a community forming to colonize this new land.

Proudly, these new landowners held their heads high, gazing up at John with mutual respect as they waited for him to speak. He bit the inside of his lip; it had been a long time since he had felt like a man. Energy surged into his exhausted body—as if all the trials in his life had meaning—a gauntlet to push him toward this destiny.

John breathed in the pure air, exhaling with a smile, and the tension in his throat fell away like the collar of his past. His words rolled from his lips. "We have won our land and this new life, denying the chains of the modern world, not out of fear, but out of choice. For many of us, our ancestors were the ones who opened the American West. They broke the land and sometimes the land broke them, but they kept coming, counting the graves as they went by, driven by that which drives us all—freedom."

Amid the sounds of the crackling fires, he spread out his arms as the rapt crowd edged forward. The faces before him were lit as brightly by the fires of passion as by the lanterns and bonfires.

"As we work the earth, we will begin to move with the rhythm of this place, and she will fold us into her breast. We will become one with this new land. We will become Antarcticans. Our children, our grandchildren, will know this continent as their home. Let's treat her with respect and care, for we are the shepherds of this New World."

As the crowd cheered, Nick placed his hand on John's shoulder, and whispered out of the side of his mouth, "Great job, son."

Then, with a broad smile, Nick raised his glass to the crowd. "Let the adventure begin!"

Part II

O' Antarctica in a post-Melt world—a new beginning for the children of Man—or the final act of treachery?

K.E. Lanning

CHAPTER 13

Flickering rays of sunlight streamed through the clear dome of the tent, teasing John awake. Half-sleep, he squinted at the pale sky, trying to remember where he was. With a yawn, he opened his eyes wide and grinned; he was a bona-fide homesteader on Antarctica.

John pushed himself into a sitting position with a groan. He massaged his head, now protesting last night's celebration. Every inch of his body ached from the grueling Land Rush. Gingerly moving from top to bottom, he stretched his neck, and then rolled his shoulders, wondering if they would ever function quite the same way again. He gazed at his bruised and scabbed knuckles, hoping that his opponents woke up in at least as much pain.

He shoved his hair back from his face, opened the medicine kit, and found a couple of ibuprofen. He popped them into his mouth, grabbed the water bottle and downed them. He flipped open the flap of the tent and waited for the medicine to kick in.

The valley lay before him, dressed in sporadic tussock grass and scrub pine. With a sigh, the wind roiled over the hills, caressing the native grasses along its way. John relaxed in the nothingness of the moment. He didn't know why, but he connected more with the quiet sincerity of nature over the incessant noise of his own species.

Ginnie mumbled in her sleep behind him. Turning with a grin, John watched her twist in the depths of the sleeping bag like a cat—perhaps dreaming of her victory over Buck—but she quieted into a deep sleep, and he didn't want to wake her. She had busted ass yesterday, moving their containers from the warehouse and setting up the tent in the dark. Last night, the two of them had sat around the campfire, staring up at the heavens bright with stars.

John crawled to the back of the tent and started the coffee brewing, dialing in "Extra Strong"—good for energy level, and perhaps a balm for his hangover. He pulled on a jacket and crawled through the flap. He stretched his arms to the blue crystalline sky, breathing in the fresh air of Antarctica.

Last night, it had been too dark to truly appreciate their surroundings. This morning, John hiked down to the gurgling brook, lined with low brush, at the bottom of the valley. He shielded his eyes from the sun and pivoted around imagining his land with trees and crops. He laughed in sheer delight. His land! Energized, he strode back to the tent to grab coffee.

In the tent, John sat cross-legged, sipping the hot brew. He picked up the tablet and checked the building plans for the next day. Tomorrow, the house crew would arrive, and everything had to be ready. The homesteaders of this sector had drawn straws to see whose house would be raised first, and by the luck of the draw, he and Ginnie would be the first to get theirs built. All the neighbors helped raise each house, getting it weathered in and functional. Like the farmhouses of the Old West, they could weather the harsh climate of the land and were independent of any power or communication grid.

He clicked on the architectural plan he had chosen and a 3D image of a utilitarian house formed above the tablet. Square in shape, it had exterior walls constructed of mega-insulating material to reduce heating needs in the brutal winters. The roof shimmered as he spun the image of the building with his finger. Environmentally, the design and function of the house was stunning. The architects and engineers had designed a self-sustaining building that didn't mar the land but created a balance between humans and the terrain.

The glass solar roof and windows provided all the power they needed during the sunlit part of the year, and also gathered power from raindrops during storms. With a voice command, sections of the roof became transparent, flooding the home with natural sunlight. Encased wind propellers built into the ridge lines provided for electricity needs during the dark time, and batteries maintained a constant power supply in between sources of renewable energy. The plumbing and septic system recycled their water, and the composting toilet created an inexhaustible supply of fertilizer.

Maybe, at least on Antarctica, humans finally had the technology—and the will—to develop a symbiotic relationship with the Earth? A great experiment might be unfolding with the colonization of this virgin land.

He sipped his coffee. Unless someone like Durant skewed the outcome.

Tilting the image, he gazed at the interior courtyard designed for a garden area. He sliced through the interior views of the house. The only extravagance was the tongue-and-groove wooden plank flooring he had ordered. It had cost him an arm and a leg to have it shipped, but he wanted something to connect him to home.

John knew by the holomaps approximately where the house would sit, tucked into the side of a hill, well-protected from the brunt of the storms, but he needed to mark out the exact location so they'd be ready for the house-raising crew tomorrow morning. He finished his coffee, put the tablet into his pocket and scooted out of the tent. In the brightening day, he walked to the site he and Ginnie had chosen and staked the four corners of the house with a GPS, and then sent the coordinates to the excavation crew scheduled to arrive this afternoon.

John pulled a pair of binoculars from his jacket pocket and scanned the valley from the house site. Years ago, naturalists had begun a release program to develop a balanced ecosystem on the continent, but today, no land creatures were in sight. In the tussock grass near the stream, John heard the seet, seet, seet call of Blackpoll warblers hunting insects. As the sun warmed, he caught the scent of lichen and moss. The sound of honking drew his eyes upward to a flock of geese flying in a V-shape over the heart of the valley.

He returned to the tent with a happy sigh. Ginnie sat on the sleeping bag, stretching her arms as he crawled in.

He rustled through the food bag, scooped a handful of nuts, and shoveled them into his mouth. He fixed himself another cup of coffee while Ginnie gazed vacantly at him. With a raised eyebrow, he shot a glance at her. "Ready to go to Amundsen?"

She murmured, "Breakfast first?"

With a smile, he ruffled her hair. "You look like you need a bucket of coffee, too." He filled a mug with a blend of coffee, hot cocoa, and powdered milk, and handed it to her. To energize her, John started a mock drum-roll on his knees.

Ginnie narrowed her eyes at him, not bothering to hide her annoyance. "You're way too chipper this morning—especially for someone who looks like they'd been run over by a train." She dug a small mirror out of her backpack and handed it to him.

He held up the mirror, staring at his face marred by scrapes and contusions, sporting a swollen left eye, now turning a lovely shade of blue. Chuckling, John shrugged. "War wounds—and don't forget that I won." Patting her leg, he said softly, "You're the one who put the key in the stake. You're my hero."

She stared at him over her mug of coffee and cocoa. "Dad, I love you very much."

He studied her face, now drawn and serious. *Was she regretting her decision to come with him?* Even he had not anticipated the level of violence of this venture, complicated by their involvement with Durant. He clenched his fist. *Why did Lowry seem to be at the heart of his troubles?*

He said softly, "Ginnie, just say the word if you ever wish to return to the States and live with your grandparents."

She replied, "Thanks, but I'm in, at least for now." She wagged her finger at him. "Just don't go get yourself killed, do you hear me?"

John nodded. "I'll try." Exhaling, he gazed at her. *It was not regret that she's come with him but worry about my safety.* He dug into the food pack and handed her a granola bar.

She examined the granola bar with disdain. "Since we're heroes, how about pancakes?"

Laughing, John said, "We'll catch lunch in town. We have a date with the UN folks to officially register our claim. Then we need to buy groceries to feed our new neighbors during the house-raising."

Ginnie dressed, grabbed her backpack, and they crawled out of the tent. John secured the flap as best he could. "Better bring any valuables you have with you."

Nodding, she said, "I'm bringing everything in my backpack." She patted her hip, and John saw a bulge, and the outline of the pistol hidden under her shirt.

"Good. It will be up to us to protect ourselves and our farm. I'm afraid it will be awhile before the cops start a beat."

They floated in the hovercar over open grassland, dotted with rocks and shallow ponds. In the distance, a plume of smoke rose from a campfire, and John and Ginnie waved toward the small figures standing outside of a tent.

Rounding a hillside, they passed a small valley filled with wildflowers, a flamboyant spectacle in the drab landscape around them.

Ginnie pointed excitedly. "Dad, can we please stop and look?"

John turned the hover and parked beside a small sign designating the valley as a bee and bird habitat. The sweet smell of the blooms drifted to them. Flowers of a dozen colors bent to the whim of the breeze, while birds and honey bees darted through the delicate stalks.

She leapt out of the hover and bolted into the field. Laughing, John rushed after her. They ran like fools through the flowers—drunk on color, perfume and joy.

Ginnie screamed with laughter when he tackled her. As his breath calmed, he rolled onto his back and she lay on his shoulder. Birds and bees flitted above them as they gazed at the luscious blossoms, inhaling a cacophony of scents.

John pointed to a small drab gray and brown bird perched on a nearby branch. "I think that's a Patagonian Tyrant."

"What a funny name."

"Yeah, but they eat whatever's available, so can survive the harsh climate—and disperse seeds."

With a grimace, Ginnie replied, "Thanks for that visual."

"You're welcome." John sat up. "I think you should be in charge of our bee and bird sanctuary." He glanced at the time. "We'd better get going."

On the way to the hover, John threw Ginnie over his shoulder, mimicking the Wicked Witch of the North's voice. "I've got you, my pretty!" and carried his squealing daughter to the hover.

Around the next hillside, sounds of the ocean drifted toward them. The new city of Amundsen came into view, with its sparkling modular buildings set in rows, like a giant's Lego set. Humans crawled over the town like ants on a sugar cube, streaming through the dusty streets, while hover pallets roamed the back alleys, stocking the stores from the rear as fast as the settlers bought goods out of the front.

When they reached the city center, a traffic jam on Main Street welcomed them with honks and shouts. They crept along through the menagerie of people and vehicles, all scurrying for scarce supplies.

In the chaos, they found the UN claim office, with a line stretching around the building. A savvy street vendor wandered along the line, hawking food to the captured audience. John bought a couple of empanadas from him, and they inched forward, eating and chatting with the other settlers.

Two hours later, they were official homesteaders, and moved into the next queue to stock up on groceries.

At the end of the day, they started back home, the hover now pulling a brand-new trailer, brimming with a barbeque pit, groceries, and supplies. The foreman from the claims office waved to them as they pulled up to their tent. He had driven out while they were in town, and had drilled the water well with a small crane and drilling unit, while the excavation crew had dug the giant cavity for the foundation that had been a field of grass just that morning.

John and Ginnie peered into the hole, marveling at the exposed layers of clay and dirt. John thanked the excavation crew, handing out the now-lukewarm cans of beer that he had purchased in town.

Ginnie fixed sandwiches on a table near the tent, while he set up the barbecue pit. He threw a match into the pit and the fire sprang up with a happy crackling sound. They ate dinner while the fire burned to glowing embers.

In the dim light of the midnight sun, two large trucks arrived, with lights blazing. Punctuated by loud beeping, they maneuvered around the building site. A man got out and waved to them, then directed the robo-arms to unload the sections of the modular house near the excavated hole. The second truck unloaded the crates with new furniture and household items.

John squinted against the flashing headlights as he placed the wrapped brisket in the barbecue pit. He flipped the little chimney open so the smoke would circulate around the meat.

Exhausted, he waved feebly at the farewell toots of the trucks, meandering back to town. He swayed on his feet, staring at the moon low on the horizon.

"Good night, Antarctica," he whispered and crawled into the warm tent.

Ginnie opened one eye. "I hope we can get some sleep now."

Snuggled in his sleeping bag, he murmured, "Who knew a barren wasteland could be so noisy." He was out when his head hit the pillow.

*　　*　　*

At daybreak the next morning, John sat in one of the chairs drinking coffee, hoping the caffeine would kick in before the neighbors arrived. The sunlight crept onto the outlines of the house and he strolled over to see if the 3D images matched the reality.

The Plasment exterior walls of the upper floor of the house were a subtle gray-brown color, resembling stucco. The material had been tested for several years at a model home at the UN station on Antarctica, and touted as being virtually indestructible. John crossed his fingers. *As long as it doesn't blow away with the first big Antarctic storm.*

The solar roof resembled slate, with a wind-propeller system cleverly designed into the ridge to disguise its true function. He strolled to the basement section—the true guts of the house. All the power, water, and recycling septic systems, like organized spaghetti, sat ready to be hooked up and functioning in one day.

He circled back around and returned to the tent. Yawning, Ginnie emerged from under the flap, and stretched her arms. Still half-asleep, she helped him set up the community folding tables and chairs brought on the same truck that had delivered the house components.

Neighbors arrived in small groups, gathering around the coffee and cookies, bundled in coats against the frigid morning air. John handed out steaming cups of coffee and opened up more boxes of cookies as the crowd grew.

Two giant robo-cranes creaked over the hill, led by the foreman from the UN claim office. The foreman got out of the hover, positioning the robo-cranes with hand signals and voice commands. He waved to John and strolled to the coffee bar.

John handed him a cup of coffee and asked, "How long do you think it will take to put the house together?"

The foreman studied the layout, his face twisting in thought. "Well, with no major problems"—his voice dropped to a whisper—"and no one does anything dumb, we should be finished by evening."

With a cookie in his hand, he stepped away from the table, waving the neighbors to circle around him. The "crew" consisted of their immediate neighbors, and this would be the first test of his new friends.

The group clustered around the foreman, listening to his instructions, but his droning voice faded from John's consciousness as a jolt went through his body. *Lowry.* He gulped his coffee, spilling it on his coat.

Lowry cantered her chestnut mare up the hill and then slowed her to a walk near the building site. Despite the incident with Durant, she'd staked her claim—the tract next to theirs.

Ginnie knew nothing of his tryst with Lowry. During the Land Rush, he had put his guilt and uncertainty in a little hole in the back of his mind, but now? He concentrated on wiping the coffee from his coat. Lowry would probably be over all the time, borrowing equipment and bringing those animals over to defecate on the lawn.

Ginnie ran over, petting the mare, and chatting with Lowry. *Why did Ginnie have to develop an unfortunate fondness for horses?* Ginnie led the mare away and Lowry walked toward him, her stride long and smooth, and his throat tightened. *How long can I hold out from touching her?*

Lowry stood in front of him as if digesting his mood of the day. Her eyes narrowed for a second, then she said, "Hello, John. Remember me?"

In the awkward silence, her lips narrowed, and the tension between them returned.

Finally, he muttered, "Want some coffee?"

"No, thanks. I had a cup earlier." Looking around, she smiled. "John, congrats—you have one of the best claims!"

"Thanks." He cleared his throat. "I guess you staked the next claim over from ours."

With a puzzled look, Lowry nodded. "Yep, still in the same spot as yesterday."

John tilted his head. "I guess I never thanked you for the information on the tracts."

She smiled. "A fair exchange for your service to Antarctica." She leaned into him, her face bright with excitement. "I wanted to be the first to tell you: the story on Durant is out and social media is eating it up. He's defeated! You can't turn around without seeing it, hearing it, or tasting it!"

"He's defeated for now, anyway," he replied. "What about your father?"

Lowry grimaced and then looked away. "He's cooperating fully with the investigation. His lawyer said he might be granted parole." She exhaled. "Dad uses the scars of his past to excuse the flaws of his present."

John wondered if Duff would still try to run for election. He didn't know if her father would get elected, but he knew plenty of elected officials throughout history who had done time at some point in their career. Luckily for Duff, his involvement in the ANT scandal was overshadowed by both the exposure of Durant and the call for Antarctic elections to be held within the year.

"What about Buck and Sergei?" John asked.

"The recruits are all being sent back to New York and the principals will be tried for racketeering. The contracts for the transport system have been kicked out and will be re-bid."

"Durant is not a man to give up with a minor setback."

"I wouldn't call it a 'minor setback.'"

"Sometimes the difference between a minor and major setback is the amount of money involved to 'fix' it."

"I hope you're wrong," she said, shaking her head.

John touched her arm. "I wish they had charged them before Hadeel—"

Lowry whispered, "I planted flowers over her grave." She met his eyes. "I'll never be able to repay you for saving my life."

"All in a day's work."

She examined his bruised face. "I hope you're healing well?"

He shrugged. "Still a bit sore." Pointing to the scrape over her eye, he asked, "Are you okay? You had a pretty hard fall."

"I've had worse." Lowry grinned. Then she gazed into his eyes. "It's good to have a friend out here."

Their eyes locked for a second, then John glanced away with a nervous cough. Ginnie had returned with a tub of lunch items.

With a nod at Ginnie, Lowry asked, "How's Ginnie adjusting to our fine continent?"

John smiled, watching Ginnie set the table for lunch. "She's a real trooper!"

"I hope she doesn't get too lonely." She turned away from the bustling activity of the house-raising and toward the emptiness surrounding them.

John scanned the landscape. In the heart of the valley, the river tumbled its way to the sea. Above them, the slopes rose to the foothills, tinted with gray rock and sporadic green tussock grass, framed with the distant, snow-topped mountains. No creatures in sight, only clouds drifting on the wind in the endless pale blue sky.

With a sigh, John asked, "Does the wind ever stop?"

"Never."

John inhaled the crisp air, and with a smile, turned toward her. "But we are free."

Lowry laughed, gesturing with her thumb toward the neighbors and the robo-cranes moving the basement of the house into the excavated hole. "Yeah, we're free to work our butts off!"

*   *   *

Lowry worked like a Trojan. She had amazing strength, which came from working outdoors since childhood. Helen would never have been able to keep up with her. Driving a tractor, Lowry dumped gravel around the exterior of the foundation, and then helped load the kitchen with the provisions they had bought in town.

Watching her, he felt himself become aroused. "Dammit!" he mumbled under his breath. He was hopeless.

By lunch, the crew had the exterior and most of the interior hooked up and running. He fixed Lowry a plate for lunch, and they chatted awkwardly during most of the meal.

Panicking that he would lose his chance to mend fences with her, he blurted out, "Lowry, I'm sorry if I hurt you after our, uh, picnic. Please give me time. I'm still a bit confused. It's especially difficult because of Ginnie—she reminds me so much of her mother."

Lowry put her hand on his arm. "John, I understand, but I wish you had figured that out a little sooner."

John stared at his plate. "I know."

After lunch, Lowry and a few neighbors moved in topsoil for the courtyard garden, while the foreman checked the power and plumbing systems. John directed the rest of the crew in moving the furniture and supplies into the house. They ended the day with a dinner of barbecue and beer, accompanied by a neighbor strumming a mandolin. The crowd waved to the foreman as he drove off, leading the robo-cranes away to be ready for the next house-raising.

After the neighbors left, John and Ginnie made the beds and except for a few minor details, completed the setup of their new home. With a cheer, they folded up the tent and stored it in the cellar. John took a hot shower, dried off with a fresh towel, and then walked into the bedroom. Sighing, he stretched out on the new bed and pulled the blankets over him, murmuring "Off" to extinguish the light. He stared at the ceiling and then flipped onto his side and re-adjusted the covers.

They would join the merry band for the next several days, until all nine houses in this sector were completed. Lowry's house was the next day. He would be near her again.

John rotated to his other side and fluffed the pillow. In the dark room, his mind returned to the day they had made love—the vision of her arms around him and the feel of her lips on his.

He was falling for her. The thought of Helen was still there, but like an old photograph, the colors were slowly deteriorating into a faded image.

CHAPTER 14

Lowry scanned the horizon. No sign of the house-raising crew as yet. With a sigh, she chewed the inside of her cheek. Was it the excitement of the construction, or being near John again?

Turning away, she busied herself with preparing food and drink for the crew. She connected the hose to the new water well spigot and cranked the handle open. Water gushed out, and she silently thanked the UN water-well crew that had drilled it yesterday. She let the system flush for a few moments before she cupped her hand and tasted the fresh clean water. She filled the water cooler, stacked the cups, and readied the coffee station.

Laughter floated up to her from below. A smile crossed her face at the sight of neighbors hovering across the valley floor, following the huge robo-cranes like baby ducks. She brought a platter of baked goods to the coffee-bar area, and said, "Start coffee," to the coffee maker. She hurriedly prepared the rest of the lunch and then waved as they reached the house site.

Ginnie yelled hello to her, but John hung back at the hovercraft, looking a bit uncomfortable.

Puzzled by his demeanor, she waved to him, and saw his visible relief at her greeting. *He's a complicated man.*

She called out, "Hey, can you help me a minute?"

John smiled. "Sure."

He helped her set up the lunch tables, and then stacked the plates, utensils, and condiments on one side. Lowry pivoted with the container of tea she had brewed and brushed against John's chest as he was passing, nearly dropping the jug.

She looked at him, breathless at the electricity jumping between them. "Sorry," she said, placing the iced tea on the table—despite the weakness in her knees.

He stood still and stared at her.

She swallowed hard. "How do you like the place? You can see where the excavators dug the hole for the house—near those stone monoliths." *Maybe if she kept talking, her heart would stop beating so fast.* "And yesterday," she continued, "I planted a few trees on each side of a path leading to the house."

Nodding, John scanned the horizon. "You have an extraordinary view. You may have the best parcel on Antarctica." He grinned. "Even better than ours. I think you were holding out on me."

They both laughed, easing some of the tension between them.

With an innocent grin, she replied, "Would I do such a thing?" and pushed him toward the crew, walking with the robo-cranes, as they moved the cellar section into the hole. "Playtime is over, mister, get over there and start building me a house."

Lowry watched him walk away. Her lips parted as he ran his fingers through his hair, recalling the touch of his hands on her bare skin. Neighbors scurried around the property, unloading items, adding more food to the tables—working hard for a fellow Antarctican. She breathed deep, trying to shake off the lingering passion between her and John. There was a house to build and a farm to grow. Life was good.

The stone for the house would be delivered next week. Lowry had planned this house for a long time. She'd hired several of the local miners to quarry stone she had found on her recon missions—brilliant white sandstone for the exterior with travertine and marble flooring through most of the house. She felt that a dwelling should blend into the environment.

She laid covered platters of sandwiches on the tables and finished the preparations for lunch. With a smile, she walked over to join the team, now with sweaty foreheads and strained sinews.

The foundation took the longest, tying the sub-floor into the bedrock, then a shout went up as the plumbing was tied into the well. Next, the robo-cranes placed the top floor on and fit it together to form an indivisible protectorate. The house had bedrooms, living areas, and a kitchen—the inner sanctuaries of a home. With the final bolt, the robo-crane lifted its arm and a cheer rose from the crowd.

The men and women laughed as they lifted furniture from the crates and readied the soil for the interior garden. Their children played in the debris around them. In this new life on Antarctica, bonds grew between these people who had been strangers, even competitors, a short time ago.

Lowry smiled. Another home on Antarctica was in place. But they were building not only a house but a community that grew where none had existed before. They would plant together and harvest together. They would live and die together. Humans had begun again, like it had been at the start of civilization when they had more to fear from the elements than each other.

As the sun approached the horizon, the troupe of neighbors waved goodbye and drifted home.

John was the last to leave and walked up with a smile. "I hope you sleep well."

"I'm exhausted. I'll sleep like a baby in my new bed, in my new house. Thanks for all your hard work. And I hear congratulations are in order—you were elected sector rep."

He raised an eyebrow. "Frankly, I wasn't expecting to be elected and I'll be glad when my term is over."

Lowry gazed at him. "You were elected because you're a leader, John. Uncle Nick told me about your speech on the night of the Land Rush. I wish I could have been there, but that was the night the new colt decided it was time to join us."

John grimaced. "I'm not sure that speech was a demonstration of leadership, or a lethal combo of exhaustion and alcohol." He raked his fingers through his hair. "Besides, a leader and a manager have two different skill sets. I had my fill of corporate management and the politics that goes with it. I'm not cut out to be a bureaucrat." He poked his thumb toward his chest. "I'm the type who needs time alone."

"Just what Antarctica needs—its first hermit." Grinning, she said, "Maybe Uncle Nick can sublet his cave to you."

He met her eyes and said softly, "Speaking of being alone, I worry about you being out here by yourself."

With a sideways grin, she nodded. "Thanks, John. I have a pistol."

"Good." He squeezed her shoulder. "Call me if you need help—I'm close by." He turned to leave, calling Ginnie to meet him at the hover.

She waved goodbye, then touched her shoulder, still warm from his hand. *Would they ever make love again?*

*　　*　　*

When all the houses in their sector were completed, the settlers focused on their own homesteads, until planting time for the major crops brought them together again.

Lowry had planted a small interior garden with vegetables and herbs susceptible to freezing, but today, she woke early to put in her main garden. She scouted around the house and found the best spot, and then led out the hover wagon, with tools, seeds, and seedlings she'd bought in town.

The community robo-tiller had arrived and introduced itself. "I am ready when you are ready." She synced the coordinates of the garden plot to the robo-tiller's software. "Thank you, I have the coordinates. May I begin?"

With an affirmative from Lowry, the robo-tiller rolled to the designated garden location, and with a beep, the tiller spun into gear with a whirr. Green light flashing, it dug into the first corner of the garden.

The rich smell of the soil drifted to her. Tears sprang into Lowry's eyes. This soil had never been touched by human hands.

The robo-tiller rumbled along, breaking and turning the soil into rows, sifting large rocks into a rear tray. The sun warmed and Lowry peeled off her sweater and ate lunch, watching the tiller progress. It took most of the day to prepare the beds, with Lowry emptying the rocks from the rear tray as it filled. When it completed the programmed garden outline, she sent the robo-tiller toddling off to the next farm, re-charging itself from the sun as it rolled along.

Lowry took a drink of water as the robo-tiller disappeared down the valley. With the long summer day, she still had time to plant the garden. She laid out the identification sticks, seed packets, and seedlings at the head of their corresponding row. She pulled on her gloves and began the back-breaking work.

As the sun reached the horizon, she lowered the last seeds into the ground, and with a flourish, set the final identification stick at the head of the last row. Exhausted, she threw the tools and trash into the wagon, peeled off her gloves, and added them to the pile. With a groan, she reached to the sky, one arm at a time, to stretch her tired back. She told the hover wagon, "Go home," and it hovered through the open door of the interior garden, back to its charging station.

With a sigh, Lowry walked to the well spigot and turned on the irrigation system. The clean water gushed down the pipe and onto the beds. The soil darkened as the moisture soaked into the earth.

Her back and shoulders ached as she trudged up the hill to the front of the house to admire her work. She slumped into one of the new Adirondack chairs and grimaced at her blistered hands. Then she gazed at the straight and ordered rows, out of place against the wilderness surrounding them. The lonely Patagonia pepper seedlings trembled in the wind, their vibrant green leaves contrasting against the dark soil.

Antarctica was a world of natural shapes—a terrain of glacial till, dotted with sporadic flowers, clumps of native grasses, and meandering rivers. *What will be the effects of human cultivation on this virgin continent?*

She had no desire to mar the landscape with the straight lines of human order. Instead of cutting her land into rows of wheat or corn, she had chosen to raise beef cattle. Tomorrow, she would begin sowing hardy grasses. Her cattle would arrive soon and they needed grasslands.

CHAPTER 15

As the sun set, Lowry gazed over her farm. It had been an exhausting month, but she was proud of her accomplishments. The land had proven to be fertile, the rains had been sufficient, and now tiny shoots of grass peeped through the earth. With the help of her neighbors and the community robo-crane, she had the stables for her horses.

Athira's white face popped over the half door of a stall and whinnied. With a grin, Lowry walked to the garden and dug up a few carrots. She broke them into pieces and walked to the stable. All the mares' heads appeared, with ears pricked, waiting for their treat. She went stall to stall, rubbing their faces as they chewed the carrot bits, chuckling as the new colt, Bashira, struggled to get his nose above the half-door. "You're too young for carrots, Baby," she said, stroking his neck.

"Good night," she called to them and strolled toward the house. She passed through the small orchard, caressing the blossoms scattered along the limbs.

She grabbed a basket in the kitchen, strolled to the interior garden. and picked some tomatoes, lettuce, and a few herbs, then returned to the kitchen to make dinner. She put a pot of boiling water on for pasta and sautéed the tomatoes with onion and garlic. When dinner was ready, she sat on the little patio, gazing at the river in the heart of the valley.

Everything she had—her home, her barn, even the food she ate—the people around her had made possible. The once-disparate souls who had competed against each other for their land were now melding into a new community. Local areas had formed small volunteer fire and police departments and elected community leaders.

Since the house-raising, she'd only seen John occasionally and usually from a distance.

Both of them had a brutal workload of building a farm out of the wilderness.

A convenient crust had formed between them.

Under the big sky, Lowry sat quietly gazing over the undulating landscape and finished the glass of wine. She set the glass on the table and caressed the stem. But work alone did not make a life.

*   *   *

A chill wind drove Lowry from the patio and into the warm house. She took the dirty dishes back into the kitchen and placed them in the dishwasher. After she cleaned the kitchen, she walked toward the bedroom, with the lights fading behind her. She showered and brushed her teeth. With a yawn, she climbed into bed and slid under the covers. She called out, "Night, night." The lights dimmed and the night shades rolled down.

In the early morning hours, her eyes shot open at the sound of Sparky's shrill barking. She held her breath to listen over her wildly beating heart, but now there was only silence. *Something was wrong.* Quietly, she slipped out of bed, threw on her robe, and tiptoed toward the front of the house.

It was an overcast morning, and she peered through the dark shades to catch a glimpse of Sparky. In the dim light, she saw a figure standing near the stable. She sucked in her breath, then dropped to her knees to hide herself below the window. *A stranger on her property.* Thank god she hadn't turned on any lights. Cautiously, she peeked over the window sill, and saw the man dragging something in the dirt toward the barn. She clapped her hand to her mouth—it was Sparky's body he was dragging.

Heart pounding, she scuttled back to the bedroom, her mind spinning in fear. With shaking hands, she grabbed some clothes from her drawers, and snatched her phone from the nightstand. She dove into the closet and punched John's number. While it rang, she jerked on her pants and threw a shirt over her head.

She crouched on a stool, whispering, "Answer, answer, answer!"

"Hello?" John said groggily.

In a hushed tone, she said, "John, this is Lowry—you've got to come quick!" Lowry choked, biting her lip. Her hands shook as she breathed deeply, struggling to control her fear. "Someone is here . . . and I, I think he killed Sparky."

"My god! I'll be right there." He paused, and asked, "Lowry, do you have your gun?"

"Um, let me see." She stood up, and stepped on top of the stool, fumbling through the clothes and boxes, until she found the pistol and a set of clips hidden on the top shelf.

John yelled into the phone, "Lowry, are you still there?"

"I was trying to find the pistol and, yes, I have it now." Her heart beat a staccato, and exhaling, she stared at the gun in her hand. In a quiet voice, she said, "I'm going to try to get out of the house, before he"—her throat constricted in fear, and in a wane voice she continued—"finds me."

"I'm leaving right now. I'll call the police on my way. And Lowry—do whatever it takes to keep yourself safe."

"I will, and thank you, John." She hung up, and sat back onto the stool, listening over her thumping heart. Voices of two men talking filtered into the closet. *God, there's two of them.*

With trembling fingers, she flipped on the flashlight of the phone. Turning the pistol upside down, she aimed the clip toward the magazine, but it slipped from her shaking hands and onto the floor with a clunk. *Shit.* She forced herself to breathe calmly. *Okay, Lowry, you can do this.* With a deep breath, she picked up the clip, and snapped it into the magazine.

Pistol in hand, she crawled to the closet door, and peered out, listening for the intruders. Nothing but an eerie silence in the house. She crept across the bedroom floor to the back window. If she could escape out the rear, she could climb the rocks and hide in one of a hundred crannies.

Lowry edged up and peeked through the window, then ducked. A man walked around the back of the house, now blocking her escape.

"I don't see the woman, but she's probably inside," he called out.

Lowry's heart beat faster and something in the pit of her stomach twisted like a knife. *They knew she was alone.* She clutched her throat at the sharp squeak of a crowbar prying open the front door. Shaking, she scrambled back across the floor and dove into the closet. She burrowed herself behind the hanging garments, pushing storage boxes in front of her feet.

Fear overcame her body under the smothering clothes and she bent forward to get more oxygen to her brain. It was the helplessness that was the worst. She didn't know if they were armed or not. She had not heard a shot killing Sparky. Maybe they didn't have a gun, but they must have some kind of weapon. And there were two of them. One man she might be able to kill, but two?

Please John, hurry. How long would it take him—maybe fifteen minutes?

The bedroom door creaked open, and she bit her lip to keep from screaming. The sound of footsteps, then thuds coming from her bedroom. He must be throwing things around in her room.

"Daddy, have you found her yet?" someone yelled from the other room.

"Nah," the intruder ransacking her room, replied.

"Her hover is by the house. She must be here."

The door to the closet slowly swung open, and her heart pounded at the sight of his dirty boots at the entrance. Light penetrated into the shadows hiding her, and "Daddy" stepped farther in and flicked on the light switch.

Lowry drew her body into a ball in the closet, staring at his red cap with an emblem of a black bear on the front. She listened to his hoarse breath as he searched for items to steal, cringing as the odor of his unwashed body hit her nostrils.

He brushed against the clothes she was hiding in and paused in front of her.

Her pulse thudded in her ears. She couldn't move, not an inch, or they would find her. A silent prayer flitted through her mind as she listened to his ragged breathing. *Please, God, if you can hear me, let them leave.*

Daddy huffed and walked out of the closet.

After several minutes of silence, she began to think he'd left the house—or at least hoped he had given up.

A clump, clump sound of footsteps coming closer again. A shadow fell across the doorway of the closet. With a shudder, she pressed herself to the wall of the closet and aimed the pistol toward the shadow. The beat of her heart pounded in her head.

Suddenly, the shadow contorted, blocking the light from the bedroom, and a hand grabbed her arm, jerking her upwards. Daddy yelled, "Looky what I found, Jake!"

The pistol became tangled in the clothes, but she pulled the trigger as he wrenched her forward. He screamed out, "The bitch shot me!" And he dragged her out of the closet.

Daddy ripped the gun from her hand. With a grunt, he threw it across the room and the pistol skidded under a chest of drawers. Lowry launched herself at him, fighting like one possessed, kicking and biting. Daddy backed away, shrieking for help. His son, Jake, leapt into the room and grabbed her by the arms, holding them tight behind her.

Lowry gagged from the body odor of the man clasping her as she faced the older man, blood dribbling down the side of his head.

Jake grunted, "Are you hurt bad, Daddy?"

With an angry stare at Lowry, Daddy jerked the red cap off of his head and pushed his finger through the singed hole the bullet had taken through the edge. He dug a bandanna out, shoved the cap into his pocket, and wiped the blood from the wound. He tied the bandanna around his head with a grunt. "Nah, just grazed me."

Lowry stared at the two men, her limbs weak with fear. Their hair was tangled and dirty, their clothes torn, and the stench in the room overpowering. They must have been sleeping out in the open for days.

Jake shoved her into the middle of the room.

Lowry shifted her eyes from one to the other. The look in their eyes revealed her danger as they rolled over her body. In a panic, she crossed her arms over her chest, holding herself together as she tried to think what to do. Without a weapon, there would be no escape unless she could outwit them until John arrived.

Glancing at his father, the younger man licked his lips. "Let's screw her—it'll serve the bitch right, shooting you like that."

Revulsion gripped her. To keep her wits about her, she breathed deeply, staring from one to the other.

The older man smiled. "Don't be so impatient, boy! Your granddad used to say, 'Work before pleasure.'" Beneath a furrowed brow, his eyes stared at her, and slowly, his mouth curled into a scowl. With one eye twitching, he stepped closer.

She shrank backwards at his leering grin.

"First, she needs to tell us where the jewelry is." In a flash, he snatched the back of her neck, jerking her toward his face. His foul breath struck her nostrils as he snarled, "Where's the good stuff? You've got to have some somewhere, at least besides here." He grabbed her crotch and squeezed.

Her heart went into her throat. Jake snickered. "Come on, let's do her now!"

Lowry shot a look at Jake, her throat closing at the look in his eyes. She gritted her teeth, staring at the older man. "Let me show you where I keep my jewelry."

The older man winked at Jake. "See, I knew she'd come around." He released his grip on her and shoved her forward, almost onto her knees.

She walked toward the bedroom door.

Daddy snapped, "Where are you going?"

"The garden. You don't think I'm so stupid to store my jewelry in the bedroom? It's the first place a thief would look."

He turned to Jake, pointing toward the side of the room. "Son, get the pistol, it's under that dresser."

Lowry sprang into the interior garden, palming a small pair of garden clippers off the table near the door. A minute later, Daddy and Jake stepped inside the garden behind her, furtively looking around.

She held the garden clippers at her side, muttering, "Now where did I bury the jewelry box?"

"We don't have all day, lady."

With a smirk, Jake followed close behind her, then gripped her butt. She twisted around and sliced at him with the garden shears.

Jake leapt back. Lowry felt the blades rip across his chest. Blood soaked through the tear in his shirt. With his teeth bared, he lunged toward her, and again she thrust the blades at him. He dodged the blow, but this time caught her by the wrist.

With a sharp twist to her arm, Jake shouted, "Drop it!"

Lowry shrieked in pain and dropped the bloody shears into the dirt. Jake pulled the pistol from his pants and pointed it at her head.

She shouted at Daddy, "Wait, let me find the jewelry box!"

Daddy snarled, "You had your chance, lady. Now it's our turn!"

Jake slapped her hard, knocking her to the ground, and she lay dazed. He knelt, raking his hand across her chest and ripping her shirt open. With a growl, she bit his hand as he tore the rest of the shirt off. He leapt on top of her, clasping her forearms with one hand, and wrenching her pants open with the other.

She rotated her leg out from under him, kicking him in the side, and he fell back, cursing. She rolled over, reaching for the leg of the garden table, but he grabbed her ankle, twisting hard. Screeching in pain, she flipped back and spat in his face.

He snatched her hair and shoved his face into hers. "You bitch!" Then he punched her in the mouth.

Flashes burst in front of her eyes, and she felt him rip the rest of her pants off. In a wave of fury, she sunk her teeth into his other hand, holding on to his skin as the metallic taste of his blood rushed into her mouth. Jake backhanded her and her face slammed into the dirt.

Barely conscious, she lay staring at the bank of windows along the front of the garden.

The older man moved over to them, spun her onto her back, and held her shoulders down. Jake stripped off the rest of her clothes and pushed open her legs. Through a haze, she could see him kneeling with his pants around his knees—and the grin on his face.

A shadow crossed the room.

"Get off of her!" John kicked Jake in mid-body, pitching him away from her.

Gaping at the shotgun pointing at him, Daddy backed up and threw up his hands.

"You animals!" John snarled, pivoting the barrel of the shotgun between the two men.

With a groan, Jake sat up, rubbing his head with his hand.

Lowry curled onto her side, covering her nakedness. From the corner of her eye, she saw Jake slip his other hand behind his back, scrambling for something in the dirt. She screamed as he raised the pistol toward John's chest. "He's got the gun!"

John spun, blasting quickly before Jake could pull the trigger.

Jake's face exploded. Bits of flesh and blood splattered across the garden. She clenched her jaw to keep from retching, staring at the bloody mass of ground meat that seconds ago had been a face. The blood oozed into the soil under Jake's body. Lowry caught the stench of body fluids and her stomach convulsed.

"Get away from her." John's voice boomed out as he aimed the shotgun at the older man's head. "Get flat on the ground or you're next." John moved closer, driving his boot into the father's chest, and he landed flat with a grunt.

Lowry sat up, plucking the shreds of her clothes with her hand.

"Are you all right?" John asked Lowry, without turning his head.

"Yes. Thank god, you came before they—" Staggering up, her legs shook. Averting her eyes from what was left of Jake, she stumbled out of the garden and into the bathroom. Her legs trembled as she sank onto the bench. She felt something on her shoulder and reached up to brush it off, but shuddered at the realization it was bits of Jake's flesh. Bile bubbled up into her throat. She got up and started to fill the tub. The hot water flowed into the bath, and swaying, she caught the edge with her hand to steady herself.

She heard John tie up Daddy with grunts and kicks.

John came into the bathroom and took Lowry into his arms, rocking her gently as he stroked her tangled hair. When the bath was ready, he slipped his arms around her body and lowered her in like a baby. The water turned pink as he washed the blood off her skin. He drained it away, then turned on the hand shower, rinsing her clean with fresh water. He helped her out and dried her off, then draped a robe around her. John shielded her eyes from the bloody scene with his body as they walked past the garden.

He sat her down in the living room. "I'll make a cup of tea," he said, and walked to the kitchen.

She heard sounds of Daddy rolling in the dirt of the garden.

"John, don't leave me alone," Lowry called out in a fragile voice.

"I'm right here, honey," he said, and glanced at the clock. "Um, let me get you some clothes. The police might be here soon."

He started back down the hall, then she heard thuds and groans.

She called out, "John, are you okay?"

"Yeah, I just had to step on the 'cockroach' again."

He returned from her bedroom with clothes and she went into the guest room to change. She laid the clothes on the bed and slid out of the robe. Cold, she shivered, and quickly pulled on the pants and sweatshirt. She stared at her trembling fingers and struggled to keep from crying. With a sigh, she staggered up and moved into the bathroom, and looked in the mirror. Lowry touched her swollen and bruised face, tears blurring her vision. She shook her head, staring at her reflected image. *It could have been worse.*

Lowry ran cool water on a washcloth and patted her wounds. Brushing her hair, she flinched as John yelled from the kitchen, "Tea's ready!"

In a daze, she walked into the kitchen and sat down at the table. With trembling fingers, she spooned in some sugar. Her face throbbed in pain as she stared vacantly out the window, sipping the hot drink.

John sat down beside her and took her hand. "Lowry, come stay with us for a few days, at least until this place is cleaned up."

"I don't know, John, I have animals to take care of." A tear ran down her face as she remembered. "They killed Sparky."

John slipped his arm around her shoulder. "I'm so sorry, Lowry." With a sigh, he stared at the table, and shook his head. "Humans are vicious animals." He paused, staring at her intently. "You shouldn't be out here by yourself. At least stay with us until you heal. Ginnie and I will help with the horses."

With a sigh, Lowry nodded.

They both jumped when someone banged on the door. John rose, picked up his shotgun, and walked to the broken door. When he opened it, a young man with a badge hastily pinned on his farm clothes stood on the steps.

The young man cleared his throat and said, "You called the police?"

"Yes, I'm John Barrous, from the next farm over." He peered behind the young man. "Are you alone?"

Shrugging, he nodded.

John said, "Well, come in," with a tilt of his head.

The young man stepped into the house and shuffled over to Lowry. With a pensive smile, he said, "I'm Lieutenant Martin Levin, from the volunteer fire and police department of this sector. Mr. Barrous telephoned that you had a couple of men break in here?"

She nodded her head but did not look at him. "Yes."

John glanced at Lowry and then turned to Lt. Levin. "Let me show you what happened," and led him into the garden.

They returned with the older man in cuffs.

"Ma'am, I'm afraid someone will have to return later to get photos and remove the body," Lt. Levin said softly. "You may want to get to the clinic and see to those wounds."

Nodding, John gazed at Lowry. "Yes, we need to make sure she's all right."

The officer shoved the older man, twice his weight, out the door.

John called after him, "Don't turn your back on him, son."

Numbly, Lowry watched John pull eggs from the refrigerator and crack them into a bowl. He set a pan onto the stove, threw in a pat of butter, and turned on the heat. He beat the eggs into a froth with a whisk, the harsh whipping sound of the metal against metal raking her ears. The egg yolks sizzled hitting the hot pan. John set the table and Lowry blinked against the noise of clattering dishes.

He sat across from her, then reached out and squeezed her hand. "Try to eat something."

Nodding, Lowry picked up her fork, staring down at the plate full of scrambled eggs, her stomach churning.

The corpse lay waiting in the garden.

CHAPTER 16

John opened his eyes in the pitch-black room. He asked softly, "P, what time is it?"

His phone answered, "Four forty-eight in the morning, John."

He grunted. With a yawn, he sat up, tucked an extra pillow behind his head, then leaned back. It was cold. He pulled the blankets over his chest.

P asked, "John, are you ready for me to roll up the dark shades?"

"Yes, please. And you can turn the alarm off. I'm awake."

The dark shades rolled up and a pale blue sky met his eyes. The sun rested on the horizon, and shadow and light played across the undulating fields, and where the sun's rays touched the frost, the landscape shimmered like diamonds.

John rolled out of bed and sat on the edge of the mattress. The room lights brightened, and he shoved his unruly hair out of his face. He scratched his head and glanced at the clothes he'd thrown over the chair the night before. *Planting day.*

He smelled coffee brewing. "Thanks, P."

"You're welcome, John. Best wishes for a successful day."

He pulled on his clothes and finished his morning ablutions, then proceeded into the kitchen. He breathed in the aroma of freshly brewed coffee, poured himself a large mug and sipped the hot liquid. The sunlight crept over the window sill and beamed into the kitchen. He jammed a muffin in his mouth, then threw on his coat and walked outside.

The summer sun had begun to rise. John gazed at the sky scattered with pale stars, like a faded pair of blue jeans with a few lingering rhinestones. It was going to be a brilliant day, with enough bite in the air to make it interesting. The fields had been prepped by removing the native vegetation and now lay waiting for seed. He walked to the barn to make sure everything was ready for the big event.

Last week, he had helped with another neighbor's farm planting barley. With four robotic tractors and several men to load seed onto waiting hoppers, they planted over a few days what would take one person a month to accomplish.

He opened the barn, stepped inside the chilly interior, and flipped on the small heater. John set up a coffee and water station and then laid out various snacks on a table. He rubbed his cold hands and checked the time. *When will the crew arrive?*

As the building warmed, the aroma of wheat rose from the bags stacked next to the wall, ready for planting. He left the barn at the sound of tractors pulling up in the yard. John directed the crew to a parking area, and then they jumped off of the robo-tractors and out of hovers.

"Have some coffee!" he yelled, gesturing to the coffee station. He poured several steaming cups and handed them around. John noticed a young man standing with the group, dressed in boots and a big cowboy hat.

With a grin, the young man stepped up to John and stuck out his hand. "Howdy, I'm Lowry's new hired hand, Chuy. Lowry had to go into Amundsen today, and she sent me over to help with the crew, in her place."

"Happy to have you." He shook his hand and gave him a cup of coffee. "Where are you from, Chuy?"

Chuy smiled. "Arizona, mostly."

John nodded, studying Chuy's honest face. "I hope Antarctica suits you and I'm glad that Lowry has help over there. You're welcome to breakfast."

Chuy walked over to the snack table and grabbed a biscuit.

John was relieved that Lowry had someone at the farm, and he hoped Chuy worked out. He smiled watching Chuy saunter to the barn—at least he wasn't wearing spurs.

The rest of the neighbors arrived. One of the more experienced farmers gathered the crew in front of the barn. John had been a minor player in the last planting and was more than aware of his shortcomings as a real farmer.

Bags of wheat were brought to the seed hopper on a hover cart. The lead farmer gestured for John to throw up the first bag. He slung the seed bag up to the hopper opening, but then stared in confusion at the mechanics of the actual loading. He glanced up and saw the grins on the faces surrounding him.

He chuckled and said, "Okay, show me how to do this!"

Laughing, they gathered around him, smiling faces from every corner of the globe, now a team of equals creating a new world: The Brazilians who had fallen into the permafrost, still with casts on their broken limbs; a lesbian couple from Australian; the tall Nigerian he had seen at the starting line; a Pakistani man; a scientist from China; and two men from Europe. The friendly faces lifted his spirits—a growing kinship between diverse people, true friendship based on loyalty and hard work. Not a hierarchy of masters and pseudo-slaves of the corporate world he had fled.

It would be a long day of planting wheat, but the only time for a human to guide the robot tractors. Once the field was programmed into the computer, the dimensions of his land was stored into the farm's virtual memory to be accessed each season, until a change in crop or use occurred. As the plows ripped into the land, John inhaled the rich aroma. In the wake of the tractors, dust swirled into the air, and birds hopped in the fertile soil for insects.

The planting went smoothly until a tractor broke down around noon. They took a lunch break while two of the men replaced the hydrogen fuel cell. John walked up to the house for cold drinks and turned at the top of the hill to gaze at the plowed rows of black earth drying in the sun.

After replacing the cell on the tractor, they returned to planting. In the warmth of the afternoon, John struggled to remove his jacket, driving the catlike tractor along the endless rows.

At the end of the day, he was pleased with their progress, but exhausted. They returned to the barn and John pulled on his coat against a chill wind. Someone called his name from afar and he turned to see Lowry cantering her mare toward him. Two furry puppy faces stuck out of a pouch strapped around her.

She halted the mare and said, "I brought Ginnie a present." She stroked their heads. "I have a puppy for me and one for Ginnie—they're Golden Retrievers."

He scratched the pups under their ears and glanced up at her. "I see." He examined her face. The bruises from the attack by the two men had faded to a pale yellow. Her smile wavered with a lingering hint of fragility. He clenched his jaw.

Her brow furrowed. "I hope you don't mind."

John shook his head. "Not at all. What's a farm without a dog?" He stroked each puppy's face. "How have you been, Lowry?"

She drew in a long breath. "I'm better. Thanks so much for letting me stay a couple of days until they cleaned up—"

He held up his hand. "Sure, no problem. And I met Chuy. He seems to be a good guy. I'm glad you have someone else at the farm."

With a broad smile, he waved her toward the house. "Let's show Ginnie—she'll love the puppy!" He called out, "Ginnie! Lowry's here with something to show you."

Lowry dismounted, pulled the sack off of her shoulder and placed it gently on the ground. She opened the top and the two puppies scrambled out, barking at John. Chuckling, he knelt and ruffled their blond coats.

Ginnie ran out of the house, screaming when she saw the puppies. "What cute puppies! Are they your new dogs, Lowry?"

"One of them is yours."

"Really?" Ginnie turned to John, who nodded with a smile.

"Pick one of them," Lowry said. "I'm taking the other one."

Ginnie played with them and then picked up the one who nuzzled her hand. "I'll take this one." She cuddled him and the puppy licked her face. "Dad, let's name him Henry—I've always liked that name."

"Henry it is."

"A great name, Ginnie. I'm going to name his brother Leo." Lowry patted him on the head. John turned to her. "It's very nice of you to give us a puppy, Lowry. How can we repay you?"

With a slight shake of her head, she smiled. "You've saved my life, let's see, how many times now? The question is—how can I repay you?"

He grinned. "I didn't have anything else to do."

CHAPTER 17

Lowry tapped her fingers against her leg and checked the horizon again for any sign of dust from vehicles on the road. She hated the waiting more than anything. Her cattle were supposed to arrive today. They should have been here this morning but had been delayed at the port by some snafu at the agricultural department. She'd sent Chuy to guide them back, but she hadn't heard from him since this morning, and then only a terse message about forms to process.

Clouds were gathering on the horizon and Lowry hoped they'd arrive before the stormy weather hit. It had been unfortunate that the delivery of the cow barn had been delayed, but Chuy had told her that cattle were used to living out.

Lowry was feeding the horses at the end of the day when she spotted the dust cloud she'd been waiting for. Six trucks came into view, the first five jammed with reddish-brown Highland cattle, but the last had only one animal—the bull. She heaved a sigh of relief and walked to the corral.

As the trucks approached, Lowry examined the pen and crossed her fingers it would hold the cattle. They had used solar electric fencing for the horses, but this new fencing system used lasers beams to hold the animals. The system had tall metal posts on four corners, embedded with a series of laser components spaced along the vertical length of the interior of the post, but no horizontal rails. Solar- and wind-powered, with a battery backup, it was touted as keeping animals inside better than any traditional fencing, but she was still a bit nervous about it. Fencing her property with conventional means, with imported wooden fence posts would be outrageous in cost, since there wasn't enough lumber available in Antarctica.

The six trucks stopped, and a cloud of dust enveloped them. Chuy jumped down and walked toward her. "All accounted for, Lowry."

"I was beginning to think cattle rustlers had waylaid you guys."

With a frown, he shook his head. "No, worse—the Antarctic Agricultural Department."

Lowry switched on the lasers to the fence, and the red beams shot around the perimeter, closing the gaps except for the chute leading from the truck ramps. Chuy signaled for the hands to get the cattle moving.

At first, the cows balked, but then ran down the chute, and circled within the red laser pen. Lowry exhaled, relieved that the lasers had held. She had chosen to start her ranch with Highland cattle, with their thick shaggy coats, their ability to survive frigid climates, and the excellent quality of their meat.

A truckload at a time, they backed up to the ramps leading to the chute, and unloaded the cattle into the pen. She counted the cattle as they barreled down the ramps—a full hundred head. The dust swirled around them and she held a handkerchief over her mouth and nose. Last was the majestic bull, with his long horns, descending the ramp into the pen. Once he reached the dirt of the corral, he threw his head up with a sniff, examining his new home. With a bellow, he ambled over to the cows, already grazing on the hay bales they had placed in the center. The herd settled in, and though several were bloodied from the long pilgrimage, they seemed in good shape. Lowry paid the drivers and they drove back to Amundsen.

She walked back to the corral and leaned on the gate. "I hope we can handle these cattle by ourselves," she said to Chuy. "Those horns are intimidating."

He smiled. "I've handled Longhorns all my life, and with my two herd dogs and those cuttin' horses you bought, these Highlanders shouldn't be any problem."

Her eyes twinkled at his youthful confidence. She had hired him through the ranch from which she had purchased the cutting horses and knew he was a good hand, but she didn't feel as confident. A young heifer walked toward the perimeter, then shied away from the energy along the laser beams. Even with the entire herd inside, the fence seemed to be holding.

Lowry grinned. *I'm a bona-fide rancher.* The wind began to rise as they settled down for the night. She zipped her jacket and walked to the house.

After dinner, the exhaustion of the day hit her and she crawled into bed and slept soundly. In the middle of the night, a flash of light hit her subconscious. The following thunder, rippling in frightening proximity, roused her awake, and she sat up in bed. She slipped out from the covers and pulled on a robe.

She stumbled to the window, calling softly to her phone, "Raise the shades, please."

The dark shades rose. With a rat-tat-tat, the rain pelted against the exterior glass. A new flash of lightning splintered across the sky, illuminating the room like a searchlight. Lowry clutched her robe as the boom of thunder shook the windowpanes.

The rain obscured her view of the corral. Even from the house she could hear their uneasy mooing. Another blast of lightning flashed overhead and exposed the wet bodies of the cows, milling about like worms in a bait bucket.

The storm was strengthening. She wouldn't be able to sleep with the wailing winds and cracking thunder. She pulled on a sweater and work pants, and then brushed her hair back with her fingers.

She returned to the window, peering out at the pen. A bolt of lightning hit the power supply panel for the fence and it exploded like fireworks. The cattle nearby jumped away as the sparks showered down on them. The red laser fence went dark.

"Oh my god!"

Another crack of lightning and the cattle bolted, running straight through the openings in the corral.

She rang Chuy's number.

His voice was groggy. "Hello?"

"The cows are out! Lightning blew the power to the pen!"

"Shit!"

Her hands shook as she fought to put on her rain gear. She bolted out of the house and into the driving rain. Halfway to the stables, lightning zipped to the earth, and the itch of electricity crawled over her body. Two more steps and the boom of thunder cracked over her. The soil oozed beneath her feet, gripping her boots as she staggered to the stable.

Lowry leapt into the stable, deafened by the rain pounding on the metal roof. She grabbed tack and ran to the stall of one the new cutting horses.

She opened the stall, and murmured, "You're okay, girl," to the trembling mare. She stroked the mare with one hand as she threw the pad and saddle over her back. She eased the bridle over her head and led her out of the stall.

Chuy ran down the steps from his room in the stable loft. He let the herd dogs out of their kennel and began to saddle the other mare.

Over the clamor of the storm, Lowry shouted to Chuy, "Follow me as fast as you can!"

Lowry swung in the saddle and kicked the mare into the driving storm. The mare hooves sloshed through the mud as they followed the wide track left by the hundred stampeding animals.

The tracks headed toward the hills, and she hoped the cattle would slow when they approached them. With the next lightning strike, Lowry's heart sunk; the cattle tracks had turned, heading toward the narrow valley that led to John's land.

"Damn!" Luck was not with her tonight.

The rain pelted into her face as she turned to follow the herd through the valley. The usually narrow stream bed was filled with rushing water and the mare slipped in the deep mud, struggling to stay on the shifting bank. The cattle had slowed through the rising water as the stream became a surging river. She clenched her teeth. It might soon be a death trap.

The cows broke away from the stream as the sides of the pass widened. Spurred by fresh bolts of lightning, the herd surged faster across the open fields on John's property. Through a surreal strobe of lightning strikes, she watched the fruit trees John had planted get knocked over by the onslaught of insane beasts.

Thundering past his house, the herd raced onto open land and she bent over the mare's neck, kicking her hard to overtake the stampede. With her ears pinned flat back, the mare stretched out, her hooves flying over the wet ground. In a fading flash of lightning, Lowry saw the lead cow, galloping at the front of the herd. Lowry slapped the reins on the mare's rear and steered her toward the cow, yelling, "Yah!" in an effort to get her to cut in front of the leader.

The lead cow raced across the flats, her long hair matted across her face, her horns wet and glistening. Lowry gave the mare her head and she leapt to the front of the herd, and cut off the leader, forcing her to the right. The lead cow broke into a trot, and the rest of the herd slowed.

Chuy galloped up behind her. The herd dogs turned the exhausted cattle into a circle.

"The storm's moving off. We should be able to head them back home," Chuy yelled.

The cattle slowed to a walk, and they turned them back toward the farm.

They walked past John's house, and her heart dropped at the sight of him at the door. She nudged the mare toward him and stopped.

She gestured with her arm. "The cattle stampeded from the storm—I am so sorry! I'll come by in the morning to look at the damage. I know they took out some of your fruit trees—"

John gripped his robe around him, his hair disheveled by the wind. "We'll see tomorrow what your crazed cattle did. I'm going back to bed." He started to turn away, then called after her, "I'm just glad you're okay."

*   *   *

Early the next morning, Lowry walked by the repaired enclosure. Most of the cattle were lying down, calmly chewing their cuds. Relieved, she walked to the stable, saddled up Athira and headed over to John's place. In the clear sunlight, the extent of the churned earth was shocking. She steered the horse to the edge of the muddy mess, onto solid ground.

After the storm of last night, the air had cleared and sunlight sparkled on the scattered puddles of rainwater. The soil had absorbed the beneficial rain and the organic smell of earth drifted on the breeze. Hardy grasses carpeted the fields— grasses she had planted.

Birds flitted through the air, butterflies gathered on the muddy ground, and wildflowers bloomed. There was a fierceness of life in the short, but intense growing season on the continent of Antarctica.

Rocking to the mare's leisurely gait, the lack of sleep of last night hit her, and she yawned in the warm sunshine. She approached the stream. The night before it had been a raging torrent, but now it flowed within its banks. Lowry nudged the mare forward into the river and let her drink from the cool water.

Lowry glanced down river and froze at the sight of a cow, lying motionless half-submerged in the water. *Shit.* She urged the mare forward, the horse's hooves made sucking sounds as they sank into the muddy, churned up bank.

When they reached the battered body of the cow, Lowry shook her head. It was one of the young heifers. The once-beautiful red coat of the cow was now matted and dull. Buzzing flies crawled in and out of her lifeless nostrils. Lowry exhaled. *Nothing to do but bury the poor beast.*

The mare nibbled on the leaves of a nearby bush, tugging the limbs toward her. Lowry picked up the slack in the reins and clucked to the mare. As the mare's head lifted, a black crow burst through the tangle of branches, flashing upwards out of the shadows. Terrified, the mare leapt to the side, jerking Lowry into the bird's line of flight. The crow's cold beady eyes stared into Lowry's and the waft from the glossy black wings stroked Lowry's face. Their beat matched the thud of her heart.

The bird flew across the stream and into the trees beyond, cawing, and Lowry shuddered at its mocking tone. She re-gripped the reins, got her feet back into the stirrups, and then stared at her trembling fingers. She scratched the mare's neck, whispering, "It's okay, girl," not sure if she was talking to the horse or herself.

Lowry tucked her hair back under her helmet and turned back toward John's farm. The cow's death and mocking crow shadowed their steps. Unease crawled up her back, like an insect between her shoulder blades. She shook her head to clear it, and when they reached solid ground along the river, she nudged the mare into a slow canter. The river flowed gently, meandering around boulders and snarled mats of brush left over from the flood. The murmur of flowing water calmed her mind, and she relaxed with the mare's smooth canter.

Lowry slowed the mare to a walk as she crossed into John's land, dreading to see the consequences of last night's stampede. Deep gouges, drying in the mud, marked the trail of destruction cutting through his land and into his orchard. John was already busy, setting the trees back up and stomping the soil into place.

Stopping near him, she dismounted and hobbled her horse. She cleared her throat and smiled, and John nodded to her, but kept working. As she walked closer to him, she assessed the damage. Maybe a third of his orchard had been bowled over.

Lowry chewed her lip and held the sapling upright while he re-staked the tree. "I'll have Chuy come over with a tractor and smooth out the ruts. And unfortunately, pick up a dead cow, trampled during the stampede near the river."

With a last blow of the hammer, he shook the tree to make sure it was stable, then looked at her. "Sorry to hear about the cow, but I'd appreciate Chuy's help." He pointed toward a field to the left, tinted green with new growth. "At least they didn't trample my baby wheat."

With a slight smile, he shrugged. "Don't worry. Besides the tracks, they knocked down some fruit trees, but I just have to straighten and stake them until they re-root." He moved to the last tree, beat the last of the stakes into the ground, and stood. "Want to come see my wheat?"

They walked over to the field and he knelt, caressing the tiny plants, grinning like a proud father as the wind rippled the young shoots. The breeze ruffled John's hair, and she glanced at his tanned face. He had become a different person since the Land Rush. His body honed to the life of farming, the stress of his former so-called easy living had fallen away like excess weight.

Lowry grinned. "Farm life suits you."

John inhaled, gazing across the fields of wheat. "Yes, I love every minute of it. I have time to think while I work in the fields." With a crooked smile, he tilted his head toward the house. "Come have coffee with me."

As they strolled to the house, John pointed out the new buildings and gardens.

"You've done a lot of work to the place!"

"Thanks, Lowry. Ginnie helps a lot when she's not in school." John opened the door and pointed her toward the kitchen.

He pulled a chair out for her at the kitchen table and called softly to the coffee maker, "Start coffee." He stepped to the counter, grabbed a couple of cups, and set them on the table. He scraped the chair on the floor as he sat across from her.

He cleared his throat. "Tell me how you've been, Lowry."

She lowered her eyes, staring at the table. The attack from the intruders had been weeks ago, but there were still nights she awoke, clutching her covers, terrified that someone was breaking in. But it was just the wind or the scratching of the dog.

He moved the sugar closer to her. "Are you sleeping okay?" he asked softly.

She breathed in the aroma of coffee and then met his gaze. "The nightmares are fading," then she touched her cheek. "And my face is healed." With a shrug, she smiled. "I'm better. Thanks for asking."

"Good." He stood, grabbed the carafe of fresh coffee, and brought it to the table, filling the cups. Their hands touched as he gave her the cup and a jolt traveled up her arm. She turned away, unconsciously caressing the lip of the cup. It had been a long time since she'd been alone with John.

John coughed, tapping his fingers on the table. Lowry glanced up at him. His face taut, he stared distractedly at his coffee. He gulped the hot brew and made a face. "Mmm, that's some hot coffee," he muttered, without looking at her.

She bit the inside of her lip. He had felt the tremor as well.

Fumbling with the spoon, she spilled sugar on the table, and then asked, "Do you have cream?"

He turned abruptly. "Sure."

Their hands touched again as he handed her the cream. Her fingers trembled as she grasped the cool bottle, pouring the fresh cream into her cup. Languidly stirring the cream into the coffee, she looked into John's face . . . and piercing gaze.

CHAPTER 18

John shielded his eyes from the bright light as he stepped onto the patio from the kitchen. He shook his head. Tonight was New Year's Eve, but somehow it didn't feel right with it being warm. At the bottom of the world, it was summer.

John walked to the garden and dully slid on his gloves. He shuffled between the rows, distractedly pulling weeds from around the vegetables. If he couldn't rid his mind of weeds, maybe he could at least do something about the ones in the garden.

The drama of the Land Rush was over. Ginnie was gone; she'd taken her finals early and had left for the holidays to be with her grandparents in the States. Within a few days after her departure, he had awoken with a touch of depression. And like a tough piece of meat, it had to be slowly, yet thoroughly, chewed.

John worked through lunch and stopped late in the afternoon. He fixed a glass of lemonade and sat on the porch, while the warm breeze dried the sweat on his body. The farm was in great shape—all he had done was work and sleep since Ginnie had left.

His mind drifted toward thoughts of Lowry. The last time they'd been alone was after the stampede, and he hadn't seen her since. With the daily survival of building a farm out of the hinterlands, the chance to mend their relationship seemed to slip away. Perhaps he was afraid to.

The creak of the rocking chair calmed his mind with its cadence. Over the months, he'd realized he no longer felt guilty about his feelings for Lowry. Helen was gone and he was sure she would have wanted him to process his grief and move on with his life. She might approve of Lowry, even though the two women were such opposites.

John stopped rocking suddenly, spilling his lemonade. Vacantly staring, he gripped the arm of the chair—he wanted to hold Lowry, to love her. *Why am I sitting on this porch, pining over Lowry, instead of trying to win her?* He wanted to spend the rest of his life with her, the two of them working together for their future.

He drank the rest of the lemonade and set the glass down. But did Lowry feel the same? When they were near each, their eyes locked for a second before they turned away. Or was he just imagining it?

Henry wandered over and placed his head on John's shoe. He bent down and stroked his head. "Are you missing your Ginnie?" he said softly.

John exhaled. Even if Lowry loved him, would she marry him? He let the idea simmer, mulling over the practical consequences of marriage with her. Perhaps they could combine their land? Regardless, it would be a huge change for him, for Lowry, and for Ginnie. His brow furrowed, staring out at the horizon. *Ginnie.* He had to discuss all this with her.

The evening cooled as the sun sank lower in the sky. John glanced at his watch, surprised at how long he'd been sitting on the porch. He jumped up and headed into the house. He'd been playing hermit too long. Tonight he was going to the New Year's Eve bash.

After a bath and shave, he dressed in the formal attire of Antarctica—jeans and a white cotton shirt. He brushed his hair in the mirror, then found himself trying to hide the strands of gray. With a sigh, he grimaced at the face in the mirror. *You're pathetic.*

John walked to the hover, glancing up at the birds dipping and darting in the sky overhead. "Wish me luck."

He cruised to the festivities, passing cultivated fields of tall wheat and barley, rippling in the wind. Over a hill, and the sparkling lights and crowds of people surrounding the new pavilion came into view. The pavilion had been designed and built by neighbors from this sector as a meeting place for families and friends, crafted out of native stone and built to last a century.

Smiling, he imagined future weddings and anniversaries. Then his smile faded on the thought of the memorials which would also be held there. Everyone who had worked on it was being honored at the dedication tonight.

A breeze picked up as John parked the hover, and he pulled on his jacket. He wandered through the crowd and steadied himself at the sight of Lowry, standing with a group of homesteaders. He walked toward her, catching tidbits of a heated political discussion.

Bill, the Australian farmer adjacent to John's land, ranted about the near-riot that had occurred at Nick's last political fundraiser. "It was a setup, I tell you, a setup!"

One of the others turned to Lowry. "I thought Durant had been run out of Antarctica. What do you think, Lowry?"

Lowry shrugged. "I heard that he beat the charges—somehow. A terrifying prospect, but rumor has it that Durant will be running against Nick for president."

Bill pounded his fist into his other hand and yelled, "If that scoundrel is running, then I'm sure it was some of Durant's men who started the ruckus."

Another farmer stepped in front of him. "How do you know it was Durant? Besides, he has the business know-how and connections to set up Antarctica. What does Nick have? He's a backwoods miner with no experience running a country—especially a new one."

He shoved the Durant supporter. He staggered backwards, then leapt forward and punched Bill in the face, knocking him to his knees. With a growl, Bill charged into his opponent. The ring of farmers closed around the circling fighters, cheering like it was a boxing match.

John jumped between them and pushed the men apart. "Settle this at the ballot box, not in the dirt," he said sharply. "It's New Year's Eve, for god's sake."

Lowry stepped into the circle, and said softly, "I know my Uncle Nick and I know Durant—we must support good over evil, my friends." She gazed at each one in turn.

Durant's supporter spat onto the ground and turned away in a huff. The rest of the farmers walked toward the drink table, slapping Bill on the back.

John turned and stepped toward Lowry. "Hi."

She shook her head with a grin. "Hi, yourself. Just had to get into the fray?"

"What's a New Year's Eve party without a fight?"

Lowry looked him up and down and straightened his jacket. "You're looking mighty sharp tonight."

He found himself getting lost in her eyes and fumbled for something to say. "How about this weather? Little dry isn't it?"

Laughing, she slipped her arm in his, leading him toward the pavilion. "What a true farmer you've become! Unfortunately, I'm already feeding hay. I hope I have enough to last through the winter."

He was out of practice for repartee and smiled.

"Where's Ginnie tonight?" Lowry asked, looking behind him. "I have steaks and a box of veggies from the garden I wanted to give you two."

He cleared his throat and mumbled, "Miss Ginnie is away at Helen's parents' house for the holidays, so it's just me, myself, and I." She narrowed her eyes at him, and he felt her studying his face. *How well can she read me?*

"I'm sure Ginnie is having fun," she said, touching his arm, "but I know the holidays are tough when you're alone."

With a grin, she dragged him toward the bar. "So, let's celebrate New Year's Eve together."

They grabbed two glasses of champagne and retreated to the edge of the crowd.

John raised his glass. "A toast to Cowgirl Lowry!"

Lowry nodded. "And one to Farmer John." Clinking his glass, she said, "Our first New Year in the New World."

"Happy New Year's Eve, Lowry." John murmured, meeting her eyes over the glass of bubbly.

At the edge of the pavilion, the mayor of Amundsen raised his arms. "Friends and neighbors, welcome."

Lowry turned to listen, smiling at the jovial crowd. John stood one step behind Lowry, swallowing hard, as a strand of hair caressed her face in the light breeze.

The mayor waved his hand toward the new building. "We have gathered here for the dedication of this stunning pavilion, and what better time to do this than on our first New Year's Eve on Antarctica!"

The crowd cheered amid pops from bottles of champagne. Laughter roared as the bubbly spewed across them and then they held out their glasses to be filled.

The mayor continued after the crowd had quieted. "We also want to announce the winner of the contest to name both the pavilion and this sector we've come to call home." A small troupe of youngsters brought him an envelope and stepped back. With a flourish, he opened the envelope and read the winner. With a big smile, he shouted into the microphone, "The winner is Ginnie Barrous, with the beautiful name of the Adélie River Region! Ginnie, if you're here, please come up to accept your award."

Clapping, Lowry turned to John with a grin. He chuckled in surprise and stumbled to the stage through the cheering crowd. He climbed the steps, smiling at the gathering. One of the children handed him the plaque for his daughter. The mayor motioned him to join him at the podium.

John stepped to the microphone, holding up the plaque for the crowd to see. "My daughter is away for the holidays. She'll be disappointed she wasn't here tonight. But I know she would want me to tell you how she came up with the name, Adélie River Region. In studying the history of Antarctica, she read about the Adélie penguins, a true Antarctic species, but who unfortunately went extinct after the Melt. In their honor, she wanted to name the river and region after them." John held up the plaque and nodded to the crowd. "Thank you, my friends."

A crowd of well-wishers descended upon them and it wasn't until the New Year was approaching that he was able to be alone with Lowry. They kissed at the stroke of midnight.

John whispered in her ear, "Let's go."

They climbed into their hovers, and Lowry followed him, floating through the soft light of evening to his farm. After she parked next to house, she opened the door of the hover and stepped out.

Henry bounded up to greet her. She knelt and petted the dog. With a happy whine, he licked her face.

John walked over to her. With a grin, he patted the dog's back, and lifted his ear, and said jokingly, "Henry-boy, back off, you're in my territory."

Laughing, Lowry stood and leaned back against the hover. He moved close to Lowry. Shyly, he pulled a lock of her hair to his lips and kissed it. He gazed into her uncertain eyes and whispered, "Are you all right?"

She tilted her head. "Yes and no—still a little fragile, I guess."

With his knuckles, John gently caressed her cheek, then pulled her into his arms with a sigh. Lowry snuggled her head into his shoulder. He stroked her hair, and his calluses caught on the strands.

He hesitated, then touched her face with his finger. "Are my hands rough?"

Smiling, she turned his hand over and kissed the palm. "They're a little rougher than the last time I felt them."

Lowry faced him, and their eyes locked together. She wrapped her arms around his neck and pulled him into a kiss.

Henry pushed between them, wagging his tail.

John frowned. "Henry, I think you need to stay in your room tonight."

John picked her up and carried her to the house, both of them laughing as he maneuvered her through the door. He stuck his leg out, blocking the dog from entering. "You go around back, through the doggy door, and get into your bed, Henry."

They entered the house and the lights brightened.

John said, "Mood lights, P."

"Yes, John. Happy New Year's Eve."

"Thanks, P, you, too. Goodnight, P." The lights dimmed, and he slowly let Lowry down.

"P?" Lowry asked.

"Yeah, P for phone—clever, I know." He stroked her cheek with his fingers.

"I've opted for no virtual assistant. Someday I'll tell you about 'Lowry's Big Adventure' and then you'll know why."

John kissed her. "But not tonight." He kissed her again.

"Definitely—"

Threading his fingers through her hair, John kissed her harder.

"—not—"

He stared into her eyes and pressed Lowry against the wall, clasping her hands and slowly stretching her arms toward the ceiling.

"—tonight," she said hoarsely.

He crushed his mouth into hers.

With trembling hands, Lowry unbuttoned his shirt, while he kissed her eyebrows. She peeled his shirt back, then ripped hers over her head. Turning toward him, she pulled his face to hers, whispering, "John, I want you to make love to me."

He grabbed the back of her hair and swung her down the hall, pressing her against the opposite wall, only steps from the bedroom.

John kissed her deeply. Her hands went to his fly and she unbuttoned his jeans, moaning as he thrust his mouth deeper into hers. They broke apart for a moment and he kicked off his pants. He picked her up and she wrapped her legs around him. Nuzzling her neck, he carried her into the bedroom.

Gently, he placed her on the bed and lay next to her. He stared at her tousled hair and the lock curled across her forehead. Her lips curved into a gentle smile. He pushed back the errant lock of hair, and her eyes met his.

Lowry wrapped her arms around his neck and pulled him into a deep kiss. He hugged her to him, and they lay facing each other on the bed. He stroked her face, then gently kissed his way up to her ear. Lowry inhaled sharply and drew his mouth onto hers.

For a second their lips parted, and in the dim light of the midnight sun, he stared at her quietly. They made love, with the same magic he had felt the first time with her.

Afterward, he kissed her gently, and then lay beside her, his breath slowing. He tilted his head to touch hers and stroked her leg with a sigh. The first time they had made love he had been an emotional basket case, but the ghosts of his past had faded into soft memories of another time, another life.

Lowry smiled tiredly and traced the shape of his lips with her finger. She shivered, and he reached down and covered them both with the sheet.

He pulled her face to him, kissing her softly. "Lowry, I love you."

She kissed his eyelids. "I love you, too."

They snuggled together and watched the sun skid along the horizon.

Lowry whispered, "The sun barely rests now."

"Yes."

She smoothed his hair away from his face. "You made it to your first New Year's on Antarctica—a time for reflection. Are you settling in, or do you ever think about going home?"

He cuddled her to him. "This is my home. I could never go back to that life. That world is so far from mine, there's no connection anymore. The few times I've talked with some of my old chums in the States, I had the vague feeling I've become more of a novelty than a friend." He chuckled. "I'm the one who went native."

He rolled onto his back, pulling her onto his shoulder. Jon stared at the ceiling with a deep sigh. "I won't deny that it's been tough. It's been a complete restructuring of our lives.

Here, you either take it or leave it—there are no choices and no conveniences. It's been especially hard on Ginnie. She'll have to make her own choice when the time comes as to whether she'll stay or not." He looked away. "But it will kill me if she leaves."

Lowry ran her fingers through the hair on his chest. "You mean *when* she leaves."

John grimaced. "Yes, when she leaves. There's no university here as yet, so unless something changes, she'll be off to college in a couple of years."

Yawning, she shifted against his shoulder, and closed her eyes.

His window of opportunity was closing. John drew in his breath and made the leap. "I know I flubbed our first foray, but I'd like to push the restart button on our relationship."

Lowry peered at him, and nestled closer. "For myself, I'll say this was a good first step."

With a grin, John squeezed her. "Back 'atcha, girlfriend." He hesitated, then started again. "If it were only me, there would be no issue, but with Ginnie—" Clearing his throat, he tapped her arm distractedly. "It has to work for her, too." He nuzzled her hair with his chin. "But Ginnie likes you, Lowry." Out of the corner of his eye, he watched her face.

"I like her, too; she seems like a good person." She pushed herself onto her elbow. "What does Ginnie say?"

He exhaled. "I haven't had a chance to talk to her."

"I think we need to include her in our discussion—it's her life, too."

He tilted his head toward her. "She loves horses; perhaps she could help you out now that our farm is in good shape." With a little cough, he continued. "And you and she could get to know each other."

After a pause, Lowry replied, "I could use the help." She tapped her finger on his chest. "John, if you really want us to 'get to know each other,' I have a trail ride that I'm planning, and I don't want to go alone."

John could see the wheels turning in her head; not sure if that was a positive or not. Facing him, she rubbed her chin with her knuckle. "A sheik has bought the colt for his breeding program, and it's a great opportunity to let him remain a stallion." Lowry brushed her hair back with her fingers. "But the sticky part of the deal is that he wants me to deliver him and they are in the middle of nowhere. With no roads, I can't trailer him, so I'll have to ride horseback and let the colt follow."

John hummed. "I agree that it isn't safe to travel alone; I wouldn't do a wilderness trek without a buddy." He stroked her arm and asked, "Who is this sheik?"

"His name is Sheik Sahail and they immigrated from North Africa, but not as a part of the Land Rush. It was a purchase agreement, acquiring the land from the UN, under the pretext of a cultural refuge. They settled in one of the Dry Valleys to get away from the modern influences on the tribe—it is a similar, albeit colder, type of climate to their homeland."

"When do you think you'll go?"

"In a couple of weeks. The colt is weaned off of his mother, but I want to make sure he's eating well and fit for the trip."

John inwardly sighed. *Why does there always seem to be some quest with Lowry?* Shrugging, he nibbled her ear. "I guess we came to Antarctica for an adventure—it might be fun."

CHAPTER 19

A week later, Lowry floated toward John's farm to deliver the promised box of vegetables and steaks. They hadn't seen each other since they'd made love on New Year's Eve. John had been swamped with an addition to a barn and she'd been out of town, meeting with Nick in Amundsen to help prepare for his upcoming campaign for president.

She turned into the pass leading to his homestead, breathing deeply to calm her heart. Skimming across the ground, an old saying clanged in her head: *Sex can kill a good friendship.* Life had taught her that love was full of traps and dead ends. The reality of relationships was that they usually don't work out. Lowry drummed the wheel of the hover. Even if John wanted a relationship, did she have the time for one? She had enough worry with her farm and the campaign for Nick.

Lowry crossed onto his land. The orchards were in full bloom and the scent of apple wafted on the air. With a sigh, she recalled the first time they had made love. Would John play the "I can't commit" card again?

She parked in front of his house and unloaded the hover. Her heart thumped as John opened the door. Lowry cleared her throat, turning to him with a slight smile, and lifted up the box of vegetables. "Veggies as promised." With a jerk of her head, she continued. "And a package of steaks in the back seat."

With a nod, he walked to the rear of the hover and grabbed the steaks. "Thanks, Lowry. Nothing like a good cut of beef."

She studied his face for any signs of withdrawal, but he simply motioned her into the house with a gesture and they walked to the kitchen. The box of vegetables slipped out of her hands and thumped onto John's kitchen table. "Sorry!"

Stuffing the steaks into the freezer, John smiled broadly. "No worries."

Lowry pulled the tomatoes, carrots, zucchinis, and cucumbers out of the box and laid them on the table. She bit her lip at the display of mostly phallic objects. *Everything I've brought is sexually explicit.*

John picked up a large tomato with a nod. "Ginnie loves spaghetti with roasted tomatoes. We'll have these for dinner when she gets home from school." He moved by her, squeezing her shoulder as he passed, then turned away, placing the vegetables in a bin on the counter.

She stared at the back of his toned body and chewed the inside of her mouth. *This silence is getting awkward. Why is small talk such a challenge when you're horny?*

She coughed, and then abruptly said, "Uh, I suppose you heard about the meeting tomorrow to start eviction proceedings on Kiki Daniels?"

John turned around, leaning on the counter. "What are you talking about?"

Lowry got control of her body. "Kiki Daniels; she and her partner are homesteaders in the sector southeast of us. She became very ill and they haven't been able to plant the rest of the land. The bureaucrats are claiming 'breach of contract' of the homesteading agreement they signed, and now the station authorities are kicking them off the property. All this happening quietly, so the rest of us don't get riled. But it leaked out."

"They can't just throw someone off their land in a situation like that! Damned politicians!" John snapped.

"I smell the stench of Durant. Despite the ANT contract scandal, he's landed on his feet, by conveniently throwing his cohorts under the bus." Lowry heaved a sigh. "And it's official—he's running for president."

He shook his head. "I knew that son of a bitch would be back."

Lowry glanced at the time. "I have to go. Chuy's waiting for me."

John tightened his lips. "So soon?"

She shrugged. "We're moving the cattle to the northwest pasture today, and he needs my help."

John touched her shoulder as they walked to the front door. "Do you at least have time for a kiss goodbye?"

With a smile, she wrapped her arms around his neck, and they kissed. *So much for getting my body under control.* Sighing, she put her hands on his chest. "I really need to go."

With a soft peck on her forehead, he opened the door. "Don't be such a stranger."

Half-way to the hover, Lowry turned back to him. "Are you going to Daniels' eviction proceedings tomorrow?"

With a grimace, John replied, "Oh, yes, I'll be there."

CHAPTER 20

The next day, John traveled to Amundsen to witness the eviction proceedings on Daniels. A buzz of angry voices hit him as he slipped into the packed courthouse. He surveyed the crowd and saw Lowry waving to him. With a smile on her face, she beckoned him toward an empty seat next to her. John edged his way down the crowded row and sat. He had a clear view of the UN authorities seated, like the Spanish Inquisition, at the center of the front table.

Lowry cocked her head toward them, and whispered to John, "Roscha, the one in the middle of the table, was appointed by the United Nations as a liaison to the farmers during the provisional government, but we think Durant handpicked him to do his dirty work."

Roscha's little pig eyes shifted over the hostile crowd. A scowl on his face, he brought the meeting to order with heavy blows of his gavel.

"I already hate this guy and I don't even know him," John murmured. Roscha had the arrogant attitude of someone who relishes the feel of power, no matter how insignificant the advantage. He had hoped to escape from all that leaving the Old World, but here it was right in front of him, just with a different face.

Roscha shouted, "This meeting is in session, quiet in the room!"

The meeting proceeded with minor items, until Roscha cleared his throat dramatically. "The final item of business is the eviction proceeding of Kiki Daniels."

Angry murmurs bubbled from the crowd. The room fell silent as a frail woman in a hover chair, followed by her partner, moved up the aisle toward the front of the hall. She coughed, and then said in a subdued voice, "I'm Kiki Daniels and I'm appealing to this board to allow an extension of my agreement due to a health issue, which prevented us from planting the required percentage of our land."

Roscha glanced at the subordinates flanking him. "Ms. Daniels, if you were too ill, why didn't your partner fulfill your contractual obligations?"

Ellie Daniels stepped closer to the table. "I had to care for her night and day—she's been very ill for weeks."

With a twitch of his nose, Roscha slowly shook his head. "I'm sorry to inform you, but NO extensions are available to fulfill your contract with the UN." Tapping the table with his finger, he snapped, "You both will need to vacate your homesteaded tract in one week." He picked up the gavel and started to swing it down to end the meeting.

Kiki wheezed as she struggled to inhale. She slumped in the chair and Ellie stepped over, placing her arm around Kiki's shoulder. The room was silent.

A growl simmered in John's throat. *This cannot stand.* He took a deep breath and stood. He raised a finger in the air. "I have a question."

Roscha narrowed his eyes at John. "Who are you?" he asked, dismissively.

John chewed the inside of his cheek, staring at the self-important man at the center of the table. *You little worm.* With a loud voice, John said, "John Barrous. I'm homesteading block NW12."

Roscha's brows furrowed, studying his tablet in front of him. Then he glanced at John, tapping the screen. "You're not a speaker on the agenda—you're interrupting this meeting!"

The room became deathly still.

John's lip curled at the sight of Roscha's arrogant chin jutting out. He breathed deep to control his anger. "You can't throw someone off of their land because of health reasons, you ass!"

Roscha slammed his hand onto the tabletop. "The contract clearly states that a homesteader must perform or forfeit their land!"

John pushed his way to the front and stood by the couple. "Aren't you also supposed to aid us in carving out a home?" John turned to the packed hall, waving his arm toward the front table. "How many of you elected these people?"

Lips tight, Roscha stood up and leaned his hands on the table. "We aren't elected. We're appointed by the United Nations and under their authority!"

John replied, "My point exactly. You have the authority to evict us from our land"—he swung his arm back to the crowd—"without the slightest representation from us."

Lowry called out, "Roscha, isn't the Daniels homestead near the proposed rail hub?"

Sinking back into his seat, Roscha drummed his fingers on the arm of the chair. He picked up the gavel and slammed in on the table. "This meeting is adjourned."

"I think he's answered your question, Lowry." John turned back to the crowd. "The time has come for us to have our own government, a government elected by us, to represent our issues, and to not allow outsiders to dictate laws and policy! It's time the homesteaders on Antarctica had rights of our own!"

Cheers and shouts sprang from the crowd.

John turned back to Roscha. "How much land do the Daniels need to have planted?"

Roscha's lip twitched. "What business is it of yours?"

John clenched his jaw. Then he repeated, very slowly, "How much land do the Daniels need to have planted?"

Roscha choked in his rage. "Fifty hectares."

John stared at Roscha and waved his hand. "You can forget about the eviction. The fifty hectares will be planted before the week is out."

The room was hushed, until a single person clapped, then spontaneous waves of clapping and hurrahs filled the hall. John turned around to the cheering settlers. Self-consciously, he rested his hand on Kiki's shoulder for a moment and turned to leave. Happy faces lined the aisle as he cut his way to the exit.

At the door, he turned back. Roscha leaned on the table, a grimace pasted on his sour face. Nearby, Lowry stood in the midst of the applauding crowd, gazing at him. Smiling, she joined him at the door. "Well done, sir."

*   *   *

That evening, John hovered to the airport near Amundsen to pick up Ginnie. He waved as she walked into the terminal from the plane. They hugged and went to the baggage claim for her luggage.

He grabbed her bag. "How was the weather in Pittsburgh?"

"It was colder in Pennsylvania than here!"

He laughed. "I got a nice tan at the beach."

Ginnie stuck her tongue out at him. "You did not."

"What did you do during the holidays?"

Ginnie shrugged. "Shopping and my friends held a belated Sweet Sixteen birthday party for me."

"Nice! And I hope you did some stuff with your grandparents."

She sighed. "Well, we visited Mom's and the twins' grave."

John swallowed hard. While he was here making love to Lowry.

With a smile, she asked, "What did you really do while I was gone?"

They reached the hover and he put her bag in the back. "Oh, nothing much." He glanced at her and rubbed his chin. He had thought to discuss his new relationship with Lowry on the ride home, but maybe it wasn't the best time. *Or maybe you're just a coward.* He put the hover on auto pilot. "Home."

As they floated over the rising plain toward the farm, Ginnie chatted about her old friends and various holiday parties.

"Ginnie, we have a project tomorrow helping one of our neighbors plant their land. The authorities are trying to kick them off due to noncompliance. But they couldn't keep to their contract because of health issues."

"Wow, I guess the UN was serious on the planting requirement, but sure, I'll help."

The following day, John and Ginnie went to the Daniels' farm. John slowed at the sight of a crowd gathered in the yard, waving at their arrival.

John spotted one of his neighbors, Kim Son, and called out to him, "What's all this?"

"Everyone's here to help you plant the Daniels' land!"

John smiled. "Let's get cracking!"

They parked and walked toward the barn. Fruit and nut trees lay roped together, ready for planting. John stopped beside a woman with a large brimmed hat, standing in front of the trees. With raised eyebrows, he asked, "Where did these come from?"

"Donations." She smiled broadly. "This will double the size of their orchards."

"Fantastic!"

They had more than enough people to plant the land. Settlers from all of the homestead areas had come to help or donated supplies. Within the first few hours, he had helped organize the planting crews and supply drops—and broken up a fight.

Mid-morning, Ginnie waved to him, pulling a small trailer with a water station behind the hover. "This is more of a festival than a planting day."

After she left, John loaded seed onto the back of one of the hovers, then he heard a vaguely familiar voice behind him.

"Having fun?"

John wiped his face with his handkerchief and glanced around.

Arms crossed, Durant stood gazing at him, with his trademark condescending look.

John flinched. He loaded the last seed bag on the cart and faced him. "You're like the cat that keeps coming back. Did you buy a 'get out of jail card?'"

Durant shrugged. "Something like that."

"What are you doing here?" John demanded. "I figured you were one of the prime reasons these folks were getting kicked off their land to begin with. I'm sure, despite any inconvenient legal obstacles you've had to remove, that you're still involved in the rail hub."

He smiled and waved toward the planting crews. "And miss this photo op? Surely you jest! These people think I'm here to help them in their struggle—I personally donated the saplings. There will be other land for the rail hub. One must be able to turn defeat into victory, my good friend."

With pinched lips, John stared at him. Leave it to Durant to benefit from someone else's tragedy and pervert it into a farce to garner votes. "I ain't your friend." John growled.

Durant lost his polite manner. "You're aware the elections are a few weeks away?"

"I heard that rumor."

Exhaling, Durant gestured to John. "I won't banter with you. I need your support. You're a natural leader, John. People's votes will be swayed by your words."

John guffawed, and then shaking his head, stared at Durant. "Why, in God's name, would I support you?"

"To be on the winning side, of course," he replied, with his signature sneer.

John's grin faded at the smirk on Durant's face. *What lay beneath that cocky look?* "Let's cut to the chase—what are you selling?"

"Your endorsement, in trade for anything you want." Durant threw up his hands and leaned toward John. "It's a waste! You're groveling like a pig in the mud, grunting with the rest. You have a brain in your head, why don't you use it?"

John leaned back on the hovercart. A master of manipulation, Durant was a con man who could be whoever he needed to be for that audience. Like a puppet master, he tugged the strings of Hope and Fear; over-guaranteeing the first and exploiting the second—a true Machiavellian.

Durant stared at him, waiting for an answer.

John studied him, and then said softly, "When a bee searches for nectar, he must beware the Venus Fly Trap. Once ensnared, the sting of the bee is futile—there is no escape."

His lips thinned. "Mr. Barrous, I assure you, I am no Venus Fly Trap."

A smile flitted briefly onto John's face. "Of course not, Mr. Durant—you are the *bee*."

Durant's eyes flickered. "Did you know that Napoleon's symbol was a bee?"

"If I remember correctly, Napoleon was defeated."

"He made some tactical errors, which I will not." Durant pursed his lips. "I know you support Nick." Shrugging, he raised his eyebrows. "But one never knows how things will turn out."

John felt a cold pit in his stomach. "What do you have up your sleeve?"

"Keep tuned to this station."

John swallowed hard. *My god, he has something on Nick.* "You're a real bastard!"

A smile flashed onto Durant's face, then faded. "First a bee, now a bastard." He stared at John with a withering look, and then said, "If you want to benefit from my election to president, I suggest you join the winners. The losers will find themselves, I'm afraid, at a disadvantage." With a dismissive wave, he walked away, and joined a nearby crowd, smiling and shaking hands with the farmers.

John found Lowry in the crowd. "Lowry," he called. Turning toward his voice, she raised her hand to him, her face white and pinched, and he realized something was amiss. He touched her arm. "What's wrong?"

Lowry shrugged. "I just heard that the older man, 'Daddy,' who broke into my house, has escaped. They were transferring him to a ship returning to the U.S. and he overcame the guard." She exhaled and stared at John. In a thin voice, she whispered, "They have no idea where he is."

John rested his hand on her shoulder. "Lowry, you have Chuy at the ranch, and you are always welcome to stay with Ginnie and I."

Lowry shook her head. "No, I'll keep a loaded gun with me until they catch him."

"And that will be soon, I'm sure." He wrapped his arm around her shoulders and drew her away from the others, whispering, "I need to talk to you about something else. Come take a walk with me."

They climbed a small hill, overlooking the fields rapidly being planted by the volunteers. Robo-tractors sowed barley in the far field, and below them, a small child waved a stick baton like a drum major, leading wagons stacked with fruit and nut saplings across a field, followed by singing homesteaders.

At the edge of the field, Durant stood on a hovercart in the middle of a crowd. And by his gestures, churning out some pretty speech. Among the innocent sheep lurked a wolf named Durant.

"Durant is here." John pointed at the gathering around Durant. "Taking advantage of the day by wooing the crowd." He looked at Lowry. "And I just had an interesting conversation with him."

Lowry squinted at Durant gesticulating to the settlers. "Once the devil gets your address, it's hard to keep him away." She turned to him. "What did his majesty want from you?"

"He wants my vote, of course, and as many others as I could round up."

"Was he serious?" She stared at John. "Why does he think you would vote for him?"

"Durant assured me that I would 'profit' by his election—his version of 'healthier and wealthier,' if I was on the winning side."

Lowry looked at John. "Nick is locked in with the miners and he has fairly good support with the new immigrants, but I'll grant you, there is a segment of the homesteaders who have bought Durant's line."

John shook his head with a snort. "There's a pretty broad swing vote, Lowry, and I'm afraid Durant has something that might be deadly to Nick."

Lowry's mouth dropped open. She whispered, "What does he have?"

John shrugged. "I don't know. But I'm sure he'll tell the world—right before the election."

"There'll be hell to pay if Durant wins the presidency."

CHAPTER 21

Tall fields of wheat and corn rippled in the wind as the summer faded, and the cattle and horses grew their winter coats. The work on the farm never stopped, and Lowry busily prepared for the harsh Antarctic winter. When John had asked Ginnie if she wanted to help with the horses, she'd been delighted.

That afternoon, Ginnie pulled up to the stables in the hovercar and parked under the shed roof.

Ginnie called out, "Hellooo," and stuck her head through the door.

"Come on in," Lowry said, brushing the colt in the stable aisle.

Henry dog-trotted up to Lowry, wagging his tail. Lowry petted the dog's back. "Henry, glad you could join us." His brother, Leo, ran up and leapt onto Henry with a playful growl. The colt shied backwards.

"Whoa, Bashira," Lowry said. "Leo, go play with Henry outside. Outside!" Lowry pointed to the exit. Leo ran out and Henry chased after him.

Ginnie scooted around the stablebot, taking a load of manure to the compost pile, then slowly walked up to the colt. "Hi, Bashira." She stroked his face and said, "Dad told me about the trek—I can't wait! It'll be a great end-of-summer trip."

Lowry raised her eyebrows at Ginnie's excited face. "This won't be an easy trail ride."

"Don't tell that to my dad."

Lowry winked. "It'll be our secret." She put the colt back into his stall and tossed him a flake of hay. "Ginnie, can you brush Kisra?"

"Yep." She moved into the stall, clipped the lead rope onto the mare's halter, and brought her into the aisle.

Lowry brought Dalal out next to Kisra. "After we finish grooming the girls, do you want to go for a ride?"

"Sure!"

"Okay, we'll take these two mares—they need some exercise." She went into the tack room, grabbed the saddles and bridles, and placed them on the saddle racks.

They tacked up, mounted, and started along the trail. Leo barked and Lowry turned back. He and Henry bounded after them, but Leo looked up at Lowry for permission to follow.

With a smile, Lowry waved. "Come on, Leo, and you too, Henry."

It was a gorgeous day as they rode over the green pastures, with the scent of wildflowers floating on the breeze.

"How is school going? Have you thought of a major, yet?" Lowry asked Ginnie.

"School's going pretty well. I'm practicing for my college entrance exams, but I'm still not sure about my major." She shrugged. "I'm thinking maybe biology."

"Antarctica needs biologists. Will you come back after college?"

"I'm not sure, but it's exciting to be a part of building a nation."

"How does your dad feel about your choice?"

"He seems fine with it."

A bevy of quail burst out of the brush nearby and both horses shied. Henry and Leo took off, chasing the birds.

Ginnie laughed, patting Kisra's neck. "You're okay, girl."

Tongues lolling out of their mouths, the dogs caught up to them after their hunt.

"I don't see any feathers, so I guess we still have to feed you tonight." Ginnie teased.

Lowry looked at Ginnie with a smile. She was a well-adjusted and bright young woman. Odd that, like herself, Ginnie had also lost her mother in a terrible incident.

"Ginnie, your dad told me about your mother's unfortunate death—such a tragedy."

She stared ahead vacantly and whispered, "I miss her very much."

Lowry said softly, "My mother passed away when I was twelve." She reached down, straightening Dalal's mane. "It would be her birthday tomorrow."

Ginnie glanced at her. "I didn't know. I'm sorry."

With a sigh, Lowry continued. "After the funeral, I came to live on Antarctica with my dad. It's been years, but you never get over the heartbreak of losing a beloved parent when you're young. It leaves a hole that can never be filled."

"Yes," Ginnie murmured.

They crossed a stream, the horses stepping carefully over the rocks. Beyond the stream, they reached a small meadow filled with flowers, and dismounted. Lowry hobbled the mares and let them graze. Lowry and Ginnie stretched out on the tender grass, gazing into a soft blue sky.

"How did your mom die?" Ginnie asked.

Lowry clenched her fists. It had been years ago, but the wound had never completely healed. "She drowned. We were camping near a river when a flash flood swept her away. I didn't even have a chance to say goodbye."

Ginnie stared at the sky. "No chance to say goodbye." She closed her eyes and tears spilled down the side of her face. "I had a dream that my mom dropped me at school one morning—a big smile on her face and she blew me a kiss. 'Have a good day, Baby,' she said as the school bell rang. I ran toward the school, but then I woke up to my alarm—just a dream."

Lowry held her breath. It had been years since she'd cried over her mother, though from time to time, a scent or snatch of a song would prompt memories of her loss. With a small gasp, tears sprang to her eyes. "I had dreams like that, too."

Henry crawled onto Ginnie's chest and licked the tears on her face. With a deep sigh, Ginnie stroked him and he snuggled into the crook of her neck.

Lowry sat up and picked a wildflower. And then with a sad smile, handed it to Ginnie. "I think our moms would be proud of us; we've kept our heads up and moved forward with no regrets."

Leo came to Lowry and leaned on her.

"Now Leo is trying to cheer you up." Ginnie said. She pushed herself onto her elbow and smelled the buttercup Lowry had given her.

"Animals know when someone needs love." Lowry smiled. "They have amazing healing powers." She shifted around to face Ginnie. "If you need to talk or feel lonely, I'm here."

Lowry stood up and unhobbled Dalal and Kisra. "It's getting late. We'd better get back."

They mounted and headed back to the farm. The horses' ears bobbed with the pace of their feet and Ginnie's face relaxed with the rhythm.

Lowry chewed the inside of her lip. Helen must have been a wonderful mother and wife, and she would never try to take her place. But what would Ginnie's reaction be to a relationship between her and John? Being a friend is one thing, but someone becoming your father's lover and possible wife was a completely different beast. Especially with a young person still mourning the loss of her mother.

Lowry pressed her fingers on her brow.

"Lowry, are you okay?" Ginnie asked, with a concerned look on her face.

With a slight smile, Lowry replied, "I have a little headache coming on."

The mares pricked their ears up as the farm came into view.

Lowry's mind whirled. A three-way relationship between John, herself, and a grieving teenager could prove complex. John thought Ginnie hung the moon, and rightly so. Was there truly a place for her in their close-knit family?

They reached the stable. Lowry dismounted and distractedly led her mare inside. They untacked, rubbed the horses down, and put them in their stalls. Ginnie tossed each of them a flake of hay. Holding Leo, Lowry waved goodbye to Ginnie as she and Henry hovered away, then they disappeared over the hill.

Lowry knelt and scratched behind Leo's ears. She wrapped her arm around him and heaved a sigh. "What odds do you give, boy?"

Leo whined and licked her face.

"Yeah, I wouldn't take that bet either."

CHAPTER 22

On the morning of the trek, John and Ginnie hovered from the farm to Lowry's place. John breathed in the clean air as they floated across fields full of wildflowers. It was a beautiful day in late summer with plentiful sunshine and a nice breeze—perfect weather to start an adventure.

When they reached Lowry's stable, they parked under the shed and walked inside.

Lowry had coffee and a box of biscotti cookies waiting for them. "Grab a cup and a cookie. Before we go, I want to show off my new cow barn."

John sipped the warm brew as they followed Lowry to the new barn.

"The UN had a contest for the perfect Antarctic barn and this design won. Lucky for me, the UN is furnishing the barn for free, but I have to submit reports monthly as to how it actually works." Lowry pointed to the exterior. "Like all the Antarctic structures, it's built of solar sheathing and roof, but this barn has double wind turbines in the ridge line."

John said, "I like the extended overhang on the shed areas."

"Yep, the cattle can hang out and not stand in the snow."

She opened the doors and they went inside. Lowry pointed to the watering and feed systems. "It's completely self-sufficient. A constant stream of recycled water flows through the barn. Hay and feed come along a conveyor belt."

John walked over and tapped the conveyor belt. "Wow, this is amazing."

Lowry chuckled. "There's an automated set of 'poopbots' collecting manure. They deposit it into composting containers, which, as it decomposes, heats the barn during the winter. And when the process is complete, we use it as fertilizer in the spring."

"Like the stablebot?" Ginnie asked.

Lowry nodded. "Yes, but this system is more sophisticated."

Ginnie tapped the floor of the barn with her foot. "This is weird flooring."

"Yeah, it's an absorbent floor with a slight incline, creating a runoff for the urine. Then it's filtered and recycled into the drinking water."

John turned his head, gazing at the interior. "This barn is an engineering marvel. But I hope they have good repair people."

"Honestly, I'm terrified it will all break down in midwinter and we're out here scooping poop!"

John gestured to the roof. "I'm worried that all of our wind turbines will ice over in a snowstorm and stop working. Then bye-bye to our heat and power."

Lowry nodded. "That would be a disaster. Battery backups only last so long. We were lucky at the mining station to have geothermal energy."

They returned to the stable and Lowry pointed to Kisra's stall. "Ginnie, you like Kisra, do you want to ride her?"

"Sure." Ginnie led Kisra out of her stall, clipped her into the cross-ties, and began grooming her.

Lowry led Dalal out and brushed her, while John finished his coffee.

With a glance to Ginnie, Lowry asked, "After you saddle Kisra, can you please saddle Dalal while I get your dad's mount?"

Ginnie nodded and Lowry disappeared out of the back doors, and returned, leading a large, spotted mule. She tied him to a post in the stable and handed John a brush. "I hope you don't mind riding Oliver, the mule, John—he's very sure-footed."

"I'll be glad for another male on this trip." John grinned. He petted Oliver's neck and then brushed the dirt from his coat with firm strokes.

Lowry brought the saddle and swung it onto Oliver's back. The mule turned his head and glared at her. "He has a few idiosyncrasies, but he's a good boy. Chuy brought him with the cutting horses and says he's a great trail animal." Oliver put his ears back when Lowry tightened the girth of the saddle.

John chuckled. "Oliver and I will be the Curmudgeon Club trekkers."

In the cool morning air, they loaded the saddlebags with provisions and strapped on their bedding.

Ginnie pulled on her gloves and helmet, then swung up on Kisra.

John put his boot in the stirrup, and began to mount, but the saddle slipped over, and he almost fell. "Oliver," he grumbled. Oliver flashed him a sardonic look as John pushed the saddle back into place. He tightened the girth again, and Oliver flattened his ears back. John walked the mule around and rechecked the tightness of the girth before he mounted. Oliver wouldn't outwit him again—he hoped.

Lowry led the colt out of the barn, keeping a tight grip on the lead rope. To distract him while she mounted Dalal, she gave him a piece of carrot. He happily chewed the carrot, but as she swung her leg over the saddle, he pulled back for an instant, jerking her backwards. Dalal stood still and Lowry got her feet in the stirrups, clucked and the mare started out. Bashira shook his head, then acquiesced, walking forward with the mare.

Lowry glanced at him as he relaxed to the rhythm of the mule. "You're bonding with Oliver."

With a grin, John winked. "I think we're distant cousins."

They followed a faint trail toward the open country between the homesteads and the wilderness area. Lowry reached down and unsnapped the lead rope, letting the colt loose. "He should stay with us now and not try to return to the farm." The colt circled around them, whinnying and picking at grass, but stayed with the group. They trotted up a long ascent to a high ridge at the border of the settlements.

A cool breeze rippled across the crest, while the animals caught their breath.

With a gasp, Lowry turned and pointed. "Look at the view."

To the east, the sparkling blue ocean stretched to the Earth's curving horizon. Behind them lay the last vestiges of civilization: the bustling town of Amundsen and the port with tall ships docked in the bay; farther inland, the homesteads—shining like square-cut emeralds lying on the umber terrain. To the west, the mountains rose like elegant queens, with their crowns of ice and stoles of wispy clouds draped across their shoulders.

Turning back to their journey, they gazed at the valley below, covered with tussock grass and scrubby brush—the beginning of the Concordia Wildlife Refuge. A meandering river spread out before them, flanked by a marsh on one side and a sandy shore of glacial till on the other.

The land of humans disappeared over the horizon as they descended into the valley. Great flocks of waterfowl filled the air with wing and call. Excited at the new scents and sounds of wild life, the animals pranced along the trail. John clenched his teeth as his mule shied at a ptarmigan flying out from the tussock grass. The bird shot past Bashira, and the colt bolted down the slope, until the mares whinnied, and he returned bucking and pitching.

They reached the slow-moving river by mid-morning and passed huge flocks of geese roosting on serene pools, while herds of caribou grazed nearby. Ginnie pointed out a bear lumbering along the brush on the far side of the river bank.

In the warmth of the sun, they relaxed into the rhythm of the trek. As they traveled deeper into the refuge, they crossed tracks of raccoon, rabbits, and fox along the sandy riverbank.

The noon hour approached and John's stomach growled loudly. "Did you hear that bear? He must be getting close."

Ginnie made a face at him. "I'm hungry enough to eat a bear."

Lowry smiled. "Okay, I get the hint." She pointed to a grove of short trees ahead. "Let's stop for lunch in the shade."

They dismounted, loosened the girths on the saddles, and hobbled the horses and the mule so they could graze. Ginnie pulled the day's lunch out of her saddlebag and handed out sandwiches. They sat on the smooth rocks under the trees, ate and relaxed in the nothingness of being.

Lowry gazed at the canopy of branches shading them. "It's amazing how fast these trees have grown since I was a child. They were tiny when Uncle Nick and I came out here on a trail ride years ago."

Lowry pulled chocolate bars out of her saddle bag, and with a grin, handed them to John and Ginnie. "I always bring chocolate on trail rides."

After lunch, the breeze kicked up. The colt trotted back and forth as if impatient to get going.

Lowry smiled at the colt and stood. "He's got the right idea—we'd better get moving, so we can make it to my favorite camping spot before dusk."

John stretched his legs before he mounted, trying to ward off the saddle soreness. "I hope there's a masseuse at this place."

Lowry signaled for them to pick up the pace and they cantered across the valley floor.

John gazed around with the feeling he had been here before, so he nudged the mule faster, and caught up to Lowry. In a hushed voice, he asked her, "Is this the same place we had lunch that day before the Land Rush?"

Lowry nodded.

He glanced at Ginnie behind them. *This could be awkward.*

They approached the narrow canyons which led to Lowry's oasis, then slowed down and moved to single file. The canyon walls narrowed and the colt balked several times at the constricted passageway.

The canyon walls widened and they rode into the small meadow with the pool of bubbling mineral waters. Once again, John felt the wonder of this secret place, inhaling the scent of flowers drifting on the humid air. After the dimness of the narrow passage they had left, the sun beamed into the blue green water with a benevolent welcome.

Ginnie asked excitedly, "What is this place? It's like something out of a fairy tale."

"This is my secret garden. No telling anyone, young lady."

"No way!"

They untacked and hobbled the animals near the cold stream of water at the edge of the meadow.

Lowry pointed to the spring. "Ginnie, this cold stream mixes with the hot thermal waters of the pool. Where they merge, the water is tolerable—you have to move until you find the perfect temperature."

Ginnie took her shoes off, put her feet in the pool, and sighed. "I love this place." She pointed to a flowering plant hanging near the water. "Those are gorgeous flowers. Do they have a name?"

"They are called Antarctic Bleeding Hearts, and this may be the only place they exist. This tiny pocket was kept warm by the geothermal waters, so some of the original flora of Antarctica survived."

John pulled a bottle of Chardonnay out of his saddle bag and put it in the cold stream to chill. "We'll have to toast Lowry for bringing us to this enchanted place."

Lowry smiled, strolled to her saddlebag and grabbed a baguette of bread and a pouch. From the pouch, she lifted out a beautiful piece of salmon. "Dinner is on me tonight. John, can you get a fire started?"

"Your word is my command."

Ginnie asked Lowry, "Can we please get in the water?"

"Sure, I hope everyone brought a change of underwear?"

"Underwear?" John asked innocently.

"Dad, you're just gross."

John started the fire, and they stripped down and slipped into the hot water. Ginnie floated around the pond, in and out of the vines that hung over the warm, fragrant water. John sighed as the warmth eased his saddle-sore body. He gazed at Lowry as she closed her eyes, leaning her head back on the moss-covered rocks.

After they grew too hungry to stay in the water, they crawled out and patted themselves dry. Lowry cooked the salmon on the coals of the fire, and the spitting sounds of the grilling fish made John's stomach growl. After a few minutes, Lowry took the salmon off of the grill and divided the fish into three pieces, placing them on the thin boards of wood she brought for plates.

John pulled the bottle of wine from the spring, opened it, and poured wine in the camp cups for him and Lowry. He held up his glass of wine. "To the best, and dare I say, loveliest chef I know."

Ginnie giggled in the awkward silence which followed. "Dad, you're embarrassing Lowry."

They devoured the salmon and the French bread, dripping with spiced olive oil.

After dinner, Ginnie took the boards and washed them in a hot pool of water, laughing as tiny fish came to the surface, nibbling the leftover salmon floating on the water. "Minnows are eating our leftovers." She set the boards out to dry and went to check on the animals.

John and Lowry sat across from each other, finishing the wine as the fire burned down.

With a sigh, he murmured, "It seems a lifetime ago since the first time—" His throat closed on his words. He coughed, staring into the embers. John took a deep breath, then gulped his wine and set the empty cup at his feet. "Grief is a funny thing; sometimes it behaves and stays in the corner where you put it . . . but sometimes it haunts you." He gazed at her. "And though I'll never forget, I've tamed the beast." He shifted closer to Lowry. "I'm a new man since we were here last," he whispered, caressing her arm.

Behind him, Ginnie gasped. "You've been here before?" She stared at John.

John jerked his head toward Ginnie. The fire illuminated the shocked look on her face. "Um, I, um, well," he stammered, then he glanced at Lowry.

Lowry grimaced. "It's my turn to 'check the horses,' while you continue your eloquent explanation." John chewed the inside of his mouth, staring at Lowry's profile as she rose and walked to the animals.

Ginnie sat where Lowry had been, crossing her arms as she stared at him.

Exhaling, he looked into Ginnie's annoyed face. "Yes, Lowry and I had a picnic here the day before the Rush." With a shrug, he grimaced. "I loved your mother very much, and you are my precious child, and I would do anything rather than hurt you." With a pinched face, John turned away and thrust a stick into the fire. "But, Ginnie, I'm also a man, and I need companionship."

She crossed her arms. "And when did you plan on telling me?"

He raked his fingers through his hair. "I feel bad that I haven't said anything to you." He swallowed hard. "Since your mother's death, I've struggled with the weight of grief, and you the same. Between heartache over your mother, and honestly, the guilt over my attraction to Lowry, it's been very hard to broach the subject with you." He leaned toward her, whispering, "I can't help it—I have strong feelings for Lowry."

Ginnie stared into the campfire. "I knew someday you might find someone else, but I hoped it would be later." With her lips tight, she shot a look at him. "I'm more upset that you haven't been upfront with me."

He grabbed her hand, gazing into her face. "When Lowry and I picnicked here months ago, I wasn't ready for a relationship." With a sigh, he continued. "While you were away, I saw her on New Year's Eve, and we reconnected." He squeezed her hand. "Ginnie, you must understand that I love Lowry."

"Are you sure, Dad?" She put her hand over his. "I don't want you getting hurt."

John raised his eyebrows. "No guarantees in life or love, I'm afraid."

With a frown, Ginnie whispered, "Now I know why she was talking about her mother's death and my mom's death." She looked at him. "I guess she was trying to bond with me?"

John stared at her. "Ginnie, I asked Lowry to get to know you."

Ginnie twisted her mouth. "Okay." She pushed her hair away from her face. "I'm just feeling weird—it's going to take time for me to sort this out." She looked at him. "I know that mom would want you to be happy, and that's the most important thing. Lowry seems nice, but we don't know her very well—you always tell *me* that." Ginnie scooted next to him, wrapping her arm around his shoulders, and sighed. "I suppose it could have been worse—like that awful bitch in Amundsen who was putting the move on you?"

Laughing, John shook his head. "Don't remind me."

Twilight was fading, and Lowry called out from behind them, "Is it safe to come back?"

He waved his arm for Lowry to return.

Lowry brought blankets, handed them around, and sat across from them. Lowry looked at their faces. "A good father-daughter talk?"

"Handled with my usual finesse." John hugged Ginnie.

The howl of wolves broke into their conversation. Sucking her breath in, Ginnie looked back and forth between John and Lowry.

Lowry's voice was tense. "I think we'd better build up the fire before we hit the sack, and maybe we should get our pistols out, just in case." She shot a look at John. "I never had to worry about predators, at least non-human ones, before the UN decided to populate Antarctica with a balanced ecosystem."

"I know; it's a double-edged sword." He shook his head. "It's wonderful to create the wildlife preserves but I hope with an adequate barrier to the homesteads."

John turned on his flashlight and pulled dead brush across the narrow opening to the oasis. He unfurled his sleeping bag on the side of the fire closest to the entrance. "I'll sleep here, so if there are any intruders, they'll have to get by me first." He got his pistol and placed it under his camp pillow. "I think both of you should sleep on the other side of the fire."

Lowry and Ginnie rolled out their sleeping bags next to each other, and placed their pistols nearby, while John stacked more twigs on the fire. The fire sprang up as they snuggled into their sleeping bags. The howls continued through the night, but fatigue overrode fear, and they awoke refreshed in the morning.

John slowly got up, stretched his sore muscles and slipped into the hot water to get his body ready for the day's ride.

Lowry brought him a mug of coffee and sat beside him, dangling her feet in the water. "I like that Camp-Brew coffee maker—really slick. Just throw a coffee packet in, dial in the strength and it brews a good cup."

"Yeah, I bought that and the Insta-Tea brewer in Amundsen."

Lowry tilted her head toward Ginnie, curled up in the sleeping bag. "Ginnie is something special. I'm sure you're proud of her."

John smiled. "Yes, she's been a delight. Helen and I taught her to think and not to just accept what was taught, but to understand why. Even as a child, we respected her views and wishes, but we also required respect in return. And she always had consequences to her actions." He shook his head. "Some people seem to treat a child like a pet, and not expect them to do chores, but I don't think that helps children become adults."

She sipped her coffee. "She's very bright." Her mouth twitched. "I will tell you that I felt a bit of resistance from her last night as we were going to bed."

"What do you mean?"

Lowry shrugged. "She gave me one of those 'I'm watching you' kind of looks."

Ginnie stirred in the sleeping bag and sat up with a yawn.

"We'd better eat a quick breakfast and get on the trail. Lowry finished her coffee and stood. One at a time, she stretched her arms upward. "We have a long day ahead to reach the Dry Valleys."

After breakfast, John cleaned up the campsite while Lowry and Ginnie tacked up the animals. Lowry filled their water bottles from the cold spring and slipped purification tablets in each one. They mounted and started out of the tiny oasis.

John looked at Lowry and Ginnie silently walking the horses through the narrow canyon. No giggling, no teasing. The tension was plain to see. He sighed, wondering if he and Lowry had a future together. The tea leaves were pretty damn vague, to say the least.

CHAPTER 23

At a brisk trot, they crossed a long stretch of flat terrain before climbing the mountain range separating the wetter side of Eastern Antarctica from the Dry Valleys. Near a rock slide, they reached the trail heading up the mountain, and slowed to a walk, threading their way through large boulders piled up at the base of the slope.

With a gasp, Lowry halted her mare. The colt threw his head up with a snort. John and Oliver came up beside her.

Her face pale, she gestured to the ground in front of her. "Look." Among the tumbled boulders and rocks, a human skull lay on the trail, its empty sockets staring casually at the sky.

John grimaced. The rest of the skeleton was strewn like matchsticks on the rocky ground. He held up his hand. "Stay back, Ginnie, you don't need to see this."

"What is it?"

"Some kind of accident and someone died on the trail, I'm afraid."

Ginnie slapped her hand over her mouth. "Yeah, I'll wait back here."

John dismounted and handed the reins to Lowry. He stepped carefully around the bones and squatted, studying the site. He stood and circled the area, then knelt and lifted up a rifle that had been half-buried in the dirt. "Maybe a hunter?" He opened the chamber and furrowed his brow. "Still bullets left." He sighted down the barrel of the gun. It had a crook in the middle. "The barrel is bent, like he used the gun as a club." He stepped a few paces from the human skeleton and kicked a jawbone laying near a pile of rocks. "This bone might be the jaw of a canine."

"Maybe he had a dog?" Lowry asked.

"Big jawbone for a dog." John scratched his head. "I think he had a fight with a pack of wolves."

An involuntarily shiver hit Lowry, staring at the scattered bones. "And the pack was so close last night." She clutched her stomach as she turned, then caught sight of a red knit cap nestled in a clump of tussock grass. Pointing toward it, she whispered, "John."

John walked over and untangled it from the snarled grass. He turned it over and looked inside, but there was no identification in the cap. He walked around the site, but only shreds of clothing remained. "I don't see anything to identify this poor guy." He shrugged. "I guess I should bury what's left of him, at least." John reached into his pack and grabbed a portable shovel.

A wave of dizziness hit Lowry as she stared at the red cap. "John, let me see that cap."

He handed it to her. Lowry held her breath as she turned it around. It had a black bear embroidered on the front—and more importantly, the shredded hole from the bullet she had shot. It was the same cap that Daddy had worn the day he and Jake broke into her home. With a tilt of her head, she exhaled. "Apparently, that pack of wolves became judge, jury, and executioner. This is the cap that 'Daddy' wore the day they broke into my house."

John shook his head in disbelief and nudged the skull with his boot. "Hope you enjoy hell, asshole." He met Lowry's eyes. "Thank god that line of DNA has been exterminated."

Lowry felt faint. "John, I think it would be better if I stay with Ginnie." Clucking to the colt to follow, she moved her horse and John's mule back to where Ginnie was waiting.

Ginnie asked, "The wolf pack killed one of the men who attacked you?"

Lowry nodded.

"Good riddance. But scary at the same time."

John dug a hole away from the trail, then gathered the bones.

Lowry flinched at the clacking sound of the bones as he dropped them in the hole. He covered the remains with dirt and pushed a rock on top of the makeshift grave.

He stuffed the red cap into a pocket of his knapsack and tied the rifle behind his saddle. "I'll drop these by the authorities." He pulled out his canteen and washed his hands. He dried his hands on his shirt and glanced at Lowry. "You don't look so good. Are you okay?"

"Not really. All this brings back too many memories." Lowry poured water into her kerchief and wiped her face. "We should get started up the trail, we still have a long way to go." She pointed up the mountain. "The trail is well marked to the top of the pass; would you mind leading the way, John?"

"Sure, Lowry."

They started up the mountain trail and Lowry tied the wet kerchief around her neck. Dalal's head bobbed in cadence as the ascent steepened. Staring vacantly ahead, the rocking motion of the horse lulled her into a daze. No one spoke as they moved along the faint trail; even the birds were silent. In the pale sky a flock of vultures circled above the valley waiting out the death of an animal.

Lowry felt bile rise in her throat.

*   *   *

At the summit, they stopped. The animal's sides heaved, recovering their breath from the climb. With haggard faces, John and Ginnie turned to Lowry.

Lowry waved toward a tiny stream of water flowing down the face of the rock. "Probably the last water until the Bedouin encampment and it's getting late. We'd better spend the night on this side before we head into the desert."

"Hurray." John dismounted. When his feet hit the ground, his legs buckled, and he leaned against Oliver. "What would I do without you, buddy?"

They unsaddled the mounts and hobbled them near the spring. The equines picked at the scant grass, while Lowry and Ginnie groomed them with a rag. John rolled out their sleeping bags near a scrubby pine tree and set out the dry dinners. Lowry filled the water bottles, dropping a purifying tablet in each, and joined the other two sitting on the sleeping bags.

Worn out, they chewed the dry meal methodically, listening to the distant hoot of an owl.

After dinner, they cleaned up and hung the saddlebags from a rock knob. As the fire crumpled into embers, they watched the sun approach the horizon. From their perch, they had a spectacular view of the valley.

A herd of caribou bedded down for the night, and across the river, a family of arctic foxes trotted along the bank in search of a meal. A torrent of bats rushed out of a crevice, darting and dipping through the crisp air. The sun's last rays spilled across the winding river, and for a breathtaking instant, the surface of the water shone like a brilliant gold necklace tossed onto the earth.

Life, intensely beautiful and horribly cruel. The cycle of birth and death never ceased. It was the one constant on Earth.

Lowry peered over the valley to catch sight of the slow wheeling vultures she had seen earlier on the trail. The sky was empty. They had descended to their meal.

CHAPTER 24

They reached the top of the pass. Lowry shielded her eyes against the sun and watched a dust devil skate across the valley floor. The foreboding Dry Valleys were the driest part of Antarctica and for most settlers, a no-man's land, but for the Bedouin tribe who had been so bold as to immigrate here, this was home.

The desert wind sucked the moisture from her skin. She pulled out her water bottle and shook it. They had filled up at the spring this morning and the purification pills should have done their job by now.

Lowry drank, then held up her water bottle. "Everyone take a drink before we head into the valley. This is the toughest part of the trek, but if all goes well, we should meet with Sheik Sahail before dusk."

After the water break, they checked their gear and the girths of their saddles and descended onto the steep slope. With no trail to follow, the animals lowered their heads and tucked their hindquarters under them, sliding around rocks and small brush. Lowry glanced back; the colt followed the horses without too much cavorting and Ginnie seemed to be fine. But she chuckled at the sight of John and the mule with the same grim expression on their faces, edging their way down the incline.

As they neared the desert floor, they paused on a ledge and rested, peeling off their outer jackets with the rising temperatures.

Lowry strapped her jacket behind the saddle. "We'll stop for a short lunch break when we reach the valley floor, then a couple more hours until we reach their camp."

"Only a few more hours, the woman says," John grumbled.

Like a solar oven, the air temperature became oppressive as they reached the valley floor. Lowry led the way toward a rock overhang for shelter against the sun while they rested. They dismounted, loosened the girths, and led the animals into the shade, to pick at the dry remnants of grass left from the spring rains.

Lowry petted her mare's neck. "Sorry, no water for you yet, but soon enough." She got apples out of her saddlebag and fed them to the animals, then left them to pick at the dry remnants of grass leftover from the spring rains.

John pulled out the dry lunch packets and handed them around. He eased onto a rock and rubbed his sore legs. "That was quite a descent. Maybe I'll get into shape before the end of this trip. Probably on the last day."

After lunch, they stretched out in the shade to rest. John and Ginnie soon fell asleep. Lowry stayed awake to watch the animals. She closed her eyes and listened to the sounds of this barren land. This was all new territory for her. The wind moaned through the rock formations with a sporadic clatter of rocks tumbling down the slope they had traversed. She opened her eyes and scanned the landscape for desert creatures, but none were out today. The UN wildlife release program had introduced high-desert species into these Dry Valleys, but most of them were nocturnal.

The sun started its downward path, and she roused the others. They tacked up, mounted, and started across the desert floor.

They approached a tall formation of rocks, covered with vultures leisurely flapping their wings—a fitting welcome to hell. As they passed, the flock of vultures took flight over their heads and the downdraft from their wings blew over them. The awkward colt jumped in fear and bucked next to John's mule. To avoid the youngster, Oliver leapt to the side, and into the flight path of the last vulture. The vulture careened away, but the tip of his wing hit one of Oliver's long ears. The mule shook his head in terror and pinned his ears back to his neck—and then bolted across the desert floor at a dead run.

"Oh, my God!" Lowry screamed. "Hold on, John!"

Lowry could see John pulling back on the reins, fighting to control the mule. He had Oliver's neck bent like a bow, but the crazed animal ran as if his tail was alight.

Lowry yelled at Ginnie, "Let's go. I'll see if I can catch up to that stupid mule and stop him."

With the colt trailing behind, they dodged rocks and jumped brush, gaining on the mule.

In front of them, the terrain was flat and wide. Lowry yelled to John, "If you can turn him in a circle, it will slow him."

John twisted Oliver's neck to the side, forcing him into a wide circle, and the mule slowed and broke into a trot. As Lowry and Ginnie reached them, Oliver halted, his sides heaving, struggling to catch his breath.

"I hate this animal," John snarled, keeping the reins taut until the mule relaxed.

Lowry sighed. "I'm sorry, he's usually very calm."

"Sure, on the farm, I'll bet he's a delight." John glared at Lowry. "I thought mules were supposed to be steady Eddies?"

"This one's name just got changed to Lightning." She tilted her head in the direction of the Bedouin camp. "Let's keep them walking, so they cool out." Grinning, Lowry said, "At least 'Lightning' was going in the right direction."

Lowry nudged Dalal next to John and Oliver. "That was impressive riding, John—you did a great job stopping him. Where did you say you learned to ride?"

"I had an extended Boy Scout summer camp one year and horseback riding was a part of the package." With a frown, he added, "But there wasn't a Runaway badge."

The valley narrowed and near a hillside, they crossed a worn path. They followed it to the other side of the hill and found a sea of Bedouin tents. Herds of sheep and goats grazed behind the camp, while Arabian horses and cud-chewing camels lounged near a small pond ringed with pearlwort and tussock grass.

A man in Bedouin robes shouted to the others, leapt on a waiting mount, and galloped up to greet them.

John mumbled under his breath, "I hope Lightning doesn't entertain our new friends with another display of speed."

Lowry raised her eyebrows. "Bedouins love a good race."

The Bedouin halted his horse in front of them. With a sweep of his arm, he said, "As-Salaam-Alaikum!"

With a smile, Lowry gestured with her hand. "Wa-alaikum-salaam!"

The Bedouin turned and waved for them follow.

Ginnie asked, "What did he say?"

"'Peace be unto you,' and I replied, 'And unto you peace.'" Trailing the Bedouin to the camp, Lowry whispered to Ginnie, "Don't touch their left hands, or show the bottom of your foot to anyone. We don't want to insult them. Follow my lead."

They reached the main tent and a tall Bedouin stepped out, bowing to them with a smile. He gestured for them to dismount, and spoke in perfect English, "Welcome! Please come have tea with us."

Lowry dismounted and bowed to him. "Salaam, Sheik Sahail." She presented John and Ginnie. "Let me introduce you to my friend John and his daughter, Ginnie, who were gracious enough to accompany me on this trip." She gestured toward the colt, nibbling dates out of the hands of Bedouin youngsters. "And here is your new colt."

Sheik Sahail bowed to John and Ginnie. "It's a pleasure to make your acquaintance." He glanced at the colt with a smile. "I hope you'll excuse me for a moment so I can greet my new stallion."

With a date in his hand, the sheik slowly approached the colt, murmuring to him. He stretched his hand out, with the date in his palm. The colt sniffed the date, gently picked it from his palm, and gobbled the treat. Then the colt sniffed his hand again and licked it, while the sheik rubbed his neck.

Sheik Sahail turned back to Lowry. "A fine young stallion for my herd. Thank you very much for delivering him." He turned to his servants and clapped his hands for them to take charge of his guests. The colt reared up in terror, but the sheik laughed. "He has a fine spirit."

The boys led the colt away, coaxing him along with more dates. Several men came up, offered to care for their mounts, and led them away. One of the sheik's servants approached Lowry, John, and Ginnie, and with a bow, waved them toward the large tent. They entered the cool shade under the awning and sank onto exquisite rugs, set with a fragrant tray of tea and sweet cookies. The sheik sat across from them, motioning them to enjoy the refreshments.

John sipped the hot tea and asked Sahail, "How is your tribe faring in Antarctica?"

Sheik Sahail smiled. "It has been a struggle to adapt to the cold, but we winter near the city of d'Urville. We immigrated here to keep our way of life pure; in this new world we can stay away from the devastating influences of civilization."

Sheik Sahail discussed the history of their tribe until a huge dinner arrived, with fresh-baked flat bread and a roasted lamb on a bed of rice, covered with a sauce of yogurt and butter, sprinkled with pine nuts. After days of camp food, it smelled delicious.

Lowry whispered to Ginnie, "Only touch the food with your right hand."

After dinner, the servants took away the platters and they lay back on the rugs, listening to a musician play a flute. Sahail asked Lowry, "How many Arabian horses do you have?"

"We have five broodmares and use imported semen from stallions around the world, but at some point, we'll have stallions here to breed with our mares. Perhaps you can come for a visit if you find yourself near Amundsen."

"I'd love to see your mares, but I am rarely near the capital city," he replied. A servant approached him with a nod. Smiling broadly, Sahail said, "If you are not too tired, we've arranged entertainment for you." He clapped his hands for the servants to bring cloaks and invited them to walk outside into the soft evening light.

Ten stunning Arabian horses with riders in full regalia pranced near the tent. The sheik handed a scarf to Ginnie. "When you drop the scarf, the race will begin."

Her eyes bright with excitement, Ginnie held the fluttering scarf over her head., then she released the scarf to the wind. The riders shouted and the horses raced around the camp. They clapped in delight as the competitors returned to the starting line, with a huge gray winning the contest.

After the riders withdrew, the sheik waved his hand to one of the men. The man walked behind a row of tents, and after a few minutes reappeared, leading a beautiful chestnut mare toward them.

Sheik Sahail turned to Lowry. "I wanted to show you a new mare for my herd—a wonderful gift from Lorenzo Durant." He smiled. "I believe he will be the new president of Antarctica?"

Astonished at this bombshell, Lowry swallowed hard. Durant had already gotten his hooks into this remote village. The election was only weeks away, but Nick hadn't visited this part of Antarctica. Leave it to Durant to bribe early and often.

Outwardly calm, Lowry smiled. "The presidential elections are coming up, but in my opinion, the more suitable candidate is Nick Walker."

Sheik Sahail raised an eyebrow. "Ah, yes, I have heard of him—your uncle, I believe?" Staring at her with a thin smile.

Lowry cleared her throat. "Yes, he is my uncle, but he's a fine man, and would make a great first president."

"No doubt," the sheik replied with a slight tilt of his head. He bowed to his guests, ending the discussion. "You must be tired—please follow my servant Bakhit, he'll show you to your tents. Sleep well, my friends."

Lowry and Ginnie were led to one tent and John to another.

"Good night." John called to them. "Don't let the Durant bugs bite."

The flap closed behind them and they sat on the hand-woven bedding. "I'm exhausted," said Ginnie with a yawn. She undressed and slipped under the soft blankets. "Good night."

Lowry slipped off her outer clothes and stretched out under the blankets. She turned out the lamp, and then lay down, staring into the darkness. What a disaster! Durant had beat them to the punch with an entire Bedouin tribe. In a close election, every vote counted, and both she and Nick had failed to get here before Durant had paid off the sheik.

With a huff, she flipped onto her side, plumping the pillow with her fist, growling "Durant" at each punch. Too angry to fall asleep, she turned onto her back, staring at the tapestries above her, shifting in the capricious wind.

CHAPTER 25

The next morning Lowry awoke to the sounds of the camp coming alive—a symphony of bleating goats, whinnying horses, and laughing children. With a yawn, she pushed herself up, and dragged her fingers through her hair. Her eyes grew wide at the smell of coffee and Lowry perused the tent for the source of the delicious aroma. Near the entrance, steam rose from a brass pot with tiny brass cups next to it. *Bedouin coffee!*

With that encouragement, she flung off the blankets, and pulled on her clothes against the morning chill. She crawled over to the coffee service and picked up a cup, admiring the Arabic floral design of lacquered black and brass. She poured herself a steaming cup of coffee and added a spoonful of honey and some goat's milk. Lowry sat cross-legged on the rug and sipped the coffee, gazing at the interior of the tent. Last night, it had been too dark to see the interior, but in the daylight, she drew in her breath at sight of lovely handcrafted items.

Painted poles held up the tall tent roof, with a brass lantern hung in the apex. For extra warmth against the cold winds, colorful tapestries hung on the inside perimeter, along with seating mats and plump pillows, covered in handwoven wool. A scattering of small wood and brass tables, storage boxes, and a few goatskin-covered chairs. Not one mass-produced item in sight.

She drank another small cup of coffee, and fortified with hot caffeine, she stood and stretched her body. She pulled on her jacket and went to the entrance, caressing the finely woven fabric of the flap as she pushed it aside, and left the dimness of the tent. The sun blinded her for an instant, then when her eyes adjusted, she gazed at the charming scene of the camp— women milking goats and beating out rugs, and behind her, boys feeding dates and dry grass to the herd of horses near the pond.

At the sound of a cough, she turned to see John sipping a cup of coffee in the shade of his tent.

With a chuckle, Lowry said, "Good morning. I didn't see you in the shadows."

He smiled. "Did you sleep well?"

She shrugged. "After I stopped thinking about Durant's 'gift' to Sheik Sahail, I did."

"Yeah, that was a bolt from the blue." He stared at her, tapping the side of his cup. "But I guess expected. Durant wants to win, and he'll do whatever it takes." He finished his coffee and tilted his head toward the tent. "I assume Ginnie is still asleep?"

"Yes, but I should wake her—we need to be on the trail soon." She slipped back through the flap.

Lowry gazed at Ginnie, dead asleep, curled in a fetal position under the blankets. It had been a big shock to Ginnie that she and her father had been romantically involved. That would have been tough for any teenager, but especially with her mother's death still fresh on her mind. *I wish John had told her earlier.*

Lowry exhaled. Nothing to do but see how all of this played out.

Ginnie shifted under the blankets, muttering in her sleep.

Lowry called out, "Come on, sleepyhead, the trail is waiting!"

She opened one eye, staring at Lowry for a moment. With a yawn, she opened both eyes, and shifted onto her back. "What, no breakfast?"

Lowry knelt and packed up her saddlebag. "I think they're getting ready to throw it out."

Ginnie stuck out her tongue at Lowry's teasing expression. "You rat, they're not throwing it out."

"Not yet, but we'd better hurry, or they might." Lowry poured Ginnie a cup of coffee and spooned in sugar and cream.

Ginnie stretched her arms and peeled herself out of the rugs. Shivering, she jerked on her clothes. With another yawn, she stood up, and shuffled over to Lowry, who handed her the coffee. With a nod, she said, "Thanks, Lowry." She sank onto one of the pillows and sipped the hot drink.

Lowry tidied her bed and then slung the saddlebag over her shoulder. She said to Ginnie, "I'd go ahead and grab your bag. I'm not sure we're coming back to the tent."

Ginnie finished her cup. "That was wonderful—my first taste of Bedouin coffee!" She crawled over and straightened the blankets on her bed.

After she grabbed her small pack, they left the tent.

John stepped toward them, smiling. "She's awake!" He joked, wrapping his arm around Ginnie.

They crossed the encampment, navigating around bleating goats, herded by a boy and his dog, and then passed a group of laughing women, weaving rugs, while their daughters smiled shyly behind them. Men and boys played soccer on a flat space near the edge of the camp, their scores punctuated with Arabic cheers.

They reached the sheik's large tent and Sheik Sahail rose to greet them, bowing and waving for them to enter. Spread before them was a large coffee service and a huge platter of fresh-baked flat bread and dates. They sank into the luxurious rugs and indulged in more coffee, and stuffed themselves with delicious bread, yogurt, and fruit.

When breakfast was finished, they thanked the sheik for his gracious hospitality. Servants brought their fully saddled mounts, and, squinting against the sun, they left the darkness of the tent. Oliver heehawed a greeting and the children nearby giggled.

Sahail grinned. "John, I think your mount is happy to see you."

John winked at Lowry. "Likewise, I'm sure."

With a bow, the sheik handed each of them a small present. "A few tokens to show my appreciation for your long journey."

He gave John a carved camel-head knife, and then to Lowry, a fly whisk with a carved horse head, and to Ginnie a beautiful woven bag. He also insisted that they take a bag of coffee, dates, and several loaves of the flatbread.

They packed their saddlebags with the gifts, and Lowry turned back to the sheik. "Please be open-minded and consider voting for my uncle. He's quite extraordinary."

The sheik inclined his head. "I'll keep your advice in mind, but I must support the candidate who will best serve our tribe."

Lowry swung into the saddle and looked at the sheik. "Of course, but I would argue that a truthful man would treat you honorably, no matter how the wind blows."

With a deep bow, he smiled. "As true a weather report as I've ever heard."

They waved to the tribe and trotted along the trail toward the mountain range, listening to the traditional ululation trilling of the Bedouin women.

The day was warm, but without the antics of the colt, they settled into a quick pace. For their return, they took another route to explore a different part of the Concordia Refuge. It was a gentler path through the mountains and they made it to the top of the pass by noon. They stopped to eat their Bedouin leftovers for lunch and John made a pot of strong coffee.

After lunch, John sipped the brew. "The Bedouins don't have anything to do with the population around them for the most part and just want to be left alone. I can't blame them, but hope all remains peaceful with any settlers who may venture into the desert."

Lowry replied, "Sheik Sahail desperately wants to preserve their way of life. When he first contacted me, he told me that it was becoming more difficult in North Africa, so their small group decided to immigrate here." She continued with a sigh. "I wonder what Durant promised him."

She stood and gestured with her thumb. "We'd better get going, so we can get down the other side before dark."

They mounted up and headed back onto the wetter side of the mountains. The animals breathed in the moister air and whinnied at the scent of fresh grass. Wildlife became more abundant as they descended the slope.

John asked Lowry, "Are we back on the Concordia Refuge?"

Lowry nodded. "I believe we are. Once we get to the bottom of the valley, this part of the refuge is known for melting permafrost areas, so we'll have to be careful. Dalal is trained to sense subterranean caverns."

As the sun dipped below the mountains, they found a small meadow overlooking the valley to set up camp for the night. They started a campfire, brought out the last loaves of flatbread, and sprinkled dried cheese and sausage on top.

John surprised Lowry with a bottle of red wine that he'd been saving for this last night of the trek. He opened the bottle and poured two glasses of wine. He held up his glass. "Here's to the Bedouin Trek!"

They clinked the camp glasses together and to Ginnie's water bottle, and then dug into their cold meal.

As they ate, Lowry asked, "Ginnie, what is your opinion of the Bedouins?"

"In some ways their life is lovely and in some ways it's really harsh." She raised an eyebrow. "I'm not sure being a Bedouin female would be easy."

Lowry nodded. "I understand the sheik's desire to 'preserve their culture,' but I hope he doesn't think that ignorance is the way to maintain it. Cultural tradition can be beautiful as long as it isn't used as a hammer against different classes."

John put more wood on the fire. "With the satellites in place, virtual schools are everywhere, but it's difficult to force remote communities such as theirs to abide by truancy laws."

After dinner, the sun slipped below the horizon and they could see a few of the constellations. They lay on the ground and gazed up at the stars, with Lowry pointing out the Southern Cross and Southern Fish.

A bright object glided across the sky.

Ginnie said, "Hey, there's the new International Space Station—we heard they were doing a polar orbit." She chuckled. "Star light, star bright, I wish upon a star tonight."

Lowry watched the pinpoint of light arcing over their heads and finished the nursery rhyme. "I wish I may, I wish I might, have this wish I wish tonight." She swallowed hard and breathed her wish: *Please don't let Durant steal Antarctica.* A cold pit twisted in her stomach as the ISS disappeared over the horizon. Was it a bad omen?

*   *   *

Cool air drifted into the camp as the fire burned down.

Ginnie sat up, shivering. She hugged her arms to her chest and scooted closer to the embers. "I'm cold and tired." Her eyes closed for a second and she twitched awake. "Before I fall into the fire, I'm calling it a night," she mumbled and crawled toward her sleeping bag.

John stood up and followed her. He knelt and gave her a kiss good night. She wormed into her sleeping bag, yanked a knit cap over her head, and with a deep sigh, fell asleep.

He grabbed a blanket from the packs and returned to the campfire, draping it across Lowry's shoulders.

"Thank you," Lowry murmured, clutching the blanket around her.

He threw a few branches onto the fire and sat across from Lowry.

The fire crackled with new life and she stared into the flames. She heaved a sigh. "I can't get rid of the nagging worry that Durant might win the election. If he's gotten to someone like the sheik, who else has he bought off?"

John shook his head. "It could be a disaster for Nick. With the small population of Antarctica, elections can be won or lost with a handful of votes."

Lowry sipped her wine and glanced back at the soundly sleeping Ginnie. "Do you think Ginnie is okay with our relationship?"

Frowning, John stared into the flames. "I think she's still pissed at me, but she'll get over it—I think." He looked at Lowry. "I should have told her earlier, but I didn't have the time . . . or balls, I guess."

John lifted the bottle of wine to the firelight, perusing the amount remaining. "Let's kill this bottle." He poured the last of the wine into their cups and set the empty bottle beside him. "I guess this is our last night out?"

Lowry nodded. "If all goes well tomorrow, we should be able to make it to the farms by tomorrow evening." She smiled. "Funny how that sounds like 'civilization' compared to this."

With a crunch, the burning twigs collapsed, and John stirred the campfire with a stick. "Civilization is a relative term." John pursed his lips. "Ralph Waldo Emerson said it best: *The end of the human race will be that it will eventually die of civilization.*"

John moved next to her, pulling the blanket around both of them. "In the wilderness you find things to replace what you lost in modern society. And sometimes you discover that the replacement far exceeds the original."

With a thin smile, he sighed. "This new life has burned away my self-delusion of a utopia in the hinterlands. The reality of living on Antarctica has been smashed into my face, fighting for basic things, like water and power." He drank the last of his wine. "But, in spite of the daily struggles, I love it—the freedom to choose what I want to do and when I want to do it." He chuckled. "I probably would have been a mountain man if I had lived in the Old West."

Lowry raised an eyebrow. "I'm glad you got rid of that self-delusion—Mountain Man."

Lowry finished her wine. She rinsed the cups, packed them away, and dried her wet hands on the blanket. She shook her cold fingers and stretched them toward the campfire, warming them with the heat of the coals. "We'd better get some rest. We have a long day tomorrow."

Lowry crawled to her sleeping bag and wriggled inside. She pulled out her hair band, shook loose her hair, and snuggled against the frigid air. Shifting in the bag, a sharp stone poked her in the side and she pivoted onto her other side. She found herself listening to John's muted snoring amid the sounds of the night as the nocturnals took the stage: the hoot of an owl, the yip of a fox.

Even the wind strummed a tune, but for Lowry, it was a song of uncertainty.

Lowry flipped onto her back, apprehension gnawing at her brain. She gazed up at the Southern Cross, coldly staring back at her. "No fortune-telling tonight, my old friend?"

CHAPTER 26

With a jolt, John opened his eyes in the pre-dawn light of the camp. Listening, he held his breath—there it was again, a deep guttural growl. Turning his head slowly, he whispered to the others, "Don't make any sudden moves—I think there's a bear in the camp."

Ginnie stirred in her sleeping bag, mumbling, "What did you say, Daddy?"

He hissed at her, "Ginnie, be quiet, there's a bear—don't move."

Lowry lay still in her sleeping bag and spoke in a low voice, "I hope the animals don't panic."

In the dimness, a dark mound lumbered behind them along the edge of the camp, grunting as it approached the packs. The hobbled animals behind them whinnied in terror; the thud of their hooves matched John's heartbeat. *Let's hope it's not a momma with cubs.*

John edged his pistol out from under his pillow and scrambled out of his bag. He crouched and aimed the pistol into the air, discharging it several times. The horses jostled each other and Oliver's bray echoed off of the stone cliffs.

The sound of claws scraping the rocks resonated behind them. John stood up, listening for the roar of a charging bear, but there was nothing. "I think he's gone."

"I'm glad he didn't want to stand and fight." Lowry said, her voice shaking.

Exhaling, Ginnie asked, "Will he come back?"

"I doubt it, but it's best to get going." John slung the holster across his shoulder, put the pistol inside, and started packing his gear.

Ginnie scooted out of her bag, shivering in the cold air as she wrestled into her clothes.

John grinned. "No coffee to warm us up this morning."

They tacked up and started along the trail, letting the animals pick the path until it was light enough to see. Before they entered the valley, they stopped to admire the view. Lowry passed around breakfast bars.

Lowry pointed toward the meandering river surrounded with a quilt-like pattern of irregular shapes. "Do you see those polygon shapes on the floor of the valley? Those are areas of permafrost and are common near rivers. The danger of permafrost is where the frozen soil thaws under the surface and gets washed away, with a bit of crust on top."

John said, "I'm assuming we can avoid those areas?"

"Yes, we'll cross where the river is narrow and stay on the opposite side of the valley."

The cold air deepened as they moved into the valley. In single file, they crossed in a shallow spot, and turned to follow the river downstream, the slow-moving water leading the way home. Brilliant red streaks from the sunrise spilled over the ridge, shimmering across the surface of the river.

The day warmed as they traveled along the river, and insects swarmed in the hazy air. Oliver shook his head to ward off the biting flies attacking his long ears.

The air became heavy by midday, and they stopped for lunch in the shade under a grove of trees. Lowry made the coffee they had missed with their hasty morning departure. The animals drank from the river and grazed on the tender grass along the bank.

After lunch, the day became breezy and conversation difficult as the wind stole their words, and they fell silent on the trail. The sunlight faded behind deepening clouds, and the wind gusted without warning, the animals jigging as sand was driven across the trail.

At a distance rumble of thunder, Lowry and John looked back, then at each other. Black clouds were building in the distance.

John yelled over the rising wind, "Lowry, we need to get to shelter. It looks like a nasty storm overtaking us."

Nodding, Lowry pointed out a grove of trees down the valley. "Let's hurry and try to reach those trees before it hits."

Lowry nudged her horse into a slow canter and the others followed her. The air turned yellow as boiling black clouds raced toward them, the rolling thunder closer with each minute. Halfway to the trees, the storm struck with fury. The wind whipped around them and lightning ripped across the sky like fingers of a skeleton.

She waved her arm for them to keep up and kicked her horse into a full gallop. Torrential rains hit, obscuring their view with a gray veil in front of their faces. John felt the muscles of the mule under the wet saddle as they ran, flat out, on the edge of the valley floor. His heart raced as Oliver galloped through the pummeling rain, following the heaving flanks of the horses ahead.

A crack of lightning hit a scrub pine tree beside them and exploded into a fireball. Burning branches of the tree landing around them, and the terrified animals bolted out of control.

Ginnie's mare raced diagonally across the valley—and into the permafrost field.

Lowry shouted, "Ginnie, follow us!"

Ginnie turned toward them, screaming inaudibly, the thunder stealing her words. She shook her head in fear. Kisra had taken the bit into her teeth and was running away with her.

Lowry's mare skidded to a stop, dropping her nose to the ground. John struggled to hang on as the mule slid to a halt behind her.

Lowry stared at the ground in front of her. "There must be cavernous permafrost ahead! Jump off, Ginnie!"

Ginnie could not hear her. Kisra careened across the karsted landscape. Lowry turned Dalal to skirt the dangerous ground and waved John to follow behind her.

"We have to get to Ginnie, let's hurry!" he yelled to her.

With a shake of her head, Lowry shouted back, "This mare is trained to sense karsting and won't cross it. We'll have to go around it and pray that Ginnie and Kisra make it through."

They galloped up the side of the valley parallel to Ginnie and the mare. Lightning drove Kisra on until she floundered in mid-gallop, struggling to stay on her feet. Then her front legs broke the fragile surface above a permafrost fissure, and she sunk to her knees. Ginnie catapulted away from her, and hit the muddy surface, spinning away from the mare. The mare panicked, fighting against the collapsing ground beneath her, but the shell of the cavern shattered under her hooves and she fell to her chest into the crevasse.

"Ginnie!" John screamed, turning the mule toward his daughter.

Lowry waved him to stop. "It's no good. We can't take the animals out there, they'll fall in as well. We'll have to go to her on foot—crawl if we must."

Lowry halted on the far side of the eroded permafrost, with John and Oliver beside her. Rain pelted them as they slipped off the animals.

Helplessly, Lowry murmured, "My god," as Kisra whinnied in terror. Dalal whinnied back as Lowry threw a hobble on her mare and one on Oliver.

Kisra struggled to rise as the ground sank beneath her, but her last cry was muffled into silence as the mud enveloped her head. Inexorably, the cavern swallowed her body into the ooze of melted permafrost.

John grabbed a rope from his saddle and threw it over his shoulder. They started across the tenuous layer of the permafrost field, with its crust squishy with rainwater. The wind and rain buffeted them as they inched closer to Ginnie.

John swallowed hard. His stomach twisted in fear at the sight of his daughter motionless on the permafrost. His only child lay there, possibly dead. "I'm sorry, Helen," he whispered, his fingers shaking.

Cracks radiated under their feet, and the ground sunk beneath them like stepping on a mattress. Lowry stopped, yelling to John over the wind, "We'd better crawl from here and you stay behind me, since I am lighter than you."

John took the rope, tied it around her waist, and threaded it through her belt loops. He wound the other end around his chest and tied it with a knot. "That way when you grab Ginnie, I can drag both of you back."

Lowry nodded and they crawled across the fragile ground. The smell of rot seeped upward as they approached the hole. A huge flash of lightning ripped across the sky and the rain pummeled them.

Ginnie lifted her head.

She's alive! John breathed a sigh of relief. "Don't move, Ginnie," he called out to her. "Stay still, we're almost there." John's knee sank into the ground. "Shit!"

Lowry held up her hand. "Let me go ahead and I'll snake across, so there isn't too much weight on the surface."

With a nod, he played out the rope as she squirmed along the muddy surface to Ginnie's foot. Lowry reached out to grab Ginnie's ankle, but the ground bowed under her.

Rain pouring over him, John held his breath.

Lowry slowly moved forward and slipped her hand around Ginnie's ankle, then cocked her head back, signaling John to pull them to safety.

Dazed, Ginnie moaned as they inched away from the rim of the cavern.

A deep yawning sound came from below her and the surface buckled under Ginnie's head, tipping her downwards into the edge of the subsiding cavity. Her arms fell into the gap and she screamed, "Daddy!"

John leapt up and sprinted backwards, his feet sinking with each step. Lowry groaned, struggling to hang on to Ginnie as they slid along the top of the collapsing ground.

John screamed, "You bastard, I won't let you win." He staggered backwards ahead of the expanding fissure, until they reached stable ground. John stood with his head down, waving to them, gasping for breath. "Crawl to me and we'll go back to the animals—we know it's safe there."

Lowry pulled Ginnie to her and then pushed her to John. Dazed and covered with mud, Ginnie crawled to where John stood, with Lowry behind her. When Ginnie reached him, John picked her up and carried her to safety next to the animals.

John eased her onto the ground and felt her arms and legs. "Are you hurt, Ginnie baby?"

Ginnie pulled off her muddy helmet and held her hand to her head. "My head hurts, but I don't think anything is broken—lucky I was wearing a helmet."

"Thank god you're alive!" He hugged her gently, and smoothed her matted, wet hair back from her face. He touched the knot swelling on her forehead. "You must have hit a rock."

Lowry wiped the streaming water from her eyes with her sleeve, untied the rope from around John's chest and rewound it. "Let's put her on my mare and we'll try to find shelter."

The thunder and lightning had passed, but the rain still poured. The animals stood with sagging ears and drenched coats. John squeezed Lowry's shoulder as they looked back at the gigantic hole. Poor Kisra had been completely swallowed by the sludge.

Lowry tied the rope to the back of John's saddle, came around to Dalal's head and grabbed the bridle. John eased Ginnie onto the horse, steadying her with his hand. Lowry led the mare through the mud and streaming water with Oliver following close to her.

By the time they reached the trees, the rain was abating and a few peeks of sunlight struggled past the clouds. John helped Ginnie off, and with his arm around her, found a flat rock for her to sit. John pulled an emergency blanket and a fire kit from his saddlebag, while Lowry picked dry grass out of a crevice. John draped the shimmering blanket around Ginnie and started a small fire.

"All of us need to change into dry clothes and warm up, before we get hypothermia," John said. He dug through Ginnie's saddlebag and found a change of clothes for her. He handed the clothes to Lowry. "Would you mind helping her change while I make tea?" He pulled out the Insta-Tea jug and gave it a twist.

Lowry helped Ginnie change and re-wrapped her in the emergency blanket, then changed her own clothes. They huddled around the fire, drinking hot tea, when the sun broke through the clouds, warming the rain-soaked valley.

Lowry glanced at John. "You need to change your clothes, too."

He nodded, walked to Oliver, and got dry clothes out of his saddlebag. He pulled his shirt over his head and saw deep rope burns across his chest. He touched them gingerly and winced.

Lowry turned at the sound. "We need to put medicine on those rope burns, John." She walked to him, then shook her head as she examined the damage. "I guess Antarctica wants to brand you, doesn't she?"

She got out the first-aid kit. "You have rope burns on your back as well." She patted antibiotic cream on his damaged skin and helped him ease the dry shirt over them. She held up his pants.

He tugged them out of her hands. "I think I can put on my own pants."

Lowry chuckled. Then she dug the last of the chocolate bars from her saddlebag and broke them into pieces. She popped one into John's mouth, a piece into hers, and walked back to Ginnie and handed her the last square of chocolate.

John came over to the blaze and squatted next to Ginnie. He swayed from exhaustion and leaned against the rock.

Ginnie nibbled the chocolate and glanced at Lowry. "You and dad saved my life."

Lowry knelt and wrapped her arm around Ginnie. "I'm so glad—you're a very special girl." Lowry sighed. "I'm afraid my poor Kisra wasn't as lucky. She was a good mare, but not the most intelligent horse in the world."

Ginnie sniffled. "I'm so sorry, Lowry."

Lowry hugged her. "It wasn't your fault, Ginnie-girl, she's the one who ran away with you and onto the permafrost, despite your efforts to stop her."

"I know, but she was a sweet horse."

"Yes, but I'm afraid Darwin won that round."

CHAPTER 27

John poked the dying embers of the fire. Then he stood and stretched with a groan. "It'll take me a month to recover from this trip."

Chuckling, Lowry said, "But the stories you'll tell when you're old and gray." She pointed at the sun, now on its downward path. "I don't think we can make it home tonight." She snapped her fingers. "I know a place where we can stay the night and it's only a slight detour off the trail. Some of the miners built stone cabins years ago, and I'm sure we can spend the night there."

With a shrug, John replied, "Possibly, but I'd like a doctor to look at Ginnie."

"It would take hours to reach the clinic near the farms. Everyone is too exhausted to travel that far."

"My head is not that bad. I agree with Lowry, Dad."

John acquiesced. "Okay, and where are these cabins?"

"They're not on any maps; besides hunting cabins, the striking miners used them during strikes to escape the wrath of the management. There's a land marker near them, so let me see if I can get a location on the GPS."

She moved into the open and came back shortly. "Looks like they are only a couple of kilometers from here, so on horseback, we could be there in less than an hour."

John said, "Let's get going."

Lowry mounted and John helped Ginnie up behind her. With a groan, he swung up on Oliver.

After the storm, the land came alive in the warm sunshine. Wildflowers and white tufts of cotton grass waved in the breeze. Birds flitted up and down, devouring the clouds of insects lingering over the fresh rainwater. Ginnie laughed as a butterfly landed on her head. John's spirits rose with joy. They had survived.

A boiling life force screamed from every corner of this wilderness where humans were just a passing annoyance or a meal. Nature was the master here and anyone who thought differently was a fool, dead, or both. His closed his eyes with a smile. *Thank you for not taking my child.*

Lowry turned her mare onto a beaten path. They rode into a clearing and she called out, "Halloo, anyone here?"

Two men approached and one recognized her. "Lowry! Where have you been keeping yourself? We heard you'd come back and homesteaded a claim."

"Hank?"

"Sure. You remembered me!" He gestured for them to dismount. "Come have some refreshments. You all coming from the back country?"

"Yep."

Cocking his head, Hank said, "That was nasty squall that raced through."

Lowry dismounted and pulled off her helmet. "Not just nasty—a killer. We were returning from a camping trip when the storm hit. Ginnie's horse ran away and fell into a permafrost cavern. Ginnie was thrown off of her, and we were lucky to pull her out." She ran her fingers through her snarled hair. "But the mare died."

"Wow, that sounds like a lovely Antarctic nature walk, but sorry about your horse."

Lowry introduced John and Ginnie to the two retired miners. "This is John Barrous and his daughter, Ginnie."

Hank shook their hands and gestured to the other man standing nearby. "This is Les. He's from Lesotho, Africa, so we call him Les." Glancing at the sky, he said, "You should stay the night—it's getting late to make it to the homesteads." He gestured with his thumb. "I'll open the other cabin."

Lowry asked, "Is there a paddock where we can put the animals?"

"Sure, we don't have any feed, but there's a little grass. No other horses have been in them this season."

"That'll be fine. But I'll need buckets of water for them."

"Les can help you while I fix up the cabin."

Hank and John grabbed the saddle bags and packs and took them to the smaller cabin. Hank said, "I'll start the stove heater going. We use meadow muffins. Plentiful in this valley."

"Meadow muffins?" John asked.

"Caribou chips—dried poop." Hank point to a bin filled with dried caribou poop.

"Ah."

After Lowry and Ginnie settled the animals into the paddock for the night, they all met back at the main cabin. John had to stoop through the low doorway. It was a rough-hewn cabin of native stone with a rickety table and a few chairs, dimly lit by a candle lantern.

Les stirred a pot of chili on the stove while Hank brought glasses of water, a large bowl of peanuts, and crackers to the table. In a faint Bantu accent, Les said, "I'm afraid it's only camp food, but it's not bad. I made the chili with goose meat."

"Goose meat?" John asked, his mouth watering from the aroma. "Smells wonderful."

Les turned to him. "Geese are the only unrestricted game we can hunt. The rest are UN-release animals." He gestured with his thumb to the back of the cabin and smiled. "We have so many geese, our solar freezer is full—it'll last all winter."

Ginnie rubbed her head with a tinge of pain on her face.

John asked her, "Are you okay?"

With a crooked smile, she said, "Yeah, but I might want some medicine."

John turned to Hank and Les. "When Ginnie was thrown off, she hit her head. Do you guys have any ibuprofen?"

Hank gestured toward Les. "Les here is a trained paramedic. Maybe he should examine her?"

Nodding, John said, "Sure, we'd appreciate it."

Les went to the back of the cabin and got a medic kit. He pulled out a cylindrical device and turned it on. Shining a light into Ginnie's eyes, he observed her reactions, then looked at the scope. "By these readings, she doesn't have a concussion." With a smile, he laid his hand on her shoulder. "You'll be fine but take it easy." He handed her a small vial with liquid ibuprofen. "This liquid will work faster than a pill."

Ginnie twisted the top and downed the medicine. She smiled. "Thanks, Les."

Les put away the first-aid kit, returned to the table and sat next to John.

John grabbed a handful of peanuts from the bowl and asked Les, "What brought you to Antarctica?"

Les shrugged. "I was an orphan and unemployed, so it was either find a job, or go into a life of crime. I heard about a ship going to the mining station from Cape Town, with the promise of good jobs. I signed up and I've been here ever since."

Hank sat across from John. "I hope you folks didn't run into an odd fellow on your trip—he had kind of a mean look. I don't know if he came with the Land Rush, or what, but he appeared to be running from something."

John thought of the skeleton on the trail and the red cap. "He didn't happen to have a red cap sporting a black-bear logo?"

Hank's mouth dropped open. "Yeah, I remember that cap. And the jerk stole some clothes and a Remington rifle, but that Remington was a piece of garbage, so good riddance—used to jam from time to time."

With a lopsided grin, John said, "The Remington seems to have jammed for the last time. We found a skeleton near the trail and his red cap stuck in the grass nearby." John pulled it out of his knapsack, holding it up for them to see. "That guy and his son broke into Lowry's house several months back."

"Son of a bitch!" Hank's mouth dropped open, and he looked at Les. "I told you that guy was no good." Turning back to John, he asked, "What happened to the son?"

John grimaced. "He tried to shoot me when I got to Lowry's house, so I'm afraid I had to shoot him." He shrugged. "Neither father nor son pose a threat to the population of Antarctica."

"This calls for a drink!" Hank chuckled. With a scrape of his chair, he jumped up and went to a cabinet. He grabbed a bottle of Scotch and glasses. Hank poured out doses of whiskey for the adults with a side of water. Les poured a glass of sweet tea for Ginnie.

Lowry lifted her glass. "To Karma—what goes around comes around."

"To Karma!" They clinked glasses.

The warmth from the alcohol spread down John's shoulders. Les returned to the stove, filled the bowls with chili, and placed them around the table. Everyone grabbed spoons and for several minutes the only sounds were clanging metal against ceramic and the crumbling of crackers.

Lowry chewed, closing her eyes for a moment. "Mmm— this is wonderful." With a nod, she grinned at the two miners. "We really appreciate your hospitality."

"You're always welcome here, Lowry." Hank lifted up his glass and made another toast, "To Nick Walker—may he be the next President!" He waved John and Lowry to follow suit. "Drink up!" He threw back the Scotch and fixed another.

Lowry pushed her empty bowl toward the center of the table. Les started to refill it, but she waved her hand. "Thanks, Les, but I'm stuffed."

John sat back in his chair, his belly filled beyond capacity, and said with a sigh, "Thanks so much, that's some of the best chili I've ever had."

Hank got up to clear the table and put the dishes in the sink. Lowry rose to offer help, but he waved her to stay seated. "I'm just putting them in the sink. You're done in, Lowry."

Les poured another round of drinks. Hank brought a lantern and set it in the middle of the table. Hank sat and grabbed his drink. He lifted his glass for a final toast. "To Antarctica!"

"Hear, hear!" They all cheered.

Lowry sipped her whiskey. She leaned forward with worry on her face. "What do you two think of Durant?"

Hank slammed his whiskey glass onto the table. "I hate that asshole."

Les nodded. "He's a crooked bastard. If he can't buy you off, he tries to intimidate you into voting for him."

Hank rapped his knuckles on the table. "Durant staged a fake fight at one of his own rallies—a band of 'miners' showed up and started a brawl, acting as if they supported Nick. They weren't miners; I'd never seen any of them."

John drummed his fingers on the table. "Let's face it, Nick is inexperienced. Durant's team has the selling of a candidate like a 'box of soap flakes' down to a T. Nick's campaigning against a prepackaged image of a confident, youthful Durant, with an onslaught of slick ads and social-media propaganda."

Lowry sighed. "Social media is filled with stories implying that Nick is a dimwitted dupe of the mining company, accusing Nick and the managers of sticking their fingers into the political pie of Antarctica."

Hank shouted, "That's crazy! Nick fought *against* the mining company!"

"God knows, cronyism is alive and well on Antarctica, but not from Nick." With a tilt of her head, Lowry said, "I've tried to talk to Nick's campaign manager, but they want to let 'Walker be Walker.' Those who don't know Nick might buy Durant's spin and fall directly into his trap."

Les nodded. "And it's working. Yesterday a new poll came out. Nick and Durant are neck and neck."

Lowry brushed her hand across her lips. "God help us."

John glanced at Lowry's pensive and exhausted face. "We'd better get some sleep for the journey tomorrow. Don't you agree, Lowry?" John got up, and staggered, knocking over his chair.

Hank laughed. "Scotch a bit strong, aye?"

John grinned back at him. "Perhaps—with a chaser of fatigue." He picked up his knapsack from the floor and draped it over his shoulder.

Lowry stood and also swayed, steadying herself with the table.

Hank guffawed. "Ginnie, you may have to help the folks to bed!" He handed Ginnie a lantern. Ginnie led the way toward the door of the cabin, while John steered Lowry with his hands on her shoulders. As he stepped through the door, he banged his head on the door frame, prompting a new round of laughter.

They stumbled to the smaller stone cabin. John hung the light on a hook, while they laid out their sleeping bags. Ginnie pulled her sleeping bag over to the other side of the heater. "Good night all." She waved.

"How is your head?" John asked.

"Much better." She crawled into the sleeping bag and looked at them with a tired smile. "I'll never forget how you and Lowry saved my life today."

"We love you, Ginnie." John said softly.

Ginnie turned toward the wall, shifted in the bag for a moment, then fell asleep.

John and Lowry arranged their bags near the warm stove. He brushed against Lowry's hand. He drew in a breath, and stood motionless, staring at her in the candlelight.

He reached out and caressed her cheek. "I believe Ginnie has given her approval of our relationship," he whispered.

Lowry smiled. He pulled her to him and tenderly kissed her eyebrows He moved down her cheek and she tilted her head back, parting her lips. He dived into the invitation with a kiss. Then he gripped her shoulders and pressed his mouth hard against hers.

They drew apart and he brushed her hair back, whispering in her ear, "Lowry, I love you." He clutched her hand, then turned it over and kissed her palm. John gazed at her. "Let's get married."

Lowry dropped her eyes. A look of anguish crossed her face. Then with a faint smile, she met his eyes. "I love you, too, John." With a shake of her head, she whispered, "But I can't think of marriage right now—I'm too nervous about the campaign." She touched his arm. "Let's talk after the elections."

Lowry would be on the road with Nick for the next several weeks.

John narrowed his eyes, and stroked the tip of her nose, trying to not show his hurt feelings.

His jaw set, John turned away from Lowry. Silently, she slipped into her sleeping bag. He knelt by the heater and shoved more chips into the little stove. The flames leapt up with new life. He slid into his sleeping bag, feeling her eyes on him.

The room became quiet. The caribou chips slumped in the heater with a soft crush.

He faced away from Lowry and clenched his fist against the searing pain in his heart. *She hadn't exactly been enthusiastic.* Had Ginnie been right? After all, he didn't really know Lowry. He heaved a sigh. Perhaps the time wasn't right for marriage— but when was there ever a "good" time to smash two headstrong personalities together?

John stared at the rock wall of the cabin. The flickering light from the stove danced on the chiseled faces of the cold stone, alive with sardonic grins and winking eyes.

But what if . . . she didn't truly love him?

K.E. Lanning

Part III

The self-inflicted thrust of the blade is the greatest betrayal.

K.E. Lanning

CHAPTER 28

Lowry awoke to the blare of the alarm. "Shut up!" she yelled, and the alarm quieted. She rubbed her eyes and stared at the ceiling. Her eyelids drifted close. The snooze jangled, louder. "Okay!" She threw the covers back and pushed herself into a sitting position on the side of the bed. With deep breaths, she tried to crank up her adrenaline. It had been a long three weeks of campaigning with Nick—she was exhausted.

Yawning, she scratched her head. She stood and looked into the mirror above the chest of drawers. *You look like hammered shit.* She dragged on her robe and slipped into her house shoes, then stumbled into the kitchen. She zapped some coffee and noticed a message from John. With a smile, she touched his face on the phone, and his image popped into 3D.

John waved. "Lowry, I'm glad you're back. Maybe I'll see you tomorrow. I'm helping at the polling station for the few primitive souls, like me, who don't vote online." He gestured thumbs up. "Best of luck to Nick tomorrow." A sideways smile came onto his face. "I've missed you. Let's plan a date after the campaign circus leaves town."

She caressed the image of his face and crossed her fingers, muttering, "We'll need the luck."

As a part of his effort to barnstorm Antarctica, Nick had attempted to get a plane to visit Sheik Sahail's community, but conveniently, any vehicle which could access the Dry Valleys either by air or land was in "maintenance repairs," or "under contract" to a private company.

Despite Durant's onslaught of dirty tricks and negative ads, the final polls had edged into their favor. Durant had the money to run a world-class campaign, but Nick appeared to have the broader base with the mining population and those perceptive homesteaders who felt Durant's hands up their proverbial skirts.

Lowry set her cup next to the phone and sighed, gazing at the image of John's face on the screen, frozen in place with his sarcastic, lopsided smile. Beneath the smile, John's pensive face revealed the tension of unresolved issues between them.

She tapped the edge of her cup and stared out of the window. When they had returned to the homesteads, she went into a full-court press on Nick's campaign. She and John had seen each other only one day in Amundsen. They had bumped into each other, and she had suggested lunch, but all through the meal, he had been aloof, perhaps hurt that she didn't jump on his marriage proposal.

Lowry swept her hand through her hair. Faced with the crunch of Nick's impending campaign, her mind was too tangled to focus on marriage and the impact on Ginnie. She had to concentrate all of her energy on electing Nick. She finished her coffee and swiped John's image away with a caress of her finger. *Repairs to the relationship are in order after the campaign.*

With a sigh, she wandered to the sink and put the cup in the dishwasher. She grabbed a bagel, dropped it into the toaster oven, and pulled the cream cheese from the fridge. She turned to the monitor and said, "Local news." The weather report aired while she poured a glass of orange juice.

An EXCLUSIVE banner pulsed across the bottom of the screen, with a reporter standing in front of the Nick Walker campaign headquarters. Lowry snapped her head around at the sight of a crowd gathered in front of the building.

The camera panned to a newswoman, shouting over the noise of the crowd, "The big story of the day is the scandal exposed this morning: Nick Walker had an illicit affair, thirty-five years ago with the wife of his brother, Duff Walker, our appointed governor of Antarctica. We've been told that Lowry Walker is really Nick's illegitimate daughter."

The newswoman's eyes glistened as she told the story of Nick's betrayal of his brother. Lowry's mind went blank as the devastating words spilled over her. Vacantly, she grabbed the hot bagel, burned her fingers, and threw it across the room.

The broadcast continued, but the blood rushing to Lowry's head blocked out the words and she saw only the newswoman's lips moving. *Maybe I'm dreaming.* She flipped to another channel and, again, the devastating report was aired.

She inhaled deeply and her brain began to function again. So this was what Durant had in his back pocket. But how the hell did he dig up the story? Durant had timed the exposure perfectly to throw a bomb into the campaign, hoping Nick couldn't recover in time. What a catastrophe!

Lowry blinked as she stared at the screen. She froze and her mouth fell open. She knew who told Durant the story— Duff. As sad as it was, there was no one else who could have or would have. The sickness never ended with him. It just boiled up, then erupted like Old Faithful. You could always count on it.

She jerked when the phone rang. A deadness sank into her as she stumbled over to answer it.

It was Nick. Taut lines creased his pale face and his green eyes stared at her, protruding like a man being strangled. He cleared his throat and spoke, his voice hoarse with emotion, "I have never lied to you, Lowry, and I never will. Your mother and I had . . ." He fumbled for the right word. ". . . Uh, an encounter, before I shipped out to Antarctica." His face wilted with the confession. "Your mother shone like a firefly with her beauty and wit, and in my loneliness, I was drawn to her light." He looked away. "In a terrible betrayal of my brother, I fell in love with her."

Tears welled up in his eyes and his head snapped up. "I only meant to comfort her after a fight with Duff, but when I touched her, something lit between us." With a shake of his head, he blinked the tears back. "But it was *my* fault, I took advantage of her raw emotions and need for love."

Lowry stared into his eyes. "Nick, are you my father?"

Nick raked his hair away from his face, shaking his head. "I don't know, Lowry. I just don't know. I'm sorry." With clenched hands, he wiped the tears from his face. He heaved a sigh and collapsed back into the chair, drained of emotion.

Lowry fell back into the chair. She had known there was something of a triangle between Duff, Nick, and her mother, but it was a bombshell to her that she might be Nick's daughter—and illegitimate to boot. God knows that was the least of her problems, but how to process this shift between fathers was beyond her mental capabilities at the moment.

Dazed, she stared out the window. Nick had been more of a father to her than Duff had ever been. Even with the political nightmare that Nick's betrayal might be, her heart lifted with the thought that the poisonous Duff wasn't her father after all. Every family had secrets, but not every family uses those secrets for personal gain. And in Duff's case, selling those secrets to the highest bidder.

"Lowry, are you okay?" Nick's worried face gazed at her.

Lowry smiled sadly. No matter how the family crashed and burned with this revelation, they had to hope that the public didn't turn from Nick and vote for Durant.

With a sigh, she said, "The problem now is how to defuse this. We'll have to have a press conference as soon as we can. You must tell them exactly what you told me. The truth is the only way out. And hope to God nobody cares who did who, thirty-some-odd years ago."

She paused and asked in a tired voice, "Nick, do you think it was Duff who leaked the story to Durant?"

"I don't know, Lowry. But Durant is the type of person to dig through years of garbage, sniff up old ashes, and make fire with it."

"I'll be by your side at the press conference."

"Thanks, Lowry."

She hung up the phone and wilted in the chair, her stomach twisted in nausea. The phone rang again and John's face appeared on the screen. She closed her eyes and opened them again. *News travels fast.* She swallowed hard and pushed the "I'll call you back" button. Lowry staggered up and walked to her bedroom to get ready to face the lions.

Durant had found the key to the closet with the rattling skeleton.

CHAPTER 29

Lowry waited in the dark. Like when she was a child, she had slipped silently through the back door into Duff's office. She wasn't even sure why she had come. The lights were dim, but she made out his form, sitting slumped over his desk. She didn't tell him she was there. A childish fear stopped her from approaching him.

She blinked at the clinking sound of glass as Duff filled the tumbler with booze. His head popped back and he downed the whiskey, then with a clunk he dropped the glass onto the desk. Exhaling, his head sagged into his hands.

Lowry shivered, recalling his frightening stories of cowering in the shadows as a child, hiding from his own father, who prowled for someone to torment as he stumbled through the house after a night of drinking. A little boy, helpless to fight the man who should have loved him.

She started at the sound of the front door opening, but couldn't see who entered—she didn't dare move or she might be discovered. Duff raised his head from his hands and straightened in the chair. He looked toward the door as if waiting for the curtain to go up on the final act of the farce. In profile, she saw the sick smile on Duff's face. He recognized the intruder. With a clip, clip, clip the footsteps came closer. Out of the shadows, a person stepped into the spotlight. Her heart beat a staccato. It was Nick.

Nick squinted as his eyes adjusted to the dim light. The revolving hologram of the Earth cast gyrating shadows on his withered face. With a smirk, Duff stood, and stepped to the front of the desk. Then he leaned back on it and faced Nick. She bit her lip at the chill of Duff's voice.

"I knew you'd come."

Nick's nose wrinkled as he leaned away from the smell of booze.

Duff threw back his head and laughed. "What's wrong? Can't face the grim reaper?" He raised a hand and continued in ecstasy. "It's finally my turn." He clasped his hand into a fist and shook it at Nick. "My turn to hurt you, to beat you, to destroy you. A tooth for a tooth, an eye for an eye."

Nick stared at him, eyes blinking in pain as if Duff had stuck him with a blade.

Tears sprang to Lowry's eyes watching Nick being crushed under the weight of sorrow—past and present.

His mouth dropped open and in a thin whisper, Nick asked, "Why?"

With his mouth like a gash across his face, Duff grunted, "*Why?* You ask *why?*" He crossed his arms and leaned toward his brother. "Mother sacrificed me for you—a pact with the devil, one soul for the other."

Nick flinched against Duff's raw hatred.

Lowry swallowed back the bile in her throat. *Sweet revenge—one of the four basic food groups.*

Swaying with liquor and emotion, Duff grabbed the edge of the desk. He stared off into the darkness and his voice faltered with the memories of his childhood. "Beating upon beating, until all that was left was a broken body and a broken heart." He ranted hoarsely, "Your past comes crying in the darkness when you can't sleep and it pins you to the bed. You can't run fast enough or far enough from the closed doors that shield the hidden acts, the acts that you never speak of in the daylight."

Lowry pinched her lips together to keep from crying out. The wounds Duff had suffered as a child had brought him to this shell of a man. No one should go through the childhood he had experienced. The act of parenting is not for the faint of heart or the damaged soul. The care of a child was the greatest responsibility of a human being.

With a twitch of his head, Duff steadied himself. The hardness came back into his voice. "Then, there was Margaret . . ." With a demonic chuckle, Duff shook his head. "You didn't think I knew? Oh, I beat that tidbit out of her, right after you left."

Nick's lips tightened. "You *bastard.*"

Duff's eyebrows rose as he pulled up his shirt to reveal a scar that went down his side. "She gave me this little memento, so I'd remember to never touch her again." A bitter smile flashed over his face.

Duff straightened. "I swore, one day I would get you, Nick—if it took me a lifetime, I would get you. Do you think I followed you to this forsaken place for a job?" He grinned. "Or out of brotherly love?" He jabbed his finger at Nick. "Just as you took Margaret from me, I took the one thing you have truly loved—Antarctica."

A spasm moved across Nick's face. He opened and closed his lips, seeming to fight for air, as if Duff had punched him in the gut. Tears welled up in Lowry's eyes. Nothing could heal these wounds; they had turned gangrenous with neglect.

"You have betrayed everything in your life and now you have betrayed Antarctica." In a tired voice, Nick said, "You're a sick man, Duff, very sick."

"Really?" Duff snickered. "Let's see . . . it only took you, what, fifty years to figure that out?"

Nick furrowed his brow. "I understand that you want to hurt me. Some of the punishment I deserve." He reached his hand out to Duff. "But why hurt Lowry?"

"Because she's yours!" Duff sneered. "Have you ever done the math?"

"No," Nick murmured, dropping his gaze to the floor.

Lowry rose and stepped from the shadows. She stared at Duff, her hands shaking with fury. "What kind of animal are you? I hope to God Nick is my father and not you." She paced between the brothers and then pivoted to face Duff. Her mouth quivered in rage as she snarled, "Instead of destroying everyone around you, why don't you just shoot yourself and put the rest of us out of our misery?"

They stared at each other and she saw a fragment of regret in his face.

Nick put his hand on her shoulder. "Let's go. There's nothing we can do here. The smell of putrefying soul is making me ill."

CHAPTER 30

The nightmare had come true. The final election results were in and Durant had defeated Nick. It didn't matter that it had been a narrow political loss. The real loss was truth and justice surrendering to greed and corruption.

It was late when Lowry walked into Nick's office. He'd asked her to meet him there, following his concession speech.

Motionless, Nick sat at his desk, staring vacantly at the wall.

With a barely perceptible cough, she stood waiting for him to acknowledge her presence. There wasn't any comforting phrase to express; they both knew the consequences of his defeat.

He glanced up at her with a slight smile. He cleared his throat and motioned to a chair. "I'm sure you are wondering why I asked you to meet me here so late."

She nodded, pulled out the chair and sat. Glancing at him, she clutched the edge of the chair at the strain evident in his face.

"I want to give you something." He lifted up a small metallic disc. "This disc contains my plans for Antarctica."

Lowry shook her head. "You can run again," tapping her finger on the desk. "That loser will so incense the public, they'll string him up in six months!"

Nick shifted in his chair. He swept his unkempt hair out of his face, staring at a photo of Antarctica behind Lowry. "I came to Antarctica as a young man. I have traveled across her and came to know her like the lover I never had."

With a grimace, he refocused his dull eyes back onto Lowry. "It would be better for her if they strung him up tonight. Durant could do a lot of damage, permanent damage, in six months." He stroked the stubble of beard on his face. "With him in charge, I'm afraid it will be the Rape of Antarctica. Durant is going to change the course of history as corruption strangles the free-enterprise system of this nation, and the world economic leaders are likely to withdraw their funds from a corrupt country. Someone said long ago, 'Ruled by shady men, a nation itself becomes shady.'"

Lowry slumped back in her chair, chewing her lip. Everything he said was true.

Nick swayed and clutched the desk. "The craziness that has brought me here. My foolish youth led me to my foolish old age." He looked at Lowry. "I want to tell you about Margaret."

Lowry inclined her head, holding up her hand to stop him, but he continued. "No, I want you to know everything." Staring at the desk, he placed his hand on the surface, as if to hold himself up. He swallowed hard, his Adam's apple bobbing up and down. "The affair with Margaret was reprehensible. Especially since Duff and I were blood brothers in the family lies." He sighed, his mouth twisting with the memories. "She came into my life when I was twenty. Their marriage wasn't going well. Duff has always had a nasty habit of drinking too much and too often. I don't even know how it happened. Her ache for love and my passion for her dragged us onto a path neither of us had meant to take."

He stared ahead of him. "It was dark. I was sitting on the bench in the garden behind their house. I heard someone crying and saw her walking along the path, escaping from another fight with her 'loving' husband. I can still see her beautiful face, streaked with tears. There was a red mark on her cheek—from a vicious slap. At first, she didn't see me. I walked over to her and touched her face. Before I knew it, we were making love in the moonlight."

Nick dropped his gaze. "Afterwards, we felt empty. Not that empty is all that bad when you're full of anger, hate, and unrequited passion. We might have fallen in love, had it been a different time and a different place."

Lowry bit her lip to keep from crying.

Tears welled up in his eyes and his mouth sagged open. "That night, I lay in bed and the guilt of what I had done buried me. So I took a job I'd had been offered in my last year of college as a geologist for the first recon work on Antarctica. I had decided against it, not wanting to spend a minimum of five years in a remote hellhole. But now, I had to leave. It was either a mental hellhole or a physical one. I packed and left the next morning."

Nick slumped back into his chair. "After your birth, your mother said they went to a cold war. Margaret raised you and Duff concentrated on his career when he had one. When you were five, I saw Margaret for the last time, and helped both of you move to Austin, and away from the floods in Houston."

His voice choked for a moment, then he continued. "Duff followed me to Antarctica for work but after Margaret died, he dragged you into a life not fit for a child." He shook his head. "He was so self-absorbed, he couldn't see what he was doing. The past has a bad habit of sticking to your ribs."

He met her eyes and reached across the desk. "I never married, never had a child to hold or love. When you came into my life, you were my salvation as a man and a human being. I taught you everything I could.

"You were a sweet child. You'd been raised by Margaret, so you didn't bear too many of Duff's scars. You may or may not be my daughter by blood, but you are my daughter by love. I want you to take these plans and keep them for the day they're needed. You'll know when that day comes."

His head dropped into his hands. "The fate of a nation, changed by a childhood gone awry." With listless eyes, he looked into her face. "Lowry, always remember, love is not a garnish on the plate. Without it, no sacrifice for others is made. No healthy children to carry on the family."

He fell silent.

Lowry reached out and touched his hand. "Thank you for telling me this. Your love is a great deal of what saved me after my mother's death."

His confession over, his face sagged with exhaustion.

"It's late. I'd better be going." She hesitated as she reached for the disc. "Are you sure you want me to take this?"

"Yes." He swayed slightly, his eyes vacantly staring ahead.

She walked to the door, paused and said, "Go home and get some sleep, Nick."

"Sure."

Distractedly, she walked to her hover and got in, sitting still for several minutes as she digested Nick's words. Lowry pulled the hard drive he had given her from her pocket, and in the dimness of the streetlight, held up the shiny disc containing Nick's vision of Antarctica. She put it back into her pocket, pondering Nick's oddness tonight. Why had he been so insistent on giving her these plans?

Something moved in front of her—Nick, coming out of his office. He walked briskly to his vehicle and jumped inside. With her brow furrowed, she wondered at his frenetic pace. *Odd that he's now so energetic.* Shrugging, she shook her head. *At least he's going home.*

Nick sped off in the opposite direction of his house. Lowry's mouth dropped open and she became alarmed. "What the—? Where could he be going at this time of the night?"

She started the hover and followed him. She had to push it to catch up, but then saw the lights of his vehicle ahead of her.

He turned to the right. She followed, but stayed back, curious as to his rendezvous.

The traffic was terrible as they approached the new convention center, bustling with Durant's victory party. The streets were packed with well-wishers and press.

Nick parked and walked toward the hall.

Lowry sat dumbfounded. Why would Nick be going to toast the newest evil since Stalin?

She found a place to park and ran, trying to catch up to him. Ahead of her, Nick opened the door to the convention center, slipped into the crowd and disappeared. Lowry raced to the door, threw it open, and the raucous sound of victory hit her in the face.

Lowry held her hand over her nose from the odor of cheap perfume and booze as she pushed through the crowd into the banquet room. She saw Nick for a second, then lost sight of him. Her eyes flitted back and forth over the gathering, ignoring the laughing faces and finger-pointing of those who recognized her. The roaches had all come out now that the election was over.

Her heart pounded as she caught sight of Durant's smile, sparkling in the spotlights of a dozen camera crews.

Nick parted the crowd as he walked up to Durant. The camera crews drew back to capture his personal concession for the nightly news. Durant had a puzzled look of amazement at Nick's appearance. Nick reached up and removed his cap to pay homage to the new leader of Antarctica.

Lowry gasped at the flash of metal. Nick had a gun in his hand. Durant's steel blue eyes pulsed with the shock of each bullet into his chest. The blood splattered Nick's face. Durant toppled over—no longer the leader of a fledging country, just a rotting corpse.

After the last echo of the shots died, an eerie silence fell. Then, with a deafening roar of screams and shouts, the crowd pummeled her, in its wild stampede out of the hall.

Swept to the side of the room in the madness, Lowry gasped as the bodyguards turned on Nick, their faces horrible in their savagery. She cried out as Nick fell under the blows. He didn't try to run. There was nowhere to hide.

Into the darkness, Durant's animals wrestled Nick outside. Lowry fought her way through the crowd, fearing the guards would kill him. As she burst through the doors, they slammed Nick onto the sidewalk, and one of the guards cracked his head with the butt of his rifle. Cursing, they kicked him in the stomach, and with each blow, Nick grunted in pain.

Lowry held her hand to her cheek, screaming, "No, don't kill him!"

One of the men shouted, "She was in on it too. Get her!"

"No, she had nothing to do with it, leave her alone!" Nick shouted through bloodied lips.

The police sirens cried in the night. The men said, "Let's go." They kicked him into the street and stomped his face into the asphalt. "Maybe the police will run over his ass." And with dirty looks toward Lowry, they ran back into the conference center to mourn the passing of their leader.

Lowry ran to Nick and turned him over, biting her lip at the sight of his bruised and swollen face, streaked in red.

Nick spit blood from his mouth and stared angrily at her. With a wobble of his head, he yelled, "Why did you follow me? They might think you're an accomplice!"

A deafening wail of sirens, then an abrupt silence, and the police leapt out and ran to where Nick lay in the street. They hesitated, looking at each other. Their ashen faces betrayed the shock of realizing who their assassin was—their friend, and for many, a man they admired. They gently picked Nick up and placed him in the squad car, with Lowry beside him, and took them to the city jail.

Nick spoke to the police officer, his swollen mouth slurring his words. "Lowry had nothing to do with this."

"Not for us to judge, Nick."

They photographed and fingerprinted Nick while Lowry was held in a cell. After an hour, they brought Nick back and put him in the cell beside her. He sat on the bed and dropped his mangled face into his hands, staring at the cement floor.

Lowry waited, saying nothing.

Nick exhaled. His face wooden as he met her eyes. "It's funny, Lowry. It was almost like a dream—the crowd surrounding someone who looked like me, like a strange, out-of-body experience. I wondered if I would die tonight. It would be ironic to split the fare of the last boat ride with Durant."

With a shrug, he continued. "Even so, my life is over. It wasn't quite the end I thought it was going to be." He tilted his head. "You pay for those evil things you do in your life, sometimes a magnitude more than the original error."

His hands shook as he blinked, holding back his emotions. Then he broke and sobbed with abandon, his shoulders quivering with grief. Lowry cried with him, tears streaming down her face, wishing she could reach him and wrap her arms around her father.

Nick got himself under control. In a voice drained of emotion, he said, "Duff must be very happy—his brother has joined the damned."

The sun began to rise. The first rays touched the high windowpane of his cell. Nick pointed at the Antarctic flag outside the jail, now at half-mast in the dim light of morning. "Thank god, the bastard is really dead!"

CHAPTER 31

The next day, the cleaning people discovered Duff's dead body, hanging by the neck in his office. In the arch of the room, he had threaded a rope around the hologram projector, still beaming an image of the Earth.

Lowry stepped into the room, her insides twisting at the sight of him spiraling at the center of the globe, like Hades, keeper of the underworld. Weather patterns revolved around him, the clouds forming a virtual shroud around the creaking body. His tongue was stiff and black, hanging down the side of his bloated face.

The two security guards shuffled their feet. She signaled and they cut him down, returning him to Antarctica in a stilted heap, his neck bizarrely twisted—a sign that his death was by a broken neck, rather than asphyxiation.

"The one time he listened to me," she whispered to herself. *Dead.* The man she had known as her father was dead.

She felt a chill of guilt, staring at his body, with the twisting shadows from the hologram making the office look like a scene from a Halloween movie. But he had sold his soul long before she was a twinkle in her mother's eye. At least he could do no more harm now, or so she hoped.

They flicked off the hologram and in the stark office light, the reality of his dead body, lying so cold upon the floor, hit her and she swallowed back the vomit in her throat. Lowry balled her fist, resisting the urge to run from the room. It was not the time to break.

She knelt and closed the half-opened lids of those sad gray eyes. Perhaps the evil haunting the family through the generations had died with him. "As we sow, so shall we reap," she whispered to the pale ashen face.

An absent father in her early life, traveling from job to job—an arrangement encouraged by her mother. After her death, Lowry had moved to Antarctica, and ironically, she now realized, Nick had become her pseudo-father.

She stroked his face in forgiveness. He had been kind to her, from time to time when she was a little girl. Yet, he could turn into a tyrant on a dime.

The two men stood in silence, waiting for instructions.

Lowry staggered up and tilted her head toward Duff's body. "Take him to the morgue."

The two men struggled to get the rigid corpse out of the door. Lowry had a grotesque impulse to shout after them, "Why do you think they call them stiffs?" She stumbled from the room to keep from giggling hysterically.

She didn't feel the bite of the cold as she left the building. Shell-shocked with the events of the last several days, her mind drained from the emotional roller-coaster ride she'd been on.

How had all this happened? Hadn't she been a good girl? Why was it her kismet to have such a vicious family history? Her mind reeled as she stumbled along the street.

Lowry reached the main street and shook herself, trying to control her emotions. In the square, crowds gathered and dispersed in waves as confusion swept through Amundsen. She pivoted toward a shout on the street behind her and saw people running down the alley. The capital was in chaos. What would happen next with no one to lead Antarctica? The government was in danger of a complete breakdown.

A special election had to be called immediately, both to stave off the panic and to prevent world agencies from stepping in and taking control. When she'd heard of the news of Duff's passing, she had called Duff's lieutenant governor and they had decided that the date for the special elections should be announced at the same time as the news of his death.

With her family tarnished, Lowry knew she had to stay out of the limelight. She herself was under investigation as an accomplice to Durant's early demise.

Gritting her teeth, she hurried toward her destination. She had to stay focused to accomplish some sort of victory from the insanity of these last days. It was a pivotal time for Antarctica and, by god, she was going to pivot it her way.

CHAPTER 32

"I nominated you."

"Excuse me?" John twisted his head and knocked over his cup of coffee onto the kitchen table. He gazed at Lowry with a bewildered look, then grabbed a towel and wiped up the spill.

She had stopped by the farm, saying she had something important to discuss. God knows there was plenty to chat about with Nick having assassinated president-elect Durant in the midst of his inaugural event. What a party crasher.

Grimly, Lowry stared at him from the other side of the table. "I nominated you."

John licked his lips and swallowed hard, not sure if he wanted to finish this conversation, or run from the house. He blinked, inhaled a deep breath, and murmured, "Nominated me for what?"

"For President of Antarctica."

He studied her face for signs that this was some stupid joke, but that resolute mien was still in place. He swayed on his feet and sat in his chair. "You must be joking."

With a fixed look, she shook her head.

Blood rushed to his brain with the rage of betrayal. His chair screeched as he leapt up, shoving it backwards. Facing her, he leaned on the table, and shouted, "How could you do that?"

Lowry stared at him; her face pinched and stalwart. She said nothing.

John paced back and forth with the table between them. "How many times have I told you that I hate politics!" Shaking a clenched fist, he turned back to her. "I came to Antarctica to escape from all that."

She jabbed a finger at him. "Well, mister, you better get a refund on that ticket, because Antarctica is getting ready to have more politics than the world has dreamed of in years!" Leaning forward, her lip curled into a snarl. "You're a self-acclaimed Old West historian. You should know that one of the most violent periods of history was during the conquering of the land. Did you think the opening of Antarctica was going to be a walk in the park?"

Lowry leaned over the table and her face softened. She said quietly, "Antarctica is in turmoil. It takes men of courage and resolve to lead a nation in crisis."

With pinched lips, John folded his arms, staring at her. "There are others better suited—what about Duff's lieutenant governor?"

She shook her head. "He's only a shade less corrupt than Duff."

His stomach churning, John gazed out of the kitchen window to the small garden near the house, slowly collapsing with each subsequent freeze as the season ended. The brown corn stalks shuddered in the breeze and leaves drifted off of the tangled and withered vines of squash.

Lowry came around the table and touched his arm. With a smile, she said, "You could build a university or plan a city." She spread her arm toward the view from the window. "You would be the one to write in the first blank pages of a new continent."

He turned back to her and gazed into her bright face. It should be her, and not him. Lowry had both the strength of personality and the desire to put up with the bullshit of jumpstarting a wilderness.

His anger boiled to a head. "Oh, sure! I'll get to all that right after the toilets work and the damn roads are in!" Shaking his head, he threw his hands up in disgust. "For God's sake, Lowry, I'll have to collect taxes!"

Lowry grabbed his shoulders and shook him. "I've thought long and hard, John—there is no one else! No one!"

He tried to turn away, but she wouldn't let him. Her eyes flicked from side to side, staring at him. Lowry brought the full force of her personality to bear. "No one else has both the support from the miners—which you do through Nick—and from the immigrants, after foiling the land scandal and standing up to the authorities in the Daniels case. You're it!"

John flopped into his chair, refusing to look at her, fuming in silence. She knelt beside him and touched his arm. He twisted away, growling, "But I don't want it! I gave up everything in my past life for this freedom."

Lowry was silent for a moment, then whispered, "Freedom comes at a price." She stood, gripped his shoulder, and made him face her. "Durant's crew is readying a new candidate. Can you imagine what it will be like if Durant's forces get in power? Your 'civilization' back in the States would look mighty good then."

John turned away, staring at the table. He felt her contemplating her next move, but he hoped she would just go away.

She retreated back to the other side of the table and sat facing him. He glanced up at her eyes, focused on him like an animal ready to attack. Lowry said in a quiet voice, "What about Ginnie? What will her future be if they get ahold of Antarctica?"

He grimaced, closing his eyes for a second against the blow. Then inhaling deeply, he looked at her. The desperation on her face was obvious. She knew the most precious thing in his life was his daughter.

The blood pulsed in John's head, katooshing in time with his thumping heart. He touched his chest to see whether he was still breathing or not. He had no idea if it had been ten seconds or ten minutes since she had spoken. His Achilles' heel was his daughter.

He glanced at Lowry, waiting for his answer, then dropped his head into his hands, and murmured, "All right."

A bright smile sprung onto her face. She wrapped her arm around him and kissed him on the cheek. "Thank you, John."

Blinking, he sat still, staring vacantly at the wall, numb to her sudden affection.

With a sweet smile, she added, "Cheer up, you'll probably lose." She bounced up from her chair, now in high spirits, wagging her finger at him. "We've got to get cracking on all the arrangements. The special election is in a month and we've got to move!" She started to leave, then stopped, and turned back. "I'll stay in the background. They're still investigating me as a possible accomplice to Nick." With a smile, she waved goodbye, and strolled from the room. "But, I'll take care of everything, don't worry."

With a thunk, the door closed.

John's lip curled, and he said hoarsely to the now-absent Lowry, "All I've ever said to you meant nothing."

In the silence of the house, he stared at the wall, surrounded by the demons who came to mock his capitulation.

*   *   *

That night, John sat across from Ginnie. "Lowry has put my name on the ballot for president of Antarctica," he said quietly, then waited for a response. There was none. "She says I'm the only choice—the only one who can win against the candidate that Durant's group will nominate."

Ginnie shrugged. "She's probably right." With a grin, she continued. "I will say—President Barrous has a nice ring to it."

He turned away with a grimace. "I don't need you to butter me up."

Ginnie looked at him. "I know you're not happy that Lowry nominated you."

"I'm *not*." With a sigh, he shoved his hair back. "I'm not cut out to be a bureaucrat." He shook his head. "I've spent my adult life trying to escape from the stranglehold of the Old

World political mess. If I'm elected president, I'll be smack in the middle of it."

"Dad, if Durant's people have control, what will our future be? Nick should have been president, but there's nothing we can do about it." Ginnie reached across the table and touched his hand. "You've always told me there are times we're called to serve."

John stared at his sixteen-year-old daughter. "You're supposed to be on my side, not Lowry's." His shoulders sagged. "It won't be easy, Ginnie. The election is a month away, and I know Lowry will want me to campaign." He gazed at her. "If, by some bizarre chance, I win, it means leaving the farm and moving into Amundsen." He hesitated. "Would you prefer to go to your grandparents, at least during the campaign?"

Ginnie shook her head. "I'll stay here and help any way I can."

*   *   *

Over the next grueling weeks, John campaigned as Lowry wished, but determined to be himself whether anybody on his team liked it or not.

As he traveled the continent, he discovered a land that he was unaware of. He hadn't realized how deeply his head had been buried on his farm. Several cult factions had set up their own territories, barely allowing anyone to enter their domain. Minority religious sects had come from across the world, escaping the persecution of the majority. The oppressed of the world once again had a chance to find freedom. Or was it just their chance to oppress others?

John studied the closed faces in the crowds. They were distant and hard to read. Most of them didn't care who was in charge; they were too busy trying to survive on a daily basis. Instability in the government was no surprise to the people from the third-world countries, and there was a distinct undercurrent of anger expressed by the expatriates from the so-called more "civilized" countries. Who could blame them, after the cold shock of the assassination?

Campaign events were opportunities for political rivals in each area to parade their positions and taunt their adversaries. Several clashes had resulted in near-riots, and in several key regions, "accidental" deaths had been reported, none of which the local law enforcement had bothered to solve. No one was taking a chance of being on the wrong side in this political fight.

Today's speech was in one of the areas where riots had been a way of life for weeks. The crowd was ominously quiet, but the chanting of "Durant" began when John stepped up to the microphone. As he started to speak, the chanting became so loud, that others in the crowd shouted for quiet. At the back of the gathering, two fellows from opposing factions began swinging their signs at each other.

John struggled to keep everyone calm, raising his hand. "Please, let's try to—"

The pop-pop of a gun blasted into the air. The two men fought over a pistol as the crowd scattered across the field, some crawling, others racing away to safety.

John's bodyguards rushed in to hustle him from the podium to the waiting car. In a rage, he shook them off and pushed his way through the panicked crowd. He stood in front of the two men, who froze in mid-fight astonished to see the candidate standing in front of them.

"Put that gun down!" John yelled.

The man who had been wrestling with the gunman backed up. The gunman didn't move. John's fury drove away any fear he had, and he ripped the gun from the man's grasp, opened the chamber and emptied the bullets onto the ground. Security guards rushed in, taking the miscreant who had fired the pistol into custody.

John turned and made his way back up to the podium. Angrily, he hit the podium with his fist, holding up the weapon. "Is this the face we want to show the world? Do we want an outside government to control us because we cannot govern ourselves?"

The crowd surged toward him, shouting, "No!"

He threw the gun onto the ground and scanned the crowd that began to reassemble before him.

When the crowd quieted, John began to speak, "We are humans. We love, hate, and hunger, just as we did thousands of years ago. We may try to separate ourselves from the dirt of the past, but it remains there, beneath our fingernails."

He pounded the podium again. "The savvy politicians know how to sway the human emotions that drive us. We must not let them control us like a school of fish. We must solve our problems with talk, not bullets, and help our neighbors as if helping ourselves and our families. For that's what we are, my friends. We are a family."

A hush came over the crowd.

John gestured with his arm. "The world is watching us. Who are we going to elect? A gang of hooligans or the people who won their tracts fair and square, alongside you—the friends who planted with you and the friends who built your homes with you?

"We are at a crossroads. We can allow the mud of corruption to follow us or we can start fresh and clean. We are the generation who will build a country for our children and beyond."

He pointed to the crowd. "And we are the ones who are going to make the choice for who will lead us in building this nation."

The crowd cheered. He left the podium, his prepared speech still in his coat pocket.

*   *   *

The day came that everyone, except him, had been waiting for—Election Day. John refused all interviews. He went to the polls early, writing in a vote for Mickey Mouse. People waved at him, but he just nodded and hurried back to the farm. For him, it was Harvest Day. With the campaign schedule, he was the last one in his sector to harvest his crop of wheat.

His mind was numb from the effort of the campaign and, he hated to admit, the fear of winning. Well-wishers had descended upon the farm to watch the election results, but John refused to play the emotional roller-coaster with the rest of them as the vote counts trickled in.

John stepped out of the house, zipped up his jacket against the chill in the air, and walked toward the barn, knowing it might be his first and last year as a farmer. His harvest crew was waiting at the barn. They were silent as he approached. He could tell they wanted to say something, but his closed face shut off any discourse. What was left to say?

Without a word, he motioned to them to start the harvesters. He climbed onto his hover and followed the great robotic harvesters as they cruised toward the ocean of yellow wheat. Four of them drove into the field closest to the house and began the harvest.

Chaff filled the air. The birds circled and feasted on the insects flushed out of their homes. His once-rippling fields were reduced to stubble. The harvesters worked through the morning, finishing one field and starting the next. The hum of the machines numbed John's ears. The tireless robots mowed down the wheat, but the humans stopped for lunch.

The day warmed, and he took off his jacket as he walked to one of the trailers, now full of grain. He thrust his hands into the wheat and let the grains trickle through his fingers. He had grown this wheat—planted, cared for, and harvested it.

He turned at shouts in the distance. Lowry rode her horse at a full gallop into the barren field. Behind her were the others, running like madmen.

She had a huge smile on her face. "We won!" she yelled.

The tension broke. Cheering, the farmers threw their hats up into the air. They ran over and pounded him on the back.

One of the farmers silenced the relentless harvesters as the crowd surrounded him. Someone pushed him up onto one of the hovers. "Speech, Speech!"

He stood on the hover and saw the shining faces, full of hope. He was lost as to what to say. He raised his hand. The group became quiet and he began to speak, "Many of you know of my hesitation in putting my name forth and it's with very mixed emotions that I hear this news." He spread his arm out at the fields surrounding them. "This farm was something I had fought for all my life, but it was not to be." He smiled sadly. "But I have had a year of grace"—he clenched his fists against the rising emotions—"a year of grace, full of good friends who have become a family."

He gazed out at the land. "The sun breathed life into Antarctica and gave her to us. And we must try our best to take care of this gift—the last unspoiled land on the Earth."

He smiled at the gathering. "We have grown our crops and our families together over this year. I will need my good friends in the next years to help us grow a nation."

They roared in unison. He stepped back to the earth—the leader of a new continent.

CHAPTER 33

Lowry hesitated at John's door. The sun hadn't yet risen above the ridge, and in the pale light, she pressed her face to the side window. John sat on the couch, and she could see by the tilt of his head that all was not well. John hadn't spoken to her since the election results.

She rang the doorbell and watched him jump at the sound. She shuffled her feet, shivering against the chill breeze, and wishing she'd worn a heavier coat than her black wool.

John opened the door. His eyes were red with fatigue and his face rough with whiskers.

Lowry smiled slightly. "Um, sorry to bother you, but I have something to give you."

He had a sneer on his face as he waved her into the house. "And you just happened to be passing by." She walked into the living room and he smirked, "Welcome to the den of fools."

With pinched lips, she took her coat off and draped it over a chair. The stress of the last weeks had worn on both of them. With furrowed brow, she replied testily, "I thought the saying was 'den of thieves.'"

He gestured with his thumb. "No, they're down the street. Remember, your uncle—no sorry, your *father*—shot one of them."

"All right, enough!" Her lips twitched. "I know you didn't want this, but now you've got it, so stand up like a man. Nick made the ultimate sacrifice—don't belittle him. He did what he felt he had to do to save Antarctica."

"To save Antarctica!" He mocked. "I guess he should have wrapped himself in the Antarctic flag and set it on fire. That might have gotten the good people to forget that he plugged your mother."

She winced against the gibe. "Look, if I hadn't been smeared along with Nick, my name would have been on the ballot. But that's not the way the cookie crumbled." She dug in her pocket and lifted Nick's silver disc up into the light. "I wanted to bring you the plans Nick gave me, before he . . . he shot Durant." She placed it on the coffee table. "He had ideas for Antarctica that you might find of use, and I wanted you to have them."

With a frown, John shrugged, and waved to the chair facing him. She sat, folding her hands, while he flopped onto the couch. He pursed his lips and stared vacantly out of the large window looking across the valley. The wind whipped across the bare fields, and the hum of the breeze through the stubble of wheat was the only sound between them.

Finally, he cleared his throat. "I used to never believe in fate, until it smacked me in the face. It's ironic that I so distrusted politicians that I felt the best solution was to shanghai some poor fool to be the illustrious leader. I never dreamed the fool would be me."

Lowry tilted her head as she started to protest, but he held up a hand for her to stop.

His gaze dropped to the floor, and a twinge crossed his face like a sharp pain had shot through him. He said hoarsely between pinched lips, "I once told Durant that ambition would ensnare him like a bee in a Venus fly trap; but it's funny, he wasn't the only one to get trapped in the flower of death." Slowly he turned toward her, staring at her with bloodshot eyes. His voice was flat, like the edge of a knife. "And guess who's the flytrap."

Her mouth parted and she exhaled. She blinked and drew in a gasping breath as the truth in his eyes washed over her.

Lowry slumped in the chair and dropped her gaze to the floor, whispering, "I know."

His shoulders sagged, and his gaze wandered away from her. Then, with a sigh, he dropped his head into his hands.

A chill went up her spine. She swallowed the bile of reality and mumbled, "I'm sorry, John—"

John glanced at her and shook his head. "Lowry, I should never have allowed my name on the ballot. I have no one to blame but myself." Closing his eyes, he sighed deeply. "I gave up everything to escape a stifling corporate system. I came here for freedom to farm my land and to raise my daughter away from an urban jungle." He lifted his eyes to her, whispering, "I came here to become a human being."

Lowry dug her nails into her palms, fighting back her anguish.

As if she was no longer there, John stared past her. "Ego was the bait in the trap of my own stupidity. Funny thing, ego. It pushes you to think you're the only one when in reality there are a dozen right behind you. As soon as the finger is drawn back, the water closes in behind it."

He swayed slightly. He rubbed his eyes and sank back onto the couch.

The wind rose again and blew dead leaves against the glass pane with a rush, and a whirlwind of dirt, sticks, and leaves danced before the window, then fell into a heap as the gust died.

Lowry turned back to John, numbly staring ahead. With his brow furrowed in puzzlement, he shook his head. "How can a man, through blood, sweat, and tears, carve his commandments on the tablet of his life: this is what I stand for, then in the next instant discard them in the dust, like a child with a forgotten toy?"

His mouth quivered and he licked his dry lips. Hoarsely, he whispered, "What will Ginnie think, a year down the road when she hasn't seen her old man in weeks? I hope she doesn't get eaten by the political machine."

Lowry's mouth twitched and she forced out, "She'll be all right."

He cleared his throat and stared at her. "Lowry, if anything happens to me—take care of her, will you?"

She glanced at him and realized what he meant. With a nod, she whispered, "Of course. I'll see to her like she was my own."

Silence fell between them.

In the valley, the rays of the sun touched the hillside facing them. With the slanted light, the shadows revealed streams cutting vertical lines down the face of the slope, rock which before had been smoothly carved by glaciers. The gradual deterioration of a mighty mountain, inevitably collapsing into the depths of the valley.

Lowry turned back and studied the anguish on John's face as he stared at the floor. He, too, had new lines cutting into his face, exposing the chaos beneath the surface.

She clenched her jaw, fighting the tears welling in her eyes. In a tight voice, she murmured, "Entropy."

With a puzzled expression, John turned to her. "What?"

She started as she realized she had spoken. Their eyes met and she smiled sadly. "Entropy." She pressed her fingers into her temple and whispered, "Entropy is a state of increasing destruction, of disorder, of decay in the world."

John tilted his head, trying to discern if she was joking or not. Then with a curled lip, he lifted an empty glass from the table and snarled, "Let's have a toast to entropy!"

Despair washed over her. Lowry turned away, clasping her arms against his hatred as nausea gripped her stomach. She was the force of his destruction, changing the course of his life with a push of her hand, sacrificing his dreams to save her version of Antarctica. And in this, she had destroyed the bonds between them.

She rose on unsteady feet. "I must leave," she said, glancing at him.

John stared at the floor. "Yes, it's time."

In a daze, Lowry slipped on her coat, walked to the door and opened it. She paused and looked back at John, frozen in place with his head in his hand. She stepped into the bright morning sun and stumbled as the light blinded her.

The End

K.E. Lanning

ACKNOWLEDGEMENTS

My deepest appreciation goes to my friends, family, and supporters, especially my author friends: Lisa Tracy and Cristina Pinto-Bailey, early readers who believed in me and bestowed great feedback, and author Sonja Yoerg, for her prodigious support. Special thanks to my wonderful editors for this novel: Heather Webb and Jim Thomsen. Thanks to Kit Foster for creating the fantastic cover and Walter B. Myers for the flooded Earth imagery. Much gratitude to my family, for supporting me during the long process of crafting these stories. Thanks to my friend and 'cheerleader' Stevie Bond for reading and supporting my writings. And a special thanks to all my reviewers and readers.

ABOUT THE AUTHOR

K.E. Lanning is a writer and scientist. Born in Texas in 1957, she grew up near Houston in the small town of Friendswood, laced with white oyster shell roads and open fields dotted with huge live oaks, riding horses rather than bikes. But nearby, NASA's space program shepherded thoughts of astrophysics into her head.

Lanning received a bachelor's degree in Physics in 1979 from Stephen F. Austin St. University in Nacogdoches, TX and a MBA in 1986 from the University of Houston.

Lanning has long been a fan of science fiction, intrigued by the multi-dimensions of the genre, allowing the author to explore society, humanity, and our future, and bringing the reader along for the ride.

She now resides in the Shenandoah Valley of Virginia with her family.

The Sting of the Bee is the second novel of THE MELT TRILOGY, and follows her debut book, *A Spider Sat Beside Her*, the first story of the trilogy. The final novel of the series will be *Listen to the Birds*.

www.kelanning.com

CPSIA information can be obtained
at www.ICGtesting.com
Printed in the USA
LVHW041032070419
613259LV00001B/159

9 780999 121023